FALSE
IMPRESSIONS

TERRI THAYER

BERKLEY PRIME CRIME, NEW YORK

THE BERKLEY PUBLISHING GROUP
Published by the Penguin Group
Penguin Group (USA) Inc.
375 Hudson Street, New York, New York 10014, USA
Penguin Group (Canada), 90 Eglinton Avenue East, Suite 700, Toronto, Ontario M4P 2Y3, Canada
(a division of Pearson Penguin Canada Inc.)
Penguin Books Ltd., 80 Strand, London WC2R 0RL, England
Penguin Group Ireland, 25 St. Stephen's Green, Dublin 2, Ireland (a division of Penguin Books Ltd.)
Penguin Group (Australia), 250 Camberwell Road, Camberwell, Victoria 3124, Australia
(a division of Pearson Australia Group Pty. Ltd.)
Penguin Books India Pvt. Ltd., 11 Community Centre, Panchsheel Park, New Delhi—110 017, India
Penguin Group (NZ), 67 Apollo Drive, Rosedale, North Shore 0632, New Zealand
(a division of Pearson New Zealand Ltd.)
Penguin Books (South Africa) (Pty.) Ltd., 24 Sturdee Avenue, Rosebank, Johannesburg 2196,
South Africa

Penguin Books Ltd., Registered Offices: 80 Strand, London WC2R 0RL, England

FALSE IMPRESSIONS

A Berkley Prime Crime Book / published by arrangement with the author

PRINTING HISTORY
Berkley Prime Crime mass-market edition / August 2010

ISBN: 978-0-425-23555-3

BERKLEY® PRIME CRIME
Berkley Prime Crime Books are published by The Berkley Publishing Group,
a division of Penguin Group (USA) Inc.,
375 Hudson Street, New York, New York 10014.
BERKLEY® PRIME CRIME and the PRIME CRIME logo are trademarks of Penguin Group
(USA) Inc.

PRINTED IN THE UNITED STATES OF AMERICA

10 9 8 7 6 5 4 3 2 1

ACKNOWLEDGMENTS

As always, thanks to my fabulous critique group, Beth Proudfoot and Becky Levine, and Jana Mcburney-Lin. I learn to write with your help.

Thanks to Holly Mabutas of Eat Cake Graphics for her wonderful stamps. You can't help but smile at her designs.

Thanks to Andrea Chebeleu of A Work of Heart studio for providing a space for messy creativity, the best kind.

And thanks to Michael Glass, for his fabulous titles.

CHAPTER 1

April spotted the box as soon as she opened the cupboard door. A beam of light caught on the red lacquer and bounced off the crystals that dotted the surface. The box was pretty, a jewel in the midst of the other plain brown shoe-box-size cardboard containers.

She looked for Deana, but she was not in the laundry room anymore. April was working in the newly repurposed room in the basement of the Hudock Family Funeral Home. Deana and Mark, her good friends who ran the business together, had moved their washer and dryer up a level next to their main bath and turned this room into storage space for their business. April had been hired to sort files and move them into their new home.

She probably shouldn't have opened this particular cupboard. In her defense, it didn't have a lock on it or anything like that. It was just that the rest of the room was covered in open shelving and curiosity had gotten the best of her. She'd wanted to see what was behind the closed doors.

Besides, she might need the space for last year's accounting records.

The box glowed. She knew it wasn't really glowing, but the paints and designs that covered the surface made it look as if it were. She had to see more than just the part that was visible. April gave it a shove with her pinky, moving it slightly. Dust rose up like fog. She coughed.

The box surface was slightly sticky from the finish used. When she got closer, she saw the lid had been collaged with faded pictures and a high school graduation program. In one of the pictures, she could see a young man holding up a trophy. Her gaze didn't rest there long but rather flicked from one image to the next. There was so much to see.

The base continued the theme. A motorcycle key graced the side. Stamped images of abstract shapes formed a border. The top and bottom of the box were tied together with a twisted braid of leather. Her fingers itched to untangle the cord.

She could make out a date on the side of the box: 2/22/09. And the initials JBH.

"Deana?" she called. No answer. This box was out of place, looking like a jeweled cup next to the plain household plates in an Egyptian tomb. It was art, with a capital A. Art among ordinary file boxes. Art in a funeral home.

Deana must have gone upstairs to refill their coffee.

The room was warm and dry, a huge old furnace keeping the place toasty despite near-zero temperatures and howling winds outside. She was happy to be inside, happy to be doing paid work. The restoration work she'd been doing had slowed and then ground to a halt as the snow and ice piled up. Aldenville was having its worst winter in years. Of course it was. This was her first January in fifteen years not spent in California.

Deana returned with two cups and two pieces of banana bread on a tray. She set it on top of an empty shelf.

"Mark told me to tell you the temperature has gone down another three degrees. It's eight now."

"He's too funny." Ever since Mark had come across a picture of Deana and April with Tom Clark, a local TV meteorologist who had come to their sixth-grade class, he'd teased her about the weather. April had had a major crush on the lanky weatherman.

The indoor-outdoor temperature gauge with digital barometer she'd given Mark for Christmas had seemed like the perfect gift, but now he was subjecting her to weather reports every chance he got.

Deana closed the cupboard door. "Oh, you needn't bother. I'll take care of those."

Curious. Nothing so far had been off-limits, although April had stayed away from the embalming room on her own. "Why? What are all those boxes? And that red box? It's gorgeous. It looks like something one of us would make."

By "us," April meant their weekly stamping group: Rocky Winchester, Suzi Dowling, Mary Lou Rosen and sometimes her daughter, Kit. And April and Deana.

Deana handed her a mug and stood in front of the door she'd just closed. She tried to make it look like a casual decision to block access, but April knew better. Deana didn't want her in there. Which, of course, drove April nuts. Deana could be so proper at times.

"Did Rocky go into the box-making business?" April asked.

She better not have, April thought as she sipped her

coffee and broke off a piece of banana bread. Rocky had her hands full as the new owner of Stamping Sisters. April wanted her to concentrate on selling her line of California Dreamin' stamps so that they could move on to the home décor line April had been dreaming about.

Deana just shook her head.

"Seriously, you've got to see this thing," she said. April reached to open the cupboard again. Deana put down her coffee and put her hand onto her friend's arm. She lowered her voice and spoke firmly. April recognized it as her business voice. Deana was quite adept at the let-me-tell-you-how-to-behave tone.

"Those are cremains, April."

April's hand drew back quickly. Cremains? April knew her best friend, the funeral home owner and part-time deputy coroner, dealt with a lot of things she did not, but cremains? What were they doing here? Didn't they have their own special room?

"Why do you have ashes of dead people stored here? Don't you give them to their . . ." She searched for the word. "Owners?"

Deana said, "I send the bodies out to be cremated. They get returned to me. Usually we have a service and the family takes their loved one home. Sometimes, they don't."

"What do you mean, sometimes *they don't*?"

April took a step away. She remembered what she'd seen inside. Six narrow shelves, two boxes to a shelf. There were at least twelve people in here. Bodies. Cremains.

She shuddered. "Why would people *not* pick up their loved ones remains?"

"It's complicated, April. Some folks can't deal."

"Like how?"

Deana looked at April, as if trying to judge how serious she was. She knew April was not a gossip and was curious about life here in Aldenville, their hometown. She made a decision and slowly opened the door.

Deana pointed to the top shelf to a plain cardboard box. April scrubbed an image of Vanna White from her head. Deana was honoring her request. She fixed her face in an appropriate expression

"This old guy has no living relatives," Deana said. She patted the box sadly and moved her hand to the next. "That one, the family moved out of the area. They left me a forwarding address, but it was wrong. They've never paid their bill. So I have Grandma."

April felt a lump grow in her throat. She didn't know how Deana coped sometimes, dealing with so much pain and anguish. Luckily, she had her husband, Mark, to partner with in the business. That helped.

But April wanted to hear about the fancy one. If that meant hearing a dozen sad tales, so be it.

The box seemed to glow inside the dim cupboard. She saw stamped images on the side, symbols meaningful to the resident that made no sense to her. Her fingers twitched. She wanted to study it.

Deana's hand was on the shelf above the red box, telling her the story of a fireman whose family was still getting used to the idea that Daddy had died in a neighbor's bed.

Deana moved down to the last row, began describing the sad tale of two sisters locked in mortal combat over their mother's remains.

"You skipped this one." April pointed to the shelf holding the red lacquer box. It was at hip height, so they had a good view of the intricate designs on the lid. Deana had just ignored it. Someone had decorated this box lovingly. How could the ashes get left behind?

Deana shut the door. "If you're just interested in gossip," Deana began, letting the sentence die an unnatural death.

Her lips were turned down almost in an unnatural shape, almost like a scowl. Deana didn't scowl.

April's hand snatched back. She was surprised by the sharpness of Deana's tone.

"You're not going to tell me, Dee?"

Deana walked out of the room, into the file room next door. She pulled open a drawer. The screeching noise hurt April's ears.

"Come on, we've got work to do," Deana called. "As soon as I'm done with the taxes, I'll want to move 2009 in this drawer here. So clear it out. Any records earlier than 2004 can go into this box and get moved onto the shelves in the other room."

Coffee break was over. April reluctantly joined her friend. It was mindless work; any drone could do it. But she needed the money Deana was paying her. The plan was to box up old records, rotating the oldest files and moving last year's files into the top drawer.

Deana came back in, carrying more files. "How are the Stamping Sisters designs coming?" she asked.

April saw her question for what it was—an effort to make up for Deana's earlier curtness.

April grabbed a handful of folders and checked the names on the files. She moved those that were out of alphabetical order. "Rocky has her own ideas, I'll tell you that."

"What do you mean?"

"That means she doesn't give a hoot about the creative side of things. She just wants me to produce."

Deana had experience as a Stamping Sisters rep. She'd sold the line of stamps and inks. "You should be glad she's a businesswoman. Don't forget she's been making a living as an artist, selling her own collages, for years. She manages to combine both art and commerce. What's wrong with that?"

April knelt down and opened the bottom drawer. "Making money would be fine, but I haven't seen any. I need income."

Deana set to vigorously dusting the drawers she'd emptied. April knew Deana was giving her space to vent if that's what she wanted. Since she'd been back in Aldenville, she'd leaned on Deana a lot.

April sighed. "I have to get out of the barn."

"I thought Charlotte and Grizz living with you at the barn was temporary."

When she'd escaped from California, her father, Ed, and his partner, Vince, had allowed her to move into their newly renovated barn. A few months after she'd settled in, Vince's parents, Charlotte and Grizz Campbell, lost their life savings and their home. Out of options, they'd moved in with April.

"It was supposed to be short term, but I don't see how things are going to change. They've lost everything. All they have is their Social Security. Vince has no choice but to keep them in the barn. Besides, I need my own place. Don't you think?"

Deana sat back on her haunches, her super microfiber cloth in her hand. She had a smudge of dust on her nose. "Your own place? Without Mitch?"

"Mitch and I don't need to live together. I've never lived on my own, you know. Well, barely, if you count the couple of months in the barn before the Campbells arrived."

"I know."

April had gone from her mother's home to college to marriage. Her first four months back in Aldenville had been the first time she'd lived on her own. And she'd been too busy to enjoy it.

"I like the idea of fixing up a house of my own. Just me, no input from anyone."

"You'd like a bedroom to bring Mitch home to."

April felt herself blush. She and Mitch had a hard time finding alone time with their busy schedules. With Charlotte and Grizz in her barn, she couldn't exactly lure Mitch up to her sleeping loft.

"I'm sick of spending the night at his place, or worse, getting up in the middle of the night and driving home. At first, it was kind of fun, but now with the bad weather, I'm only doing it once a week."

Deana chuckled. "Like an old married couple."

"We're busy," April protested. "If I had my own apartment, I could cook him dinner and he could hang out for as long as he wanted to."

"Before driving home in the middle of the night," Deana said. "I thought you were more liberated than that."

"It's not a question of liberation. I don't mind being the one to drive home once in a while, but not every time. Shared responsibility."

"Have you started looking?"

April nodded. "Mary Lou's on the case." Mary Lou Rosen was the top-earning local Realtor. She sold most of the homes that went on the market in Aldenville. "She left me a message, saying she might have one or two for me to look at. She's bought up a few foreclosures in the last couple of months."

"I heard about that."

April sighed again. "Have you noticed this valley shuts down in the winter? No one moves in or out. Everyone's in a holding pattern until spring. It's driving me nuts."

"Well, it's kind of tough with forty inches of snow on the ground," Deana said. "I like the slower pace. We take this time to reflect on life and other matters. Like end-of-year cleaning." Deana smiled at her. "Besides, you're the one who thought you missed it. Winter."

It was true. Living in San Francisco, April had often bored her California friends with fabulous winter wonderland scenarios. She'd called Deana once a week for a weather update, and during big weather events, she'd be online following the local TV coverage.

"In those fantasies, I had plenty of thermal underwear."

"I heard you and Mitch went cross-country on Saturday." Deana lifted her fingers into air quotes.

"No, we went cross-country *skiing*, no quotes necessary," April corrected.

"The story I got was that you two were out for about an hour before you gave up and spent the rest of the day in front of the fire at the club."

April looked up from the pile of files she'd been sorting. "Damn this small town. Who told you that?"

Deana grinned. "Not saying. Just know eyes are everywhere and on you."

"Why me?"

"Hey, you're the girl who's got three fathers and one mother, who just moved here from California. You're interesting."

Deana shoved a full box marked with her neat block handwriting onto a metal shelf. The number of files, the dates, the years.

She didn't need April here. She was just throwing her some work to keep her busy and help her pay her grocery bills. Plus, Deana knew that April would go crazy without something to focus on besides the cold weather.

April unfolded herself from the cross-legged position she'd taken on the floor. She dragged a box closer. A noise from inside the wall startled her and she knocked the box over, spilling files onto the floor.

Deana opened a small metal door that was cut into the wall opposite. The noise got louder. Deana caught April's

eye. "Dumbwaiter. From the kitchen. My father's father
had it installed so he wouldn't have to stop working. My
grandmother sent food down to him. Mark wants company
when he eats so he just sends messages." She plucked a
piece of paper off a plate and read it, laughing.

"Come and get it," she read.

April grabbed a handful of files to put back into the
box until after lunch. A familiar name on the tab caught
her eye: Rosen, Mary Lou. She opened the file, blocking
Deana's view with her body.

Inside was an order for cremation. A copy of the death
certificate for a Joseph Bartholomew Hunsinger.

An invoice for the funeral expenses marked "Paid."
Made out to Mary Lou Rosen.

April stood, her voice squeaking as she spoke. She
couldn't hide her excitement. "I knew it. I knew I recognized that style. That's Mary Lou's box."

Deana's fingers froze holding the note in midair.

April asked, "Why are there cremains belonging to
Mary Lou in your basement?"

CHAPTER 2

"April, dang it."

Deana's version of cussing. "I told you to leave it alone. Mark says the panini are ready for lunch."

April crossed her arms over her chest, casting a loaded glance at the file. "I don't want panini."

Someone's stomach growled.

April covered her belly and said, "Well, I mean, of course I do want lunch, but I want to know why Mary Lou paid for this cremation."

Deana ignored her question and started up the stairs. Built into the side of a hill, the funeral home had many levels, most of them secret from the public space. This part of the basement was accessible only by these stairs that led straight into the kitchen. As they climbed, April could smell basil and tomato and toasted bread. Her stomach did a flip-flop at the promise of food. Cleaning out basements was hungry work.

Deana was already at the sink and offered April a pump of soap. She squirted some into both their palms and they washed up, elbow to elbow.

"I'll find out; you know I will," April said.

Deana dried her hands, remaining mute. Mark, burly and handsome, had dished the sandwiches on plates. He and April exchanged cheek kisses.

Mark was the public face of Hudock Family Funeral Home. He met with the families, sold the services, and talked money with grace and compassion. He left the scientific stuff to Deana. It was a system that worked well for them.

He pulled out a chair for his wife and one for April. She sat down. "Thanks, Mark."

"My pleasure," he said. "You're doing my job. I'd much rather be up here cooking than cleaning out files in the basement."

Deana said chirpily, every note a false one, "I don't know what I was thinking, getting him that panini maker for Christmas. I've gained ten pounds from all the carbs."

She avoided April's eyes. April watched her as she cut her sandwich with a knife and a fork.

April picked hers up with two hands and dug in. She took a big bite and chewed slowly, letting the hot meat and cheese warm up her innards. Mary Lou had paid for a cremation and boxed it up in a fancy container but left it in Deana's basement. It didn't make sense.

April waited for Mark to finish his first sandwich. He ate quickly, smacking his lips when he was finished. Deana offered him a napkin, which he took with a smile.

April saw her opportunity. "Mark, what do you know about Mary Lou's family?"

"I know she has one," he said.

Deana frowned over a mouthful of salami and cheese.

Her eyes widened. She shook her head. Her husband stood up and smiled at her. She didn't need to tell Mark not to talk. He was well versed in the discretion it took to be a funeral director in a small town.

April persisted. "There are cremains down there . . ."

Mark screwed up his face as though he was thinking hard. "Cremains, huh? Was that the guy who was abducted by aliens? What a mess that was. You try making a face look presentable to the family after it's been peeled off by tiny little creatures. Not easy. Cremation was the only answer."

April smirked at him. "Funny." She sometimes thought of Mark as the brother she never had. He liked to tease her.

"Or was he the poor fellow that peed on the exposed wire in the last ice storm? We had no choice on that one. Talk about fried . . ."

Deana swallowed hard. "Mark, please. This is not exactly a conversation I want to have over lunch."

April frowned. "I know you two have had far more graphic conversations over all kinds of meals. I just want you to take me seriously. I'm not looking for gossip."

Mark put a piece of bread on the grill and opened a package of cheese. He dangled the yellow mass. "Come on, Dee. It's April."

"Yeah, only me," April said. "I'm practically an employee now."

Deana said, "Enough." She didn't have to say more. The moral high ground was hers. Mark turned back to his sandwich making. April took another big bite.

"Mary Lou doesn't like to talk about what happened to her brother. I'm trying to respect that," Deana said.

April slowed her chewing, trying not to react to the slip Deana had made. A brother. It was Mary Lou's brother in the box.

April considered what she knew about Mary Lou Rosen. She'd only met her when she'd moved back to Aldenville last June. She couldn't remember Mary Lou ever mentioning a brother. He would have been dead for several months by then, based on the invoice. To be fair, most of their discussion lately had centered around Mary Lou becoming a grandmother for the first time. Kit's twins were just about six months old.

Her curiosity was really piqued now. Deana didn't seem to notice that she'd misspoke. April would like to know more. But if Mary Lou wasn't ready to talk about it, she'd have to respect that.

Lunch was finished quickly. Twenty minutes later, they all went back to work.

Deana left her alone in the basement for the afternoon. April left around four, wrapping her granny-square scarf around her neck three times. Charlotte Campbell had made it, and April, while grateful for Charlotte's efforts, had thought she'd never wear it. But the colder the weather got, the less ugly the hideous orange color seemed. The scarf was delightfully warm and soft.

Still, her chin felt brittle from the cold, and she sat on her hands in the car, waiting for it to warm up enough to drive.

Mark waved to her cheerily from behind his snowblower as he drove past her. He was clearing the parking lot. Most of it was down to the bare asphalt, but it was rimmed by the piles made by the plow. Those had to be disposed of.

Winter weather had been a lot more fun when she was a kid, although Mark seemed to be enjoying himself.

A huge pile of snow slid off the roof of the funeral home and banged down next to where she'd been walking just a moment before. April jumped, but Mark just grinned. She rolled down her window to hear him.

"Guess I've got to get up on the roof and take care of some of that," he said with glee.

"No one should be that happy about snow," she yelled at him. He laughed.

April turned her car around so she didn't have to back out their long driveway. She let three cars pass before she felt comfortable pulling out. Her tires hit a patch of ice and spun before releasing her into the road.

April stopped at Rocky's office on the way home. Rocky had rented a space in the small business park across from the grocery store. She was trying to make a go of the Stamping Sisters business that she'd bought from Trish Taylor. The former owner had met with an untimely death a few months earlier. Rocky was recruiting new people to sell the line.

It was awkward working for Rocky. April was dating her brother, Mitch Winchester. April still had to find the delicate balance needed to work for one Winchester and date another.

Rocky had asked for this meeting. Rocky considered April her employee, despite the fact that April had sold her line of California Dreamin' stamps to Trish with a deal that cut April a percentage of royalties. Not exactly a partner, but not an hourly worker, either. A subtle distinction that Rocky chose to ignore.

Maybe the California Dreamin' stamps were ready. April pulled open the door. Rocky was seated on a stool in front of the bar-high kitchen table that served as her desk. She was a woman who understood how to grab power in any way.

She had a Spanish-English dictionary in front of her.

"How do you say 'celebrate' in *español*?" she asked when April let herself in. "I'm thinking I need to do a line of Spanish word stamps."

"I don't know. I took French in high school."

"There's no market for French stamps," Rocky said as if April had just suggested there was.

April rolled her eyes and settled across from Rocky, laying down her portfolio but leaving it closed. "You should ask Vanesa for help. She'd be glad to give you a hand."

Vanesa Villarreal was the eldest daughter of the family that had moved into Mitch's first Winchester Homes for Hope, Mitch's pet project. A custom furniture maker by trade, he'd started building homes for the less fortunate.

"Especially if you can pay her. I know she needs an after-school job."

Rocky leaned on her open palm. "I need an after-school job. This business is all outlay and no payback so far."

Rocky had no idea what it meant to need money. Not really. She always had the Winchester fortunes, for backup. Or she could go to her brother, Mitch, for a loan as she had before. He was already a part owner of Stamping Sisters.

April had no fallback. Her mother worked in the country club kitchen and paid her expenses but had little left over. Her marriage to Clive Pierce, aging pop star, made her financial life more secure, but April would never ask him for money. Her father and Vince's historical home restoration business, Retro Reproductions, had had a few financial setbacks in the last couple of years, and with Vince's parents' losing all their money last year, Ed and Vince were more concerned than ever about finances.

She'd been paying her bills and had paid off all the obligations she'd left behind in California. At least the finality of her divorce from Ken meant she was no longer responsible for any debts he piled up now.

But just when she was starting to feel more comfortable, work had dried up. The snow and the ice meant the restoration of Mirabella had halted. Mirabella, the mansion owned by Mitch's aunt Barbara, was the biggest job Retro Reproductions had. April had been working at the house as part of the Retro Reproductions team, stamping the walls with her historically accurate designs, since June. January 1, Ed and Vince had escaped to the time-share in Florida they'd bought years ago, spending their days at jai alai and the dog track. Her pleas to restart the jobs fell on deaf ears. Deaf and tanned ears.

"I've been looking at your home décor drawings," Rocky said, laying aside her sketchbook and clearing a space on the table for April to open her portfolio. April felt her spirits lift. This was what she was truly interested in.

She could see her designs stamped on walls all over the country.

"This is my favorite," she said, pointing to a William Morris chrysanthemum.

"Too complicated," Rocky said. "How am I supposed to manufacture that? It would take six separate stamps. The price point would be too high. We've got to keep these simple."

April sighed. Making simple stamps was not her strong suit. Interesting did not translate well to a few lines.

"Keep it simple, stupid," Rocky said. At April's quick look, she said, "You know. KISS. Keep it simple. Not that you're stupid. I know you can do this. Just bear in mind the amount of cutting we'd need to do to make the stamp. Then reproduce it."

"But I like complicated," April said.

"I know," Rocky said. "But complicated means costly to manufacture. Expensive means fewer people can afford it. That's why you're lucky to have me to remind you."

April closed the book. She rubbed the front of her portfolio, the smooth leather soothing her spiky feelings.

"We can't make these stamps now anyhow," Rocky said, her mouth in a straight line.

"But you said—"

"I said once we start making some money, we could expand into home dec stamps. We're not there yet. I need more of the cute kind of rubber stamps. People like those."

"But there's twenty lines in that catalog." She indicated the Stamping Sisters catalog. Her California Dreamin' stamps were just one of many.

The business model for Stamping Sisters was the same as that for Tupperware. The sellers were all independent contractors who made money in two ways: by selling the stamps themselves at parties held in private homes or by recruiting others to become salespeople. Rocky was revamping the business she'd bought from Trish, but the basic premise remained the same. The more people selling the products, the more money everyone made. And since April was to receive royalties on the stamps she designed, the same went for her. It was in her best interest to help Rocky sell stamps. But she'd never been a good salesperson.

"The public is always demanding new stuff. We have to keep up. I need you to design four more lines of coordinating sets by the next catalog, which I will send to the printer next month."

April hadn't signed on for this. She'd designed a line of seven stamps that she'd sold to Trish. Trish had promised to pay her royalties. End of story.

"Are you going to pay me for my time?" April said.

"We're all going to have to make sacrifices. I don't make money until your stamps sell. The more stamps you've got out there, the more money you can make. Make sense?"

April buried her face in her hands. Yes, it made sense, but is that what she wanted to be? A designer of stamps for the Stamping Sisters line? Was that her career path?

She did stamping on walls for historical renovations. Her wall stamps were unique to the project, based on historical architectural research. Rocky had promised a line of wall stamps in the catalog. Eventually. She had to earn the right to get there. She lifted her head, leaned on one palm.

"All right," April said. She wanted that home dec line more than anything. She'd have to pay the piper in the meantime. Rocky being the piper.

"Okay. So how about a new line of stamps from you?" Rocky's tone was reproachful. April felt like a first-grader being scolded by her teacher for not turning in her homework. Homework she hadn't known was due.

She said, "What do you mean?"

"How about a winter wonderland line? I've decided to sell the Stamping Sisters at the Ice Festival."

The Ice Festival hadn't been such a big deal when she was growing up. From what Mitch had told her, twelve years ago, after a few extra cold winters, the borough council had created a January event to break up the doldrums caused by too much snow, not enough sun, and way too much time indoors with family members. It had grown to a special all-day event. The money raised went to fund recreation programs.

"I thought they told you no selling allowed."

"That's why you and I are going to the council meeting. Tonight."

April's shoulders started to creep up. Her neck tensed. She sighed, flexing her fingers. It was easy to get tied up in knots around Rocky and her healthy disrespect for authority.

"Okaaay," April began.

Rocky looked out the window as a Turkey Hill truck drove by, on its way to fill up the gas tanks at the nearby convenience store. The air brakes squealed as it slowed on

the hill. The sound hurt April's ears, and she worried that
the driver wouldn't be able to stop. Where the sun hadn't
reached it, the road was still icy in spots. The truck shuddered to a stop.

"So I want you to develop a new line of stamps for the
event," Rocky said. "We'll roll out the line there."

"That's next weekend," April said. "I need more time
than that."

"I'd love to give you more, but there's a captive audience
at these things. Just develop the line. You know the drill.
Ice crystals, snowflakes, snowmen."

April's mind did begin working on ideas, despite the
fact that she felt the deadline was too close. Welcome to
the new Stamping Sisters. Rocky wanted to catapult the
Stamping Sisters brand into the national eye. For that,
April would have to step up her game.

In the past, she'd developed one or two large stamps for
a customer's needs. Before October, she'd never designed a
whole line before. Designing the California Dreamin' line
she'd made for Trish had been easy. The stamps came to her
in a flood of nostalgia for the life she'd left behind. She'd
sold the line to Stamping Sisters after it was complete.

Now Rocky was asking for a new line in a week. She
didn't know if she could do it. She couldn't plead that she
had no time. Rocky knew she wasn't working right now.

"I've got no place to work," April said. She was peril-
ously close to whining. "You know the Campbells are at
my place."

Rocky pointed to the empty corner. "Bring your drafting table over and set up in here. I'd love the company."

April hid a grimace. Working in such close proximity
to Rocky would not be fun. She needed quiet and solitude.
Things that were in short supply at the barn, too. She'd

tried working at Mitch's, but he was so distracting she never got anything done.

"What are you smiling about?" Rocky snarled.

April composed herself. Mitch's distractions were always a lot of fun.

"I'll think about it." There was no way she would be able to share a studio with Rocky. This was just another reason to find a place of her own. If she had her own house, she could designate a room as a studio.

"Just to be clear, I can't work your booth at the Ice Festival. I'm going to help Mitch with his ice sculpture."

Rocky let out a short bark of a laugh. "Really?"

"He's coming over tonight. Something about a chain saw," April said, nodding.

Rocky looked at her sharply, smiling. "I swear that boy gets a new chain saw every other year."

"He said something about new controls and a lighter weight."

"Blah, blah, blabbity, blah. It's all just rationalization for a new toy. He'll try anything to do better than he did last year. He came in second. As good as last to him."

Rocky put her hand under her hair on her neck and lifted. The swoop across her eye, across her scar, stayed in place as though hot glued there. Rocky was a beautiful woman, but a scar that ran through her eye and onto her cheek marred her good looks, and she made sure it was hidden. April wondered when she would learn the truth behind the scar. Mitch had already made it clear he wouldn't be the one to tell her. Rocky would tell April when she was ready, according to her brother.

Maybe soon. Maybe I should just mind my own business, April thought.

But . . . "Rocky, did you know Mary Lou's brother?"

"Which one?" Rocky's computer dinged, and she looked at the screen.

"She has two?"

"Yeah. J.B. and Gregg. Gregg just moved to California." She smiled at something and began to type.

J.B. Joseph Bartholomew. That's him.

"J.B."

Rocky looked up at her, something in April's voice signaling that she was interested. "He was killed last year. Why?"

April knew better than to share Deana's secret with Rocky. She shook her head. "Nothing. I just heard her mention brothers and I didn't know she had any."

Rocky studied April. April kept her face neutral, meeting her gaze.

April decided to stop talking before she gave away too much. Like the fact that Mary Lou had never claimed her brother's ashes.

"So what time is the council meeting?"

CHAPTER 3

April left, promising to meet Rocky at the borough hall. The afternoon sun was so weak the air temperature seemed to have dropped another twenty degrees since she'd left the funeral home. She shivered as she tried to get her key into the frozen lock, and once inside, prayed that the car would start. Last week she'd been stranded when her car had sat too long outside Perkins and wouldn't start after lunch. That never happened in San Francisco.

April knew dinner would be waiting for her when she got home, but a steady diet of veal chops, pierogies and meatloaf was leaving her feeling overstuffed, slow and cranky. She'd dreamt last night of a giant green salad of organic arugula with Sonoma County goat cheese and grilled Alaskan salmon. Fat chance that was on the menu tonight.

Barring that, she'd have liked nothing better than to microwave herself a frozen diet dinner, but Charlotte wouldn't hear of it. She'd have spent all afternoon cooking dinner, starting preparations almost as soon as the breakfast dishes were cleared.

She stopped at the mailbox at the end of the road, pulled out the day's offerings and then continued up the drive. Parking next to Charlotte and Grizz's snow-covered sedan, she ran for the door, telling herself that Charlotte's homemade bread made up for her tasteless, greasy fried chicken. She stamped her cold feet and let herself in.

"Hi, Charlotte. Hi, Grizz." April yelled to be heard over Fox News. Charlotte bustled over to take her coat, brushing it with her hand and hanging it in the closet. April sat down to take off her boots and lined them up on the plastic tray Charlotte had set out.

Grizz was ensconced in the middle of the barn, his corduroy recliner looking as faded as his flannel shirt. Charlotte had tried to cover the worst of the stains with her homemade afghans, but still the chair was an affront to the discerning eye. Any eye that was open, really.

"Dinner in fifteen minutes, dear," Charlotte said. Grizz grunted. It was only five o'clock, but April knew he'd have eaten earlier if it weren't for her.

The barn used to be wide open and too big for her. Her lowly futon had sat in the space like a forgotten garage sale item. She could have ridden her bike in there when she'd first moved in. Heck, she could have parked her car in the open floor plan.

Now every available bit of floor space was taken up with the Campbells' stuff. A large bed sat in the far corner. Huge carved dressers, one with a fancy mirror, sat where April had had a TV and her futon. A card table with a puzzle on it was permanently set up in the dining area. Two couches and two recliners and a ten-year-old large-screen TV filled the rest of the space.

April had been relegated to the loft.

She seated herself at the kitchen table, her hand automatically rubbing the grain. She loved feeling the softness of the wood. The table was the one piece of furniture her father had left behind when he and Vince moved out of the barn. It wouldn't fit in their new place. Mitch had been commissioned to make it, before she knew him. It was the first piece of his she'd ever seen, and she loved feeling the warmth of it beneath her fingers. She sorted through the day's mail, separating hers and the Campbells'. A prettily adorned blue envelope caught her eye. The back flap had been embossed and stamped with a white crystal snowflake design.

"Fifteenth Annual Mid-January Blast Event," the front read. Inside were directions to Mary Lou's house and the time and date. Sunday, in the late afternoon.

Mary Lou had talked about this party last week at stamping. A party would be a nice break in the routine of winter. Good conversation. A warm fire. And Mary Lou probably had access to great food.

Grizz sat down next to her. April looked up, surprised to see him in the unfamiliar spot. Was she sitting in his seat? She checked, but no. He was seated in Charlotte's usual chair. That was disconcerting enough, but he seemed to want to talk to her directly. Unprecedented.

His mouth worked, as if he couldn't quite get started. April looked over his head at Charlotte. Grizz was the silent type. She knew he and Charlotte communicated, but she didn't see it often. He seemed to use a series of hand gestures and grunts to tell her what he needed. After sixty years of marriage, they didn't need to say much.

Grizz talked even less to April. He sometimes asked Charlotte what April was doing or why she was doing something but rarely seemed satisfied with the answer.

She'd gotten used to his ways and didn't take it personally. He was in his eighties after all and had had little contact with women her age. He didn't seem to know how to behave.

But here he was.

"Come here," he said gruffly. "I want to show you something."

Charlotte was smiling, her soft face crinkling around her eyes, her cheeks ringed with wrinkles. April looked to her for some kind of clue, but Charlotte pressed her hands in front of her lips and shook her head.

April pushed away from the table self-consciously. Both sets of eyes were on her. When she turned to look into the barn, she saw a draped shape on the coffee table.

Charlotte clapped her hands once in excitement. Grizz shot her a look, but she ignored it.

"Go ahead," he said, urging April forward. "It's for you."

April looked questioningly from one to the other. Charlotte swept her hand toward the thing with a grand flourish. Grizz tapped his toe impatiently.

April pulled off the tablecloth. Underneath was a lovely wooden lap desk. No, a drafting table. It had a slanted top. A lamp was clamped to one side. The top was made of a combination of woods, reddish cherry and oak, so that the colors were rich and deep with the hues of an old wood forest.

"For me?" she said.

Grizz grunted. He must have used up his quota of words.

Charlotte couldn't contain herself any longer. "He made it for you," she said. She looked at Grizz with pride. "He didn't even tell me he was working on it. He's been out in the shed for weeks. He could only do a little at a time because it's been so cold."

Grizz was watching April. She let the joy she felt show on her face so that he could see how pleased she was. Her old drafting table, her favorite possession in the world, had been dismantled when the Campbells moved in. There wasn't enough floor space.

"You made this?" April said. "Grizz, this is beautiful."

This could go up to the loft with her. She would be able to work on the bed, sitting with this on her lap. The slanted top would make it easy to draw on. No more leaning on her knees to sketch.

"Open it," Grizz said.

April complied. The top was hinged and opened to reveal a series of cubbyholes inside the desk. He'd gouged out pencil holders and a place for erasers.

"He does wonderful work, doesn't he?" Charlotte said. She was so proud. It was cute.

"I love it," April said. "Thank you so much."

She couldn't believe Grizz had built her this gift. He'd obviously spent a lot of time, not just on the building but the planning as well. Grizz had really thought out how she worked and figured out a way to accommodate her needs. She hadn't thought he'd been paying any attention to her at all.

April took two steps to Grizz, her arms extended for a hug. He frowned and looked down. Charlotte made a noise, and he lifted his head. April moved in and enveloped him quickly. He stepped back and patted her shoulder awkwardly.

"You're welcome," he said.

Charlotte moved in and took April into her arms, pulling her close to her cushiony bosom. "You work so hard, and you've been so good to us. We're happy to do something nice for you for a change."

April felt tears prick her lids. She hadn't wanted the Campbells to move in. Now she felt selfish and silly for her complaints.

They were really a sweet couple who were caught up in a terrible situation. It was the least she could do to help them out.

"Dinner," Grizz said. April laughed and went to set the table.

After supper, she met Rocky outside the old building that housed the Aldenville borough government. The room that held the public meetings was up a flight of stairs. Hospital green paint, which looked as though it had been applied long before April was born, covered the stairwell walls and continued into the meeting space.

Two long tables pushed together at the front of the room made a dais of sorts. Rows of chairs were set up facing the front, giving the impression that a twelve-step meeting was about to take place. There were posters tacked to the wall exalting people to "Thrive" and "Strive" and to "Drive Slow Now That School Is Back."

There weren't many people in the seats, so she and Rocky sat down near the door.

April felt the hairs prick on her neck as if someone was staring at her. Officer Henry Yost was leaning against the back wall in the corner, one foot propped up behind him. She had never seen him in civilian clothes. In a flannel shirt and thermal Henley, he looked almost normal. When she caught his eye, he was leaning over to say something to the woman next to him.

Henry Yost had probably been telling her what a pain

in the butt April was. April had stepped into two of his investigations in the last year, and rather than appreciating that justice had been done, he channeled his energies into harassing her. He liked to stop her for minor traffic infractions. Last week he had cited her for going too slow, even though she was following a piece of snow-removal equipment that was blocking the roadway.

She nudged Rocky. "Yostie's got himself a girlfriend?"

Maybe if he had other interests in his life, he'd leave her alone.

Rocky looked over. "Could be. He had a wife and kids once upon a time, but I think she ditched him."

April snuck another look at the woman next to Yost. She might have been pretty once, but she was too thin now. Her pronounced jaw was bracketed by ears that stuck out through hanks of wiry hair. Her hands were jammed into her pockets. She was wearing an oversize navy peacoat and pegged pants tucked into furry boots. She looked a little familiar, but since returning to Aldenville, April often saw faces she thought she knew. Younger brothers of schoolmates, former teachers grown old, and all sorts of others whose vaguely familiar appearance was probably the result of DNA that had been replicated too often in this small town.

A woman with a laptop sat off to their right under an American flag. The county seal was painted on the wall, along with the Aldenville crest. Four council members filed in from a small room at the top of the stairs.

One of them was Mary Lou's husband and business partner, Peter Rosen. He straightened the legal pad in front of him and took out a pen. He nodded at someone to April's right. She looked back and saw Yost nod in return.

The meeting was called to order. April tuned out as the old business was dispatched. She pulled out a sketchbook and pencil from her purse. She'd had some ideas since this afternoon and began work on a border stamp of tumbling snowmen, trying out different proportions.

A sharp noise brought her out of her trance. The council chair had pounded the gavel. The atmosphere in the room was charged, as if everyone had rubbed their feet on the carpet and built up static electricity.

Rocky bumped April's arm as she sat forward, leaning her elbows on her knees. Something in the proceedings had changed. Voices were raised, and someone clapped, once.

"What's going on?" April asked. She glanced around as if she'd just woken up. Sketching could do that to her. She looked down to see she'd filled several pages but had no recollection of time passing.

Rocky hid her hand behind her curtain of hair and spoke into it. "It's a dang blessed tie. Two members want to vote out the local police and two want to merge with the other townships."

A council member was speaking. She was a large woman who hadn't taken off her white fur-lined cape when she sat down. She looked like an ice princess from a Russian fairy tale.

"While we understand the beauty of having someone local policing our streets, it's a luxury we can no longer afford. The economic strain that it puts on our budget disadvantages all the citizens."

Her chins sunk into the depths of her collar when she finished speaking.

Peter Rosen said, "Aldenville is a safe place because of our local police force. Our youth are church-going, studious children. Drugs are not a problem."

"What about the meth-lab explosion last year?" someone shouted from the audience. April, looking behind her, didn't see who said it, but she caught sight of Yost as he shifted his posture. He no longer slouched. Cop mode. He put a hand on his hip, as if going for his gun. She couldn't tell if he was actually armed. His expression was guarded.

"Meth-lab explosion?" April whispered.

Rocky shifted in her chair. She ignored April's question. "We're never going to get our hearing if they keep going on about the police."

"Don't you care?" April said. If there were bad guys making illegal drugs in the valley, perhaps getting rid of the police was not such a good idea.   •

Rocky shrugged. "Not really. The state police do most of the heavy lifting. Yost and the chief do more traffic control than anything. I just want the council to quit pussyfooting around and *do* something."

She raised her voice with the last couple of words. In response, Peter's head snapped up, and he whispered to the chair sitting next to him.

The chair banged his gavel and said, "We are at an impasse. I'm tabling this discussion until next month when Councilman Monroe returns from the Caymans. Let's get an update on the Ice Festival."

The small crowd shifted and stopped their chatter.

"We've had a request from one of local businesses to sell her wares at the Ice Festival."

The cape woman said, "We don't sell goods at the Ice Festival."

Rocky said loudly, "What about the hot chocolate booth and the chili?"

"Run by the Girl Scouts and the Friends of the Library, respectively. Nonprofits. The money goes to help those organizations." She looked to the chair as if asking him to move the conversation along to the next agenda item. "No for-profit businesses allowed.

"Chuck's Sporting Goods is always there," Rocky contended.

The chair said, "He gives demonstrations and hands out free samples. Do you have giveaways?"

"Heck, no," Rocky said. "Stamping Sisters can barely afford to stay in business. I'll go under if I give away stuff."

"You may display your products and hand out whatever information you want, but no sales."

The chair banged his gavel and called for the next order of business. Rocky and April beat a hasty retreat as the council took up the question of a noisy dog groomer.

They clattered down the steps. "Well, that was interesting," April said.

Rocky was not in the mood for small talk. "Whatever. Listen, I'm going to call a special meeting of the stampers. We'll do samples of cards, three or four collages. Suzi can do some burn-out scarves with the stamps."

Rocky had her phone open and was composing an e-mail as she talked.

"Let's meet at my place on Wednesday. Bring the new stamps. I can decorate the booth with the samples. I'll garner some attention for Stamping Sisters one way or the other. Nobody said I can't recruit new folks to sell the stamps at the bleeding Ice Festival."

"Wednesday?" April said. It was Friday. That gave April only five days to work up a line of stamps. That wasn't much time to think up ideas that were original, distinctive.

Rocky looked up, surprised. "Welcome to the world of retail, girlfriend. We have to take advantage of this opportunity. What's the problem? I once did fourteen collages in a day to satisfy a customer. You do what you have to do."

April sighed. Rocky was right. The more stamps Rocky sold, the more money April made. She needed to fill the tank with heating oil in another three weeks or so. Each fill-up cost nearly a thousand dollars and lasted two months. The barn with its senior residents was not exactly energy efficient.

They parted ways in the bank parking lot, and April turned on her phone.

"I got the new chain saw," Mitch crowed on April's voice mail. "You're not going to believe how lightweight it is. And it starts so fast. I can't wait to see you with this baby in your arms. Where are you?"

CHAPTER 4

When she got to the barn, Mitch was in her driveway, carrying a faux leather bag. She could see how excited he was, walking back and forth. April held out her phone.

"Is that what you're on about? You got a new chain saw?" she said. It was tough getting excited about a new chain saw, but she was trying. That's what it meant to be a girlfriend: get excited about stuff you had no interest in whatsoever. Like ice sculpting. At least he wasn't into stock car racing or Dungeons and Dragons.

"I did, and while I was there, Chet showed me this." He held up the bag as if it were a prize turkey in the annual Thanksgiving hunt. "It's so light, you'll be able to handle it with no trouble."

She took the bag from his outstretched arm. She zipped open the large industrial zipper and peeked inside. Whatever it was, it was pink. Hot pink. This was her day for unexpected gifts.

She looked up at him for an explanation.

He was grinning like a kid. Her first response was a weakening of the knees because his smile changed his face, making all of his features fit together in a new way. His dimples got deeper, and his eyes twinkled. The cleft in his chin deepened. She liked a happy Mitch. Liked it a lot.

She pulled out the little chain saw. Mitch admired it. "This is going to be a snap for you. You carve stamps all the time. This isn't that much different."

April was dubious. "My X-Acto doesn't have a plug. Or chains. Or make noise."

"That's the best part. You rev this baby up, and varoom, you know you're alive." He shouted the last couple of words because he'd pulled the lawn-mower-type cord and started the motor. He held up the saw like a psycho from a slasher movie and grinned.

April had to laugh. Mitch was as far from Jason as you could get. "Mitch, I don't know anything about carving ice."

"Homework, baby, homework. We'll have to study every night." He sidled in for a kiss, still revving the chain saw. April leaned back until he turned it off and then kissed him quickly.

She could see this was not a fight she was going to win. She might as well embrace it.

"It's going to be fun," Mitch said, his voice unfortunately sounding a lot like Jack Nicholson's in *The Shining*.

"I'll try," she said. "But it sounds cold."

"We have ways of warming you up," Mitch said.

A thick layer of clouds meant that night had arrived by four o'clock when the party started, but Mary Lou's house was ablaze when Mitch and April pulled up. Paper bag

luminaries lit up the walkway to the front door of her center hall Colonial. The porch columns were barber-poled
with twinkle lights.

The night air was so cold that April grabbed Mitch's
arm for comfort when he opened her door. He hauled her
out of the Jeep and tucked her hand under his arm. She
pushed the other one in her pocket and put her head down.
Mary Lou's house sat on a rise, and the wind was howling.
April began to rethink her prejudice against earmuffs.

"Why don't you have more clothes on?" she asked him.
Mitch was dressed in a turtleneck sweater and jeans. No
coat or hat. April felt the frigid air bite through her full-
length wool coat as though it were made of seersucker.

"Not cold," he said simply.

She gave him a gentle shove but pulled him back quickly
as she needed his body heat.

"Am I going to know anyone at this party?" Mitch said.

"You'll probably know more people than me," April
said. Mitch's ties to the town and valley were generations
deep.

"But it's a newcomer party," Mitch said.

"The stampers will all be here."

April had been here for stamping events, but this was
the first time Mitch had been to Mary Lou's. He only knew
her through April and his sister.

Mary Lou's husband, Peter, opened the front door and ush-
ered them in, telling them to lay their coats in the computer
room just off the foyer. It was a cozy room, walls filled with
wood built-ins. Framed citations told of the couples' success
as Realtors. They'd been members of the million-dollar-
listing club for years. Not an easy feat when the average
home price in the valley was under two hundred thousand.

From the sounds of the noises coming from the other
room, the party was well under way.

April pulled Mitch in for a quick kiss.

"Let's do this," Mitch said with forced enthusiasm.

The entire first floor was filled with people. The formal living room was to their left, and the two couches that flanked the fireplace were filled. People stood around the dining room, picking at the stuffed mushrooms and spanakopita. April spotted chocolate-covered strawberries. Leave it to Mary Lou to find berries in the dead of winter. She felt herself salivate.

April and Mitch followed the flow into the kitchen where he set down the bottle of wine they'd brought. April hoped it suited Mary Lou's taste. She'd picked it because she liked the label. Selection at the state liquor store was shockingly meager. And expensive. As a girl used to cheap California wines, she suffered severe sticker shock.

April waved to Kit, who was standing next to a group of women her age across the large family room that opened off the country kitchen. The twins were nowhere to be seen. Kit waved back.

A waiter dressed in a white shirt and black pants offered them drinks. April took a sip from her glass. It was some kind of punch. It tasted good, so she'd have to watch herself. Drinks that tasted like Kool-Aid were her downfall.

A tall man nudged Mitch, nearly spilling his drink. He'd been given a drink that was brown and manly, not pink.

"Winchester, you up for a rematch? Ready for me to kick your butt?"

The florid man took Mitch's proffered hand and managed to turn it into an elbow twisting greeting that Mitch endured with a tight smile.

Looked as though Mitch knew someone here after all. April didn't recognize the guy but figured it was a club thing. The members of the country club seemed to love tournaments as much as they did cabernet. There were the

spring and fall golf classics, and tennis tournaments every
weekend in the summer. Even in January, there were Risk
or Scrabble tournaments. Mitch was a competitive guy, but
April hadn't thought he'd signed up for the latest tournament. She thought she'd heard it was a video game round-
robin. Not his thing.

Mitch had manners, though. "April, this is Buck Sienstra. He's the holder of the Aldenville Cup. For now."

Buck took her hand and pumped it. "Your buddy here
has never managed to beat my team. Too bad."

Mitch smiled. "This year I have a secret weapon, Bucko.
Don't you worry about me."

"Chain saws at dawn, my man. Chain saws at dawn.
See you on the twenty-fifth." Buck jiggled Mitch's shoulder
heartily and disappeared into the crowd.

Rocky and Suzi came up and exchanged hugs and kisses
with Mitch and April. Suzi had dressed up for the occa-
sion. She was wearing a cardigan with a garden theme,
blue corduroys and a red turtleneck. A charm shaped like
a trowel dangled from a gold chain. Spring couldn't come
fast enough for Suzi.

Rocky was all in black, except for a swath of color at
her neck.

"Quite the party, yes?" Rocky said.

April surveyed the room. Mary Lou's family room was
massive, at least thirty feet long and twenty feet across.
A huge brick fireplace dominated the far wall. The fire was
lit with tiers of candles. Mary Lou had cut snowflakes from
bright white paper and hung them from the ceiling in a
faux blizzard.

The end of the room closest to the kitchen had a bar top
and five stools, which were all occupied. Two red leather
sectionals were covered with bodies. People seemed to be

standing on every available inch of hardwood. The noise of conversation made it necessary to shout.

"Do you know any of these people?" April asked Rocky.

Rocky was wearing a hand-knitted long scarf as a shawl. She draped one end across her neck as she spoke, winding the ends around and around. The wool was gorgeous, pinks and reds, boucles and mohair. April snuck a touch as the piece passed her. It was as soft as it looked.

Rocky said, "Most of them are people Mary Lou and Peter sold a house to."

"This year?" April said. There were at least sixty couples here. It seemed unlikely that that many new people had moved in since last year.

"No," Suzi said. "Once you're on Mary Lou's list, you never get taken off. She just keeps adding."

That explained the number of people. Some were young couples, probably just starting out in their first home. Others were older, probably retirees who'd downsized.

Mary Lou steamed toward them, carrying a casserole dish. The tangy smell of barbecue sauce followed her.

"April," Mary Lou said, stopping briefly. "I haven't forgotten about looking for a rental for you. I downloaded a list. Come by the office tomorrow."

Mitch's head snapped around. "A rental?" He didn't look angry, just surprised.

Mary Lou powered on past them into the kitchen. April stuttered. "I'm . . ."

Kit came up behind them, throwing her arm around Suzi and forcing the three women into a group hug. She didn't know how grateful April was for the interruption. Mitch hadn't been kept in the loop about April's plans. She'd been waiting to see if anything was available that she liked before having that talk.

Suzi said, "What's this your mother tells me? You've got a new house?"

"A foreclosure, right?" Rocky said. "I bet she got a sweet deal."

April pulled back to look at Kit. Mary Lou had been talking about all the foreclosures in the valley for months.

Kit's face grew troubled. "Yeah, Mom and Logan surprised me."

She didn't look too happy to April.

"Where is it?"

"Out Dowling Road, in fact, a couple miles past your farm," Kit said.

"Way out there?" Rocky said.

Kit's mouth twitched. Rocky'd hit a nerve. "I'd been hoping to be closer to town. With the twins, you know. But it's nice. Three-bedroom ranch." Her shoulders slumped. "It needs a lot of work."

Mitch said, "Well, if you need any help . . ."

Kit smiled, glancing at her mother, who'd just returned with a silver ice bucket. She turned her smile up a watt, but it still looked fake. "We'll get it done. Logan and I are going to be working night and day for the next week. The babies are staying with his mother."

Rocky directed Mitch to a waiter carrying a plate of stuffed mushrooms. The two of them followed him into the family room. Suzi drifted away, following a conversation about the borough council meeting.

Kit looked guiltily at her mother across the room and leaned into April. "I know I should be more grateful but the place was trashed by the last owners. They pulled out the stove, smashed the bathtub."

April put an arm around Kit. Kit took a deep breath, swiped at the tears that had leaked through, and leaned away. "It's just not the place I'd pick. I wanted a two-story farmhouse on a town lot." She took another breath, then said quickly, "I'll be fine."

April looked to see what Kit had seen that had changed her demeanor. Mary Lou had noticed their heads together and was heading their way.

She didn't look happy. "Kit, please refill the punch bowl," she said. Kit moved away and went into the kitchen. Mary Lou turned away.

April muttered, "Why do I feel like *I* did something wrong?"

Suzi, standing nearby, overheard April's remark and said, "She's a bear when it comes to her family."

And yet her brother's ashes live in a beautiful box in the funeral home's basement, April thought. It just didn't make sense.

CHAPTER 5

The door opened and a cold wind blew in. April felt Rocky stiffen next to her. "Oh, lordy, let the good times roll," she drawled.

April looked around the crowd of partygoers and saw Officer Henry Yost enter. Her favorite neighborhood cop. She sighed.

"I wonder why he's here," Mitch said.

"Following me. Everywhere I go, I run into him," April said. "He was at the council meeting last night giving me the evil eye. Did I tell you last week he gave me a ticket for going twenty in a twenty-five-mile-an-hour zone?"

Mitch patted her arm. "Henry just needs more to do. This town is too quiet for him."

"Is that why the council is voting to get rid of him?" she asked.

Mary Lou appeared in front of the fireplace. She clapped her hands twice. The loud sound was lost in the din of conversation, but as people noticed her standing there, they quieted. April looked around. The crowd was suddenly all women. The men seemed to have vanished.

Mary Lou spoke earnestly. "I have a special treat for you tonight. Most of you know Officer Yost, the town's preeminent law enforcement officer. He offered to speak about the safety of our community. He has years of experience with neighborhood policing, and he has joined up with Rosen Homes Realty to offer his services to you individually. His feeling, and mine, is that if he knows you, knows your name, learns your children's names, he can offer his best services."

"I'd keep him away from your sixteen year old daughters," Rocky whispered.

April laughed. She knew she was being mean, but Yost had never been a friend to her family and was an easy target to boot. He was incompetent and inept, with an overinflated sense of importance.

Yost took his place in front next to Mary Lou. He was wearing his dress uniform with black leather knee-high boots like a motorcycle cop would wear. His hat was a version of the Smokey the Bear hat worn by the state troopers. His badge was shiny, as was his leather belt and holster. Image was everything to Yost. Considering he had to pay for all of it himself, it was an impressive outfit.

Mary Lou asked people to find a seat and get comfortable. Her son, Connor, home from college, had set up a computer to display a slide show on the wide-screen TV. A title card flashed: "How to Be a Good Neighbor."

The newcomers seemed to be impressed.

"He's working hard to save his job," April said. "Maybe if he frightens the housewives into calling the cops every time they see a stranger, he can change the council's mind."

He started by talking about the dangers of not being aware of one's surroundings. Self-defense was key. He just happened to be offering a course for women in protection techniques.

Rocky said, "Ranger Rick is milking it. Or is he more Dudley Do-Right?"

A woman with a tall ponytail turned and shushed Rocky. April giggled. The thought of Yost being more interesting than Rocky was ridiculous.

But she had to admit the crowd appeared to be fascinated. Yost was pandering to their fears. He talked about the two break-ins as if the Jesse James gang had suddenly come alive and started robbing houses. Not that a traveling salesman had left his laptop in his car in plain sight. Or that a boyfriend had broken into his girlfriend's apartment and taken the TV he'd paid for. Not exactly like living in the Tenderloin.

Yost said, "You need to make sure to secure your premises. Don't leave your garage open when you're at home. If you're working in the backyard, lock your front door."

Most people in Aldenville were more in danger of a raccoon trashing their house by coming in through the cat door than an actual burglar. But Yost wouldn't be in business without fear. Fear was what drove people to call the police.

"Secure premises," Rocky said in a funny voice.

"Got it," April said, laughing.

The older generation in Aldenville didn't lock their doors most of the time. April had come home many times to find Grizz and Charlotte asleep in their recliners with the front door wide open. She couldn't decide if she felt more or less safe because they never bolted the door. She didn't want to invite trouble, but it was nice to feel it unnecessary to lock up tight.

"Is there a drug problem in town?" an earnest-looking woman with long earrings and a sparkly headband asked. Her brow was deeply furrowed as she sipped her red wine. The oversize glass was filled.

"Drugs have not been an issue," Yost said. He'd succeeded in scaring the natives.

"What about the meth house that exploded last winter?" April said, not quite loud enough to be heard by Yost. A woman close to her reared back and shot her a look. Rocky smiled, full of teeth.

"Let's get out of here," Rocky said. She'd heard enough.

"Outside?" April asked hopefully.

"Have you forgotten its five degrees out?" Mitch said, putting an arm around her shoulder and pulling her close. "You'll freeze your cute little California butt off."

"That's true." She had forgotten. It was going to take more than one winter for her to forget that going outside was not an option for several months unless there were skis strapped to her feet and down enveloping her body. And, quite possibly, earmuffs.

"We can go in the basement," Rocky whispered. "There's a huge rec room downstairs."

April followed Rocky, trying to sneak away without Yost noticing. He wouldn't be above heckling her like a comedian calling out to a bathroom-goer. People parted reluctantly, craning over their heads to see the next slide. A big-haired woman grumbled as Mitch stepped on her foot. Finally they saw the carpeted set of stairs leading from the kitchen to the lower level.

The threesome clambered down the steps as if someone were after them.

The stairs ended at a wall covered in blue denim. They turned the corner and went down three more steps. April couldn't believe her eyes. The room was filled with guys.

"Wow," April said. "So this is where all the men got to."

"I didn't get the memo," Mitch said. "This is unbelievable."

They stopped in place, overwhelmed by the space. To say the rec room was decorated in a sports theme was like saying the Taj Mahal was ornate. Every sport was represented. There were pennants from Penn State strung prayer-flag style from the ceiling. The walls were painted in Yankee blue and white pinstripes. A Philadelphia Eagles helmet had been made into a lamp. Hockey jerseys were framed like precious art.

They heard the crack from the pool table before they noticed it. Mitch practically skipped into the room. "What an awesome man cave," Mitch said admiringly.

"Maybe we should start doing team logo stamps," Rocky said, her head swiveling.

"Thanks, but no." April shuddered. There was probably money to be made, but she didn't want to be the one making stamps like that. There was no room for creativity in that world.

April's eye roamed over the velour pit sofa, the gigantic television that was playing a pregame show, sound muted. The neon lines of the jukebox played across the ceiling. An antique Pong arcade game stood in one corner, the ball bouncing mesmerizingly across the screen.

The effect was the design equivalent of a dog whistle, a décor appreciated only by the male gender.

Rocky nudged her, pointing with her chin. Across the room, an old-fashioned pine bar with a tufted, nail-headed red pleather front had empty bar stools. A kegerator was barely visible through a thicket of men holding beer steins. Mary Lou would never allow that upstairs.

"No wonder Yost has a captive audience," April said.

They made their way across the room. Mitch tripped over his feet as he tried to take it all in.

They sat at the bar, catching their breath. No one was bartending, so they helped themselves to glasses of wine from the open bottle.

Rocky grabbed a pool cue from the rack on the wall and sashayed over to the pool table. "I've got winner," she said to the two guys playing.

"You can play now," one of them said, checking Rocky out thoroughly. She grinned at his perusal. He was young for her and married, judging by the ring on his finger, but that wouldn't stop her from flirting.

The other bowed with a flourish. "By all means, break," he said as the married guy racked up a new game. Rocky grinned and put a ten-dollar bill on the table's edge.

"Winner takes all," she said, wriggling herself into position. Most of the men in the room stopped to take notice of her butt. She stayed there longer than she needed to, then stroked the cue.

"Think there's any unattached men in the room?" April whispered to Mitch.

"Let's hope so," he said.

April and Mitch were on an active hunt for a boyfriend for Rocky. She was spending too much of their time with them. April looked around. She hadn't been single long enough to develop any instincts for who was married and who was not, but she looked for wedding bands and well-pressed shirts.

She saw Kit's husband. He was dressed in a fisherman's knit pullover with neatly pressed jeans. His hair was swooped up in the front with gel. April left Mitch watching his sister play pool and went over to say hi.

She slowed as she got closer, realizing she was interrupting a conversation about guns.

April had forgotten what a staple a gun cabinet was in a Pennsylvania home. Lovingly made of the finest hardwoods, decorated with brass hardware and leaded glass, the locked cabinet had a permanent home in many living rooms, like a breakfront or hutch. Logan had this one open and was showing another guy about his age a pair of pearl-handled small revolvers.

He pointed one down at the floor and said, "You never know what kind of whackos you'll meet out at a property. Mary Lou has had to run off more than one squatter. She told this one guy she would shoot him. First in the right one, then the left one . . ."

He stopped when he saw April approach. "Don't worry; they're not loaded."

She took a step closer, and he offered her one of the guns to hold. She picked one from his upturned palm. It was lightweight. And pretty. A vine design twined around the barrel.

"Twenty-two?" she asked. Ed had taught her to use a gun as soon as she'd turned thirteen. She'd been to a range in Marin a few times when she lived in California, but not for several years.

"Yeah, girly guns," Logan said disparagingly. "If she ever shot this, that mother-of-pearl on the handle would crack."

He opened the cabinet and put away the guns in their wooden case and set it back on the shelf. He took out a shotgun.

"My new pump action," he said, laying the gun lovingly in his friend's arms, who grunted in admiration. "Just got it."

"Looks expensive," April said, wondering how he'd afforded it with new twins.

"My wife's telling me I have to leave it here when we move into the new place," Logan said with the exasperation of a newlywed unused to compromise. "She doesn't want any guns in the house." He took it from his friend and locked the gun cabinet, using a key on a chain heavy with keys. His friend wandered off after offering to bring Logan a refill. Logan refused.

April asked, "How long have you and Kit been together?" He must have always been interested in guns.

"Off and on, since high school."

She could ask him about Mary Lou's brother. There was no chance down here of Mary Lou overhearing and getting the wrong idea. "So did you know Kit's uncle? The one who died?"

Logan shrugged. "J.D.? Sure I know him. I spent most of my senior year of high school in this house. He was living here back then."

Kit was twenty-one, so that was about four years ago.

"Didn't he work?" April asked. She kept an eye on the steps for signs of Mary Lou. She didn't want her to know she was asking about her brother, but this was her chance to find out.

"Off and on. He was working at the lumberyard for a while. Then at a gas station. He was good with motorcycles, not much else. He never had much of a career or anything. Mary Lou kept him busy. She always has odd jobs to do at her houses. Ripping out old carpet, putting down new stuff. Shoveling the walks in the winter, keeping the lawn green in the summer. I do the odd jobs for her now."

A roar went up from the pool table. Mitch called her over. "Rocky's run the table."

She walked over. April raised her eyebrows at Rocky's success. "Why doesn't that surprise me?" she said.

Logan joined them. "Rocky is pretty coordinated," Logan said. "She beat me at Donkey Kong the last time we had a party here."

April said, raising her voice, "She has a major advantage. She's old enough to have been around for the original game."

"I heard that," Rocky said, mock threatening her with a pool cue. "Rack 'em," she said to her brother.

"I'm not playing you," Mitch said. "I like to keep my money."

"I know, brother, I know." She made a challenge to the room, but no one was willing to take her on, so Rocky played by herself, methodically sending the balls into the pockets.

The sound on the TV suddenly came up, with the familiar music that meant the game was about to begin. A popcorn machine had been started, and the pervasive smell filled the air. This was about to become a serious football-viewing venue. April wanted to get out before the coin toss.

Mitch came over and kissed her neck, his eyes on the TV.

"You want to watch this?" she asked.

"I don't have to," he said, straining to hear the announcer. "It's the Steelers."

"You can," April said. "I'm going to go see if Mary Lou needs help."

"I'll be up in a while," Mitch said. April laughed. She didn't believe him. When she was ready to go home, she'd have to drag him out. He'd already followed Logan to an empty spot on the couch with a direct view of the TV. Not that there was any place in the room without a view of the TV.

Rocky downed a shot and raised the glass to April as she left the room.

Upstairs, Yost had thankfully finished his lecture on staying safe in Aldenville. April, for one, felt so much safer knowing he was on the job.

She joined Mary Lou and Deana in the kitchen. "What can I do?"

"I'm out of forks," Mary Lou said. "Everyone seems to be using two at a time. Is it too much to ask that people hang on to their forks for dessert?"

Deana and April looked at each other. "Probably," they said in unison.

Mary Lou smiled. "You're right. That was a little crazy."

"Everything okay?" April asked as Mary Lou handed her a pile of silverware to dry. "You seem out of sorts."

"I'm fine," Mary Lou said.

Deana caught April's eye and shook her head slightly. She was washing a glass plate that had held crudités. A pile of cream puffs was waiting to go on it. Mary Lou, opening a cupboard and the refrigerator simultaneously, grabbed a pile of paper doilies, indicating they should go on first. Deana complied.

Mary Lou went out of the room carrying a plate of deviled eggs and a basket of pretzels.

"What's up?" April said as she disappeared. "What's with the evil eye?"

"Were you going to ask Mary Lou about her brother?"

April popped a slice of jicama into her mouth. "Jeez, no. I'm just concerned about her. She and Kit are fighting. She bought a house for them that Kit's not crazy about."

Deana said, "She probably just wants the best for her grandchildren."

"Sounds to me like she needs to back off and let the kids find their way."

"I guess it's easier for those of us without children to see the right thing to do."

April looked at Deana and saw the sadness in her friend's stance. She knew that Mark and Deana had been trying to get pregnant for months now.

April put an arm around her friend. "Is it hard to see Kit and Logan, so young, with twins?"

Deana dried her hands. "I don't begrudge them, you understand."

"I get it." April said, her voice catching. Deana deserved babies, lots of them, and it did seem unfair that she wasn't getting pregnant as easily as she wanted. She and Mark were settled, making a good income at jobs that they loved. Their home had plenty of bedrooms waiting to be filled. Logan and Kit were living on the edge of poverty. Kit had a two-year degree in medical transcription from Penn State Lynwood but hadn't worked for nearly a year. April was sure Logan didn't make much. She did know that if it hadn't been for the foreclosure Mary Lou found them, they wouldn't be getting a house at all.

"I wonder if we waited too long," she said quietly. Mark, big and silent, appeared in the doorway. He seemed to know exactly when his wife was in need of a hug.

April smiled at the sight of the two of them. Mark didn't say much. He just took the dish towel from her hand and pulled her into his chest.

"You two will make pretty babies," April said. "How many, six?"

"At least," Mark said over Deana's head. She giggled.

"Pretty and smart," April said. "Girls, so that Mark can be all wrapped around their fingers and I can teach them how to carve stamps and flirt with boys."

"They won't be allowed boys until they're thirty-one," Mark said.

"If my parents followed that rule, you and I would never have married," Deana said. She gave him a push and went back to filling the plate with desserts. April put the silverware into the special holder Mary Lou had set out.

Deana offered Mark a cream puff. He ate it off her

fingers, smacking his lips. She grinned at him and handed him the full plate with instructions to put it on the dining room table. She washed her hands again.

April said, "You're just tired. You need a vacation. You and Mark need a week off. Can you take one?"

"That would be nice. I thought Dad was coming up for a few days next week to give us a break, but he's stuck in Florida. A bridge tournament. Mark and I will go to the city for an overnight or something."

She straightened her shoulders and smiled brightly at her friend. The tears in Deana's eyes stayed there, willed not to fall.

"We'll be okay. I'm starting a new yoga class. That'll help."

April saw the opportunity to lighten the conversation. "Help what? With the relaxation or is this about some sexual positions I don't want to know about? Like in order to get pregnant, you'll have to be able to put your legs over your head."

Deana giggled. April knew she could get her to laugh outright if she kept going. She grabbed the heel of her foot and twisted it around her back, shifting to her left hand and grimacing wildly. She leaned against the counter so she didn't fall.

Deana howled with laughter. Her eyes danced as her gaze shifted to the doorway. Mark was back, the empty platter in his hand. His eyes were wide.

April said, "Deana was just telling me about some of the sexual positions you two have to utilize to get pregnant."

"I wasn't!" Deana said, although she was laughing.

Mark didn't miss a beat. "Did you tell her about the one where I have to hang onto the ceiling fan? First I have to grab her like this . . ."

Mark pulled Deana onto his shoulder and picked her up, caveman style. She gasped for air, and wriggled.

"And then what?" April said, egging Mark on. She knew Deana wouldn't really protest; she was having a good time.

"That's enough, you two," Deana said. She let out a yelp as Mark deposited her on the kitchen counter. He pretended to mash on her, snuffling into her neck like a rutting elephant. April's side hurt from laughing.

"Looks like all the fun is going on in the kitchen," a snarky voice said from the doorway. April wheeled to see Yost filling the space.

Deana jumped down and pulled on her shirt, which had come untucked from her jeans. Leave it to Yost to spoil the mood.

Mark was undaunted. He pulled himself up on the counter and laid a hand on Deana's thigh. Her breathing calmed, and she leaned into Mark's legs.

"Just showing April how we old married couples keep it spicy," Mark said.

Deana hiccupped. April giggled again. Yost frowned, getting the fact that he didn't belong.

April said, "Did you get everyone equipped with mace and stun guns? Tell them to triple lock their doors and get a burglary alarm system? When are you running the next gun safety class?" she asked.

"Would you like a lesson?" Yost said. "I could take you out to the range, and we could fire off a few rounds." He made his offer sound dirty.

April looked from Mark to Deana. Suddenly, their play felt over-the-top and slightly ridiculous. Sexual, not just innocent fun. Yost made everything he touched turn unseemly.

"I'm sure the newcomers appreciated your view of life

here," Deana said. She didn't like Yost, but as she was the newest deputy coroner, she did have to deal with him. Deana believed that everyone had a little good in them, if they just had a chance to shine.

"Unless they turn tail and leave the neighborhood," April said.

"Well, as long as Mary Lou gets the business, right?" Yost replied snidely. "Sell them the house on the way in and sell the house when they leave. Isn't that how real estate works?"

April said, "Is that why you don't mind a house explosion or two? Keeps the local Realtors happy?"

Her heart sank as she saw Mary Lou stop, just outside the door. She was carrying a pile of dirty plates. She stared at April, her mouth hanging slightly open as if she couldn't believe what she'd just heard.

April felt ashamed. She always let Yost push her buttons. "Mary Lou, I didn't mean you." She searched for an explanation. "I've heard meth is a problem."

"Not around here," Yost said. "Maybe back in Californication where you come from."

April felt her face flush. "What about the explosion last year? Wasn't that because of someone making methamphetamine?"

Mary Lou's face froze with her hostess smile in place. Her eyes darkened. She glared at April.

Rocky and Mitch had come up from the basement and stepped into the already crowded kitchen. April saw Peter, Mary Lou's husband, behind her.

Deana leaned in and whispered in April's ear, "Maybe you should dial it down a notch."

"Why? If there's meth around, shouldn't people know? What about it, Officer Yost," she said, raising her voice so all could hear her. This sanctimonious prick.

"There was no evidence of a meth-making operation," Yost said.

"No evidence because it all blew up," April said.

Mary Lou was shooting daggers at her now. April knew she shouldn't talk about it here. She was messing up Mary Lou's perfect soiree. People didn't buy bigger houses and move their friends into neighborhoods where there were drug problems.

But it seemed to her that if Yost was really concerned about doing his job, he'd be concerned about all illegal activity.

Rocky pulled on her sleeve. "Leave it alone," she said.

"Are you quite positive that no one else has started making meth?" April wondered if Yost would know how to break up a ring of meth makers. Meth had been a hot-button issue in California. April remembered reading about damage done in the rural forests of Northern California, streams ruined by the toxic runoff.

Yost was glowering at her now, and Mary Lou's newcomers had begun to back away. Yost left her with no reason.

"April," Rocky said. April had just taken in a deep breath, ready to go one more round with Yost. She could show him up for the fool he was. Something in Rocky's voice made her stop. She let the air out of her lungs and faced Rocky.

"What?"

Rocky leaned over her, blocking April from view with her hair. She whispered softly, "That's how Mary Lou's brother died," Rocky said. "In that house."

April glanced up at Mary Lou, who was escaping into the dining room.

She'd had no idea. "In the meth house?"

That did explain the cremains. Certainly there couldn't be much left for burial.

April felt her stomach churn. She hadn't meant to hurt Mary Lou. She looked up, but Mary Lou had turned her back and was disappearing into the crowd. April heard her voice, low and purring, but she could see from the stiffness in her shoulders that she was furious.

She turned to Rocky. She glanced at Deana and Mitch. Their heads were hung low. "Are you telling me her brother was making meth?"

"Not really. I think he was more of an errand boy. He was never a druggie, just a drunk."

Mitch came up behind her and kissed her ear. "Ready to go?" he said.

"I need to go say good-bye to Mary Lou first," April said, watching her friend as she herded her guests into the family room for a nightcap.

"Maybe not tonight," Mitch said. "You can call her tomorrow."

April glanced from Rocky to Deana and Mark. They all looked disappointed in her.

"I didn't know," she said. "I didn't know."

CHAPTER 6

"I didn't know," April said to Mitch *for the tenth time since* they'd gotten in the car. They were only a half mile from Mary Lou's place. April kept looking behind them, as if she could still see the house and know what was going on.

"There was no way you could have. You were in California."

"Deana could have told me, instead of making it seem like a state secret."

Mitch repeated himself. "You couldn't have known. Mary Lou's just hurting. She won't stay mad."

April wasn't so sure. Mary Lou could hold a grudge. There were several Realtors in town that she'd cut out of her business because of their sketchy dealings. April didn't want to be cut out of the stamping group. She liked Mary Lou, Suzi, Rocky, and Deana. They were her closest friends here. If she didn't have those women in her life, Aldenville wouldn't be a fun place to be.

Mitch put a hand on her thigh, reminding her of one big reason Aldenville felt like a great place to live. He smiled at her, chucking her under the chin, a move that would have warranted a slap away if attempted by anyone else.

She grabbed his fingers and squeezed. The returned pressure felt like sustenance.

"She can't stay angry with you," Mitch reiterated.

"*You* can't stay angry with me," she countered.

He sensed a change in her mood and furthered it along by kissing her fingertips. "So true."

He drove with one hand, twirling the steering wheel with his pinky. April felt herself softening. She didn't want to think about what she'd just done to Mary Lou. She wanted to obliterate the reaction she'd seen on her friend's face.

Mitch was at the end of the road. "Right or left? Are you coming home with me?"

They'd planned on ending their evening in front of his fireplace. Now the decision had to be made. Left to Mitch's. Right to the barn. Left to mind-altering ministrations from Mitch. Right to home and nonstop recriminations. There was really no choice.

"Promise to ply me with drink?"

"My best scotch is at your disposal."

"Promise me to make me forget what a jerk I just was?"

"I have the method in mind," he said.

"Promise to drive me home in a few hours?"

"I will." With his right hand, he tapped out a rhythm on her knee. "You won't be sorry. I built a fire. It's all ready to go." His voice grew low and teasing. "Just one match, and whoosh . . ."

April's thigh heated up where his fingertips now rested.

His touch held a lot of promise. They'd be at his house in a few minutes. The house would be toasty, warm enough to get rid of the layers of clothes she was wearing.

"Drive faster," she said.

April woke up late. Mitch had dropped her off at about two A.M. What sky she could see from the clerestory windows high above her in the loft was pale. The sun might not make an appearance at all from the looks of the cloud cover.

She could hear the usual midmorning noises coming from downstairs. The TV was on. Charlotte opened the refrigerator slowly, trying to be quiet as she got their early lunch started. She'd hate it if she knew her attempts to stifle herself were more annoying to April than a steady stream of noise would be. She held her breath waiting for the refrigerator to make the final squeak. It took forever.

April had hoped that ideas for the stamps for Rocky's new line would come to her in the night. She often set her mind in gear before falling asleep and came up with wonderful ideas in those moments just before she fully woke up. Last night was not one of those times.

Maybe it was the subject matter. Winter was not an inspiration to her. This winter had been too harsh, too restrictive, too cold for her to enjoy and want to memorialize in stamps. She tried to come up with pictures in her head that reflected the beauty, but nothing was coming.

The real reason was how badly she felt about mouthing off at Mary Lou's. She couldn't stop thinking about it, wishing she had said something else.

But it was curious. Mary Lou was the last person she'd expect to have a brother who had died in a meth-lab explosion. It was hard to believe Mary Lou had a criminal in the family. She was so straight.

The purse guns that Logan had showed April took on a new meaning now.

Even so, she hadn't meant to rub Mary Lou's nose in it. She couldn't have known the facts, but still, she had hurt Mary Lou. She needed to make amends quickly.

She would go to Mary Lou's office for the list of rental houses and talk to her there.

April threw off her duvet. The loft was too warm, victim of the seniors downstairs in charge of the thermostat. She tried not to think of the heating oil they were burning as she started down her ladder.

Charlotte greeted her with a smile. She got up out of her recliner and headed to the kitchen, trying to beat April to the counter. "I didn't know if you wanted coffee," she said.

"I'll get it," April said. "Sit down."

Charlotte parked herself at the kitchen table, watching April as she got down a mug and a cereal bowl.

"Want eggs?"

April held her hand up. "I'm just going to have instant oatmeal."

Charlotte settled back like a cartoon bird on a nest. "Are you having dinner with Mitchell, dear?"

"Yes, he's cooking."

Grizz harrumphed from the other room, whether at Mitch's cooking or something Maury Povich said, she wasn't sure.

April finished off the soy milk. A trip to the store was in her future. Since the weather had turned so cold and snowy, she did all the shopping. Charlotte and Grizz hadn't left the house in probably three weeks.

"Do you have a grocery list for me?" she asked.

Charlotte produced one from her apron pocket.

"I've got some work to do, and then I'll run errands."

"Thank you, sweetie pie."

April went back up to the loft after her shower and drew for an hour. She never hit her stride, feeling like she was trying to force something that wasn't coming.

She gave up and headed out for her errands.

Mary Lou's real estate office sat in an old home at the edge of the development she and her husband had built twenty years earlier. Her own house was visible on a hill that overlooked both. April pulled into the small asphalt parking lot.

The door opened into a small reception office. A middle-aged woman with tightly controlled curly hair smiled at her.

"Can I help you?"

"Mary Lou here?"

"No, I'm sorry, she's not."

April was disappointed. She'd hoped to get to Mary Lou right away and apologize. She didn't want this to fester. "Okay. Do you have an envelope for me? April Buchert? She said she would pull together a list of rentals for me."

The receptionist looked through a pile of papers on her desk. The door to the inner office opened and closed. Logan, Kit's husband, came through.

"April? You taken care of?"

The receptionist shot him a look of pure resentment. "Got it covered, Logan," she said, not looking up from her task.

"You working?" April asked.

"Yeah. Going out to make the rounds. Make sure no pipes burst over the weekend."

"That's nice," April said. From the exasperated expression of the receptionist, April got the feeling Logan was padding his importance.

"I don't see anything with your name on it, Miss Buchert."

Again, April was disappointed. She wanted to get started looking for a new place.

Logan came forward, perching himself behind the receptionist on the desk return. He ignored her pointed look and swung his legs. "Whatcha need?"

"Your mother-in-law said she had a list of houses for rent. I want to start looking at what's available."

"I can take you to a few."

"I'd rather go by myself. Mary Lou said she'd give me the lockbox key."

She didn't need an escort. Especially Logan.

"Wait here," he said, jumping off the desk and going back into the inner sanctum. April could see a giant mahogany desk and credenza. Pictures of Kit and the twins filled the walls. Mary Lou's office.

The receptionist smiled slightly. The phone rang, and she answered it. April knew when she was being dismissed. April had thrown her lot in with Logan, and the receptionist was miffed.

"Here you go," Logan said.

The receptionist looked over, trying to see what was in his hand. He palmed the page and gave April a key.

"I put my cell number up on top. If you need anything, just call. This key will get you into all of these. These are all foreclosures, so they're empty."

April glanced at the list. There were ten houses listed. A lot of the descriptions were abbreviated, and she wasn't sure what they meant.

She could go home and look at them on Google Earth and see if any suited her needs. Perfect.

"Thanks, Logan." She nodded to the surly receptionist and let herself out. On to the IGA.

She was only about halfway through Charlotte's grocery list when she heard her name being called.

"April? April Buchert?"

April turned her head. She'd not gotten used to how

small Aldenville was. She must not have changed much
since she was sixteen; she was always running into people
who knew her parents and recognized her.

She plastered a fake smile and prepared to meet yet
another aging friend of her parents. Last week, it had had
been Dumpy, the Presbyterian minister. The week before,
she'd been mortified in the frozen food aisle by her kin-
dergarten teacher gushing about April's artistic talents at
age five.

The woman in front of her looked to be at least fifty. Her
hair was lank, and there were scabs on the backs of her hands
that appeared to have been picked many times over and never
allowed to heal. When the woman opened her mouth to talk,
April was shocked to see broken and brown teeth.

Alarmed, April took a step back.

"It's me, Violet."

April shook her head. She didn't remember this person.
She started to walk away, but the woman wasn't finished.

"Violet Wysocki."

Violet *Wysocki*? April could barely keep her jaw from
dropping. Of course she should have made the connection.
Not too many people were named after a crayon. But this
person was so far from the girl she'd known.

Violet had been her very first best friend. Daughter of
the town's most popular general practitioner, she'd been
pampered and cosseted her entire life. Naturally blonde
and predatorily perky, she'd ruled every class they'd ever
been in together, starting in first grade. She and April had
been inseparable until about fifth grade, when Violet began
to change. By the time they got to high school, Deana and
April were tight, and Violet, queen of the mean girls,
wouldn't give her a second glance. When Ed had come
out, ruining April's senior year, Violet had ignored April
entirely.

She had been the most talented kid in the school. She'd nailed the highest pikes in cheer, got the best grades in math, and sang the lead in all the school plays.

What had happened to her? She looked older than her own mother. Take that back. Her mother, who April remembered as a tight frosted-hair version of her daughter, would never let herself look like this. Not this.

"I saw you at the council meeting," Violet said.

April struggled until she realized this was the woman Yost had been with. She'd blended into the woodwork there. Violet's hand shook as she offered it to April. She was so thin, April was afraid to press too hard as she accepted.

Was it anorexia? Violet had been overly concerned about her weight in high school, but April didn't think anorexia could do this to a person.

A woman in a disability cart beeped at them to get past. Violet drew her over to the side of the aisle.

"How are you?" she asked, but her eyes wouldn't light on April's, and she didn't really sound like she wanted to know everything. She glanced over her shoulder several times.

"Well, I've moved back."

"I heard."

"It's great," April said, trying to end the conversation as fast as she could. The smell coming from her mouth of rotting teeth was awful. Standing this close to her was not an option. "But I'm in a hurry. Catch up another time?"

"Call me," Violet said, wagging her thumb and index finger. "I'm at my dad's." April nodded politely. The woman walked away. Her steps were mincing as though her feet hurt. It was painful to watch her.

April didn't think she was going to be calling her anytime soon.

April went home, helped Charlotte put things in the

cupboards, and went back up to the loft to work. She tried to get the picture of a ruined Violet out of her mind but couldn't help but notice her sketches of icy mountains resembled broken teeth. Doggedly, she put her mind on hold and drew without thought. An angry Mary Lou made a mental appearance. April kept drawing until finally she was lost in the process.

Her cell phone rang, breaking her hard-earned concentration. From the backlit readout, it was nearly four o'clock. She had managed to work for several hours. She paged through the sketchbook to see if anything was worth keeping as she answered.

"April, can you come over?"

April didn't recognize the voice at first. "Kit?" she asked.

While April liked Kit, Kit was not the kind of friend that she expected to get a call from. She saw Kit sometimes at stamping, although since the twins had been born, she hadn't seen much of her at all. And after the scene at the party last night, she'd figured none of the Rosens would be talking to her.

"Are you at your mother's?" April asked. She still needed to talk to Mary Lou. She'd left a message that so far hadn't been returned.

"I am over at the new house. I'm sanding the kitchen cupboards."

"Do you need help?" April asked. Perhaps Kit wanted her expert opinion on decorating.

"I've got something I want you to see. Can you come over in a half an hour?"

April realized the girl sounded excited. Maybe she'd found something to like about the house after all.

"Okay, give me the address."

April clicked off her cell phone. Kit must be really

bothered by her trouble with her mother. April was glad the girl had called her for some advice.

She had the computer open to Google Earth in antici-pation of looking up the addresses Logan had given her. She searched for directions to Kit's house. She thought she knew where she was going but wanted to make sure. It was a rural route address. Like Kit said, the house was isolated, set back from the road and with a pig farm on one side and fields across the street. Looked like the nearest human neighbor was a quarter mile away.

April grabbed her purse and her keys. She followed the directions she'd downloaded from the Internet. Kit's new house was several miles on the Dowling Road, past Suzi's nursery. The homes thinned once past Suzi's. Long stretches of empty snow-covered land appeared, prob-ably farms. The road was cleared, although piles of snow encroached from the shoulders and made the road more narrow than usual.

A pair of deer crossed the road in front of her. Her foot came off the accelerator. Ed's voice rang in her ear. If there's two, there's more. Slow down and watch carefully.

Her father was right. A smaller deer bounded across the road, leaving fluffy bursts of snow in her wake.

She drove slowly. The snow looked deeper out here, and the road wasn't cleared to two full lanes. If she met another car head on, she'd wind up in a snowbank.

She could see how a young mother wouldn't want to be this far away from town. Still, she wouldn't mind living out here. It was quiet and peaceful. She caught sight of a cardinal, sitting on a snow-covered branch. He flew off as she approached, and snow flew up in bursts.

Mitch's house was only ten minutes away across the valley. After being in close quarters with the Campbells for the past three months, April relished the idea of no neighbors. She could work all night if she wanted, play her music loudly. She missed being able to blast her MP3 player. In the nice weather, she could work outside.

She found Kit's place, but there was no car in the drive. April was early. She had to pull in as mounds of snow made it dangerous to park in the street. She left plenty of room for Kit to park behind her.

The house was a long redbrick ranch, probably built in the sixties. Not much in the way of charm. Just a functional space. The walk was neatly shoveled, the last snowfall piled high along the drive. Logan's doing. April walked to the back of the house, following a neatly shoveled walk around to a windblown deck. The property seemed to go back several hundred yards. Woods stood at the far end, and she imagined she heard water. A babbling brook.

Something colorful stood out against the deck railing. April went to investigate. She found several brightly colored pieces of paper. Rocky was always looking for odd bits of texture to add to her collages. April picked up the papers and stuck them in her pocket. They were an odd shape, but she couldn't figure out what they were.

Why wasn't Kit here? She checked her watch. It'd been thirty-five minutes since she called. April stomped her feet. Her toes were beginning to get cold. She tried to force some blood into them by doing a little shuffle step.

She heard a car door slam and went back to the front of the house. Kit was getting out and hurried up the driveway. She put a key in the lock of the front door and let them both in.

"Sorry, April," she said. "I just ran out to get a few things. Have you been waiting long? You must be freezing." Kit was talking quickly. April couldn't tell if the color in her cheeks was from the cold or excitement, but she seemed pent up about something. The kid looked much happier than she had at the party.

April hurried inside. Kit closed the door quickly. She was carrying several IGA bags. They took off their boots and went into the kitchen. The house was cold, and Kit turned on a space heater as soon as she'd laid down her packages on the plywood countertop.

Gold-patterned linoleum covered the floor, curling up under the kick plate of the cabinets. The doors to the cupboards were off, standing in rows, leaning against each other and the back wall. They were in various stages of being stripped. A small hand sander was plugged into the socket and lay on the floor.

That wall still had the original wallpaper, a green and brown design featuring coffee grinders and other old-fashioned kitchen tools divided by rows of cross-stitched exes. A wooden sawhorse had been set up in the middle of the room. It was topped with a full sheet of plywood and covered with paintbrushes and other tools.

"Welcome to our humble abode. I'll be appearing here all week. Logan and I are going to pull an all-nighter. He'll be here in a couple of hours after he puts the kids to bed at his mother's."

"Are you liking it better?"

"Not really. I just decided I don't care."

She didn't look like someone who didn't care. Something else must have happened to make her this happy.

"But that's not why I called you. I wanted to talk to you about my uncle."

April's face fell. Her inexcusable behavior last night had hurt Kit, too. "Listen, I'm sorry. I didn't know. I've been trying to call your mother all day to apologize.

Kit pulled out a kielbasa and a hunk of cheese from the

grocery bag. "My mother needs to stop trying to control everyone's behavior."

April pointed to the food. "You didn't need to feed me. Mitch is expecting me for dinner. This looks like an expensive snack."

Kit had bought a new paring knife and was unwrapping it. "It *was* expensive. Logan's going to have a fit when he sees the charge. But it's not for you."

She twirled around. Her eyes were lit with excitement. She was brandishing the tiny knife. April stepped back.

"It's for my uncle. He's coming here."

"Your uncle's dead," April said slowly. She looked at Kit's pupils. The light wasn't great in here, but they didn't seem to be dilated. She decided to say something harsh, to snap her out of it. "I saw his cremains at Deana's."

Kit shook her head. "That's just it. He's not. He's alive."

CHAPTER 7

Kit had slashes of bright color high on her cheeks and her eyes were glowing. Was she on something? Did she even know what she was saying? Did she think J.B. was truly alive?

"Kit, really. I know it's not easy to accept his death, but . . ."

Kit sighed and began slicing the sausage, using a paper plate for a cutting board. "I know it's kind of silly. He loves kielbasa and cheddar. With beer, of course. But he's not drinking anymore, so no beer. I thought about getting the nonalcoholic stuff, but then I thought why even tempt him?"

April watched, growing more dismayed as the girl rambled. What if this was hormonal? Kit had six-month-old twins. It might be some kind of postpartum depression or something. April was the last person equipped to deal with that. She mentally ran down a list of people she could call. Deana might know what to do.

"You must miss him terribly," she said quietly. It seemed like speaking softly was the right thing to do.

Kit looked up and said at a normal volume, "Listen. I'm not crazy."

"I'm sure it feels like your uncle is everywhere . . ." April began.

"No, seriously. April, he's alive. It wasn't him in the meth-lab explosion."

"How can that be? Didn't they find his body?"

"They found his truck and his license in the glove compartment. The house had burned to the ground. They didn't find much that was identifiable," Kit said.

She looked away, staring at an icicle outside her kitchen window. Her gutters must have been blocked because the icicle was as thick as her forearm and tapered to a sharp, dripping point. April thought about how much it would hurt if it fell on someone.

"My uncle wasn't making meth, April, he wasn't. He'd started going to AA as soon as he knew I was pregnant. Said he wanted to be awake and aware to enjoy my babies."

Kit's voice broke then, and a sob escaped. She stuffed her hand into her mouth. April put a hand on Kit's shaking shoulder.

"Kit, do you want me to call your mother?" She took out her cell phone and began scrolling for Mary Lou's number.

"No!" Kit took April's cell away from her. "We're not telling my mother about this. He won't come if we do."

Her face was like a young child's. April could see what Kit must have looked like as a five-year-old, throwing a tantrum at the IGA because her mother wouldn't buy her an Elmo balloon. Her lips were pursed, her eyes steely.

"What do you mean?"

Kit opened her eyes. "He wants to talk to me. Only me."

April searched Kit's face. Her cheeks were flushed,

and her fingers nervously scratched the surface of the cell phone. Underneath the ruddy blush, her skin was as pale as the icicle hanging from the roof.

"No one can know he's coming," Kit said. She laid down the phone out of April's reach and went back to arranging circles of kielbasa on a paper plate. "He's waiting until after dark. If Yost or the state police catch him, he'll get thrown in jail. We have to do this on the q.t."

April looked out the window. Darkness came quickly and early on these cloudy days. The sky was already dusky outside. Within the half hour, it would be inky black. The darkness unsettled April even more.

"How can you be sure it's him? What if it's some kind of hoax?" April couldn't hide her concern.

"It's not." Kit was calm, her hands busy with the snack she was making. She stopped suddenly and looked around the kitchen. "We've got no place to sit. There are some folding chairs in the basement. Would you go down and get them?"

Kit pointed to a door off the kitchen. She grabbed a wipe from her purse and cleaned off her hands. "I've got an empty five-gallon pail we can use for a table."

April looked at her in amazement. Kit was acting like her mother. The perfect hostess. The fact that the house was in a complete uproar didn't stop that entertaining gene from surfacing.

Why wasn't Mary Lou here? April paused in front of the door.

"Why me? Why ask me to come here?"

"I promised J.B. I wouldn't tell anyone yet. But I didn't want to be alone. You see things that others don't see. You have insights."

April blushed. Kit was flattering her, she knew. But it was somewhat true. She had had a knack for getting to the bottom of mysterious doings around Aldenville.

She wanted to kick Kit for making her a part of this. Mary Lou would have a fit if she knew. April found a light switch and went down the basement stairs. The stairs were wooden, and the walls were plain cinder block. She stepped slowly, scanning for the promised folding chairs.

The room was a sea of black plastic.

All she could see were trash bags, filled to capacity. Wow. These kids really have been busy, she thought. She finally spotted the chairs against the wall at the bottom of the stairs and wrestled three upstairs.

Kit had covered the bucket with a piece of fabric and stuck a candle in the middle on a small plate. She'd lit the candle. April was touched by the effort to make the place look fancy.

She took one of the chairs from April and set it up, fussing with the position. April set the other two out and let Kit arrange them. She looked to April, her need for approval nakedly apparent. "How'd I do? These are the old curtains I found in a closet, and the candle was left behind in the bathroom."

April smiled. "It looks great."

Headlights raked across the ceiling. Tires crunched on the driveway.

"He's here." Kit flew to the front door and yanked it open.

"Be . . . careful," April finished as Kit flipped on the porch light. Outside, it was as dark as the deepest night, even thought it was barely suppertime.

She looked back at April and beamed. "It's him. I'd recognize him anywhere."

She flew outside to meet the man getting out of the car, even as April tried to grab her back into the house. The temperature had dropped again, and the porch steps might be icy. But Kit was young and impervious to the dangerous cold as she flung herself into the man's arms.

He'd parked behind Kit's car. With the door open and the dome light on, April got a glimpse of a man slightly taller than Kit.

Out on the road, a car slowed. April couldn't see the driver, but she was suddenly aware that a supposedly dead man was in Kit's front yard. One wanted by the police.

"Come in here, you two," she hissed, holding the door open. "Now." They complied.

"Are you okay?" she heard Kit say as they crossed the threshold.

"I'm so sorry, Kitten. I never meant for you to suffer."

They ignored April as J.B. wrapped his arms around Kit. Kit rested her head on his shoulder and sighed. April hadn't sighed like that since she was in high school. She shut the door behind them.

Kit broke away from him. She held on to his hand and turned to April. "This is my uncle," Kit said. "J.B. Hunsinger."

He was skinny legged, with a belly bulging under his plaid shirt. He wore a red thermal Henley shirt underneath, probably for warmth as the flannel looked thin and worn through in spots. His jeans were Wranglers. He had inexpensive fur-lined ankle boots. This was a man who did his shopping at Walmart. Unlike Mary Lou, who traveled to Philadelphia to shop.

J.B. reached over and shook April's hand. He seemed a bit nervous to find someone else with Kit. He looked around her. "Is there anyone else here? I asked you not to tell anyone."

"Of course not. April's different. She won't tell anyone. I wanted her to hear your story. She can help you with the police, maybe."

April cocked her head at Kit. Seriously? Did this kid think she had a good relationship with the Aldenville police?

Kit directed them to the kitchen where she shyly pointed J.B. to the vignette she'd set up. He smiled at her, but J.B. didn't sit. He wandered around the room, touching the half-stripped wallpaper and testing the crooked miniblinds over the window. He walked on the balls of his feet, so he was in a jigging motion much of the time. He looked like someone who found it impossible to relax.

"So this place going to be okay for you?" he asked.

Kit laughed. "I guess. It's not a Victorian on Main Street, my dream house. But I guess those don't go into foreclosure that often."

His face changed, a storm cloud moving across his forehead quickly. Kit didn't notice the anger April saw. J.B. got himself under control, testing a kitchen drawer, keeping his face turned away from his niece.

"You look good," Kit said.

"I'm doing good, real good."

"Where have you been?"

"Not far away," J.B. said. "In Mountain Top."

Kit had just sat down, but she bounced back out of her seat. She faced him, her hands on her hips. "You've been, what, fifteen miles away this whole entire time? I thought you'd left the county at least."

J.B. used a soothing tone. "No, I've been staying with a friend."

Kit's eyes were huge. She settled back in, grabbing J.B.'s hand, pulling him away from the construction zone and over to where she sat. He sat in the folding chair opposite her. "But did you have money? Where did you live?"

"There was a little money, yes. It's been okay."

"Who died in the fire?" April asked.

Kit jutted her chin at April. She clearly didn't want April talking about the explosion.

J.B. lifted his eyes to hers. He didn't seem to miss much, and he was probably wondering what her role was. He glanced at Kit, who hadn't taken her hand out of his and was stroking it in her lap like a cat.

"Got pictures of the babies, Kit? I really need to know if the young'uns got my nose." His tone of voice was light, but to April's ear, a bit forced.

Kit laughed and grabbed her backpack off a hook on the wall next to the basement door. She pulled out a pocket-size photo album. The cover had been stamped and embossed. She pulled open the ribbon that bound the book and handed it to him.

The pain of losing her uncle was etched on her face. Rocky had told April she'd been in a precarious stage of her pregnancy when the explosion happened and very nearly miscarried. The joy and excitement of having twins had been tempered by the death of her favorite relative.

They bent their heads over the pictures. The two looked alike. Their hair color was almost exactly the same. J.B.'s hair was still thick, despite his forty-plus years, and it had natural highlights that April would have paid big bucks for. He wasn't overly thin. He looked like he'd had been well cared for.

April sat down in the third chair. They were in an awkward little circle with Kit's snacks untouched in the middle.

He hadn't answered her question about who had died in the fire. It would have had to have been a major conflagration to burn bodies down to ash, with no identifying remains. Of course, in this small town, no one was going to do DNA testing. It would be easy to misidentify the remains.

But if J.B. were alive, then some other family was missing their son.

"Everyone was so sad," Kit said, pointing at a picture of the babies' christening. "We missed you that day."

"Not everyone," J.B. said. J.B. picked up a round of kielbasa and ate it. "Your parents were happy to be rid of me. And your husband."

"No one wanted you dead," Kit said.

J.B. hung his head. "I was such a loser. I wouldn't blame them if they did."

"Why didn't you die that day?" April asked.

"I wasn't there when the house exploded."

"Your truck was there." Kit's voice was small. She was understanding something she didn't want to know.

J.B. sat back in his chair. He sipped the water Kit had poured for him. "I got involved with the wrong people. I got myself in a situation."

He wasn't being clear. April wanted him to tell Kit everything. She'd be better off if she knew exactly what he'd been doing.

"Were you making meth?" April asked. Kit looked up sharply. April might as well have smacked her across the face.

J.B. didn't look at April. He put his hand on Kit's knee. "I made some bad choices."

April made a snickering noise. J.B. glanced her way and sat back in his chair. He propped one leg up on the other and held on to his ankle.

"Look, I got to a position where I couldn't say no when people asked me to help them."

"People?" April asked. She was not going to let him get away with this obfuscating. He owed Kit an explanation.

He closed his eyes. "A gang. A meth-making gang,"

he said. He spoke slowly as though the truth was painful. "There were two other guys that cooked in that house. I was the smurf, the one who buys the legal drugs they need to make the stuff. Cold medicine, over-the-counter stuff. Not a big deal to buy, unless you want quantity, which is what they needed. The drugs are regulated, so I would drive all over to different stores. I'd go into New York, New Jersey and get the stuff. It took me all day most days to obtain enough cold meds. They needed a lot."

April watched Kit carefully. She was hearing directly from the source. After this, she could have no doubt that her uncle had been involved in making meth.

"Didn't you use your truck?"

J.B. shrugged. "Sometimes. But I didn't want my truck to get known, so usually I took one of the cars they had laying around and left mine behind. That's what happened that day."

Kit was not reacting, just watching her uncle closely.

April said, "No one said anything about a missing car."

He laughed. It was curt. "It's not like they were registered or anything. The, um, gang always had a couple of cars around the place. Stolen with fake plates."

Besides, April thought, no one was left to complain. It's not like gang members could call the police. "Did you know who died?"

"Yes. When I left that morning, two guys were in the house. They were both Cretins—gang members. They knew the chance they were taking."

April said, "One person was identified. What about the other? Someone's family is missing that guy."

J.B. dropped his feet to the floor and leaned forward. April sat back, startled. "Look, for all I know they'd gone to the diner for food. Maybe no one was inside. Besides, those bangers had no family. They'd taken an oath to the gang. That's their only loyalty. Most of their families think they've been dead for years."

Nice justification. April knew he might be right, but still. Someone was dead who people thought was alive, and someone else, J.B., was thought to be dead but here he was living a life. Of some kind.

"Why didn't you come forward when you knew people thought *you* were dead?" April asked.

J.B. stiffened, and his chin jutted out. He looked like Kit when she'd told April about her uncle. Determined. Wrong, maybe, but in the moment, sure of their convictions.

Kit said, "April, leave him alone."

J.B. seemed to make a decision. He pushed off his knees and stood. "I'm going to get out of here," J.B. said, squeezing Kit's shoulder.

Kit jumped out of her seat. She gave April a hard look. This was her fault. "No, please don't go. Can't we just talk some more?"

She hugged him hard. He patted her back. "Let me go. Just for a little while. I'm going to be around, Kitten. I promise. I want to go tell your mother that I'm here."

"You're going to Mary Lou's?" April asked.

"You know my sister?" he said.

"I do," April said. "She's my friend." And she's really going to be shocked, April added mentally.

"Well, I'm taking a risk coming back into town, but I need to talk to my sister. Please don't tell anyone I've been here. I'll be able to come back for good real soon."

"You promise?" Kit asked.

"I do, Kitten, I do," J.B. said. "With all my heart."

He kissed Kit on the cheek, looking into her face. "You've grown up a lot in the last year," he said.

Death and pregnancy will do that to a girl, April thought.

She felt so protective toward Kit. She was angry at this guy for making everyone so miserable.

"Let me go straighten out a few things with your mother. We have a lot to talk over."

A flash of pain crossed his face. It looked as though his sister still had the ability to hurt him after all these years. He reached up to rub his eyes.

"See that?" Kit said, nudging April and pointing to a string bracelet on J.B.'s skinny wrist. It was faded and shabby. "I made it for him in tenth grade. I used to have one just like it," she said.

J.B. stopped as he was going out the door. He spoke slowly, as if just remembering something. "This was a foreclosure, right?"

"Yeah, my mother bought it from the bank."

"Did she know the family that lived here before?"

Kit shrugged. She pulled up the collar of his jacket in a touching maternal gesture. She patted his jacket front. "I don't know." She held his gaze. "You'll come back, right?" The competent mother of two was gone, replaced by a little girl afraid of the dark but soothed by her uncle's presence.

"I promise."

She hugged him close, her face hanging over his shoulder like a moon. April could see streaks of tears and felt her own throat close up.

J.B. went out the door. They heard the crunch of his boots on the snowy drive and his car starting up. Neither of them moved until they heard him pull away.

April went to Kit's side. She smoothed her hair, pushing it behind her ears and looking into Kit's face. "You okay?"

Kit nodded, rubbing at her face to dry her tears. "Feels like a dream."

"A good dream?"

Kit sighed. "Yes. A complicated one, but ultimately

good. My mother is going to be so mad," she said with a
little laugh.

"Mad doesn't begin to describe what your mother is
going to be." April thought a moment, then asked, "What
will you do now?"

"Work on the house. Even faster. Logan and I need to
get it ready." Kit grinned. "Just think. When I host my first
family party, my uncle will be here."

*April said good-bye and left. J.B. wasn't dead after all. Kit had
her uncle back, and soon Mary Lou would have her brother.
The twins would know him now. He seemed sober enough;
maybe he could clean up his act for good. He'd said he'd
stopped drinking, and if he could do that, who knew?
Maybe he could be the guy they needed.*

April pulled out, careful to watch for icy spots where
the water had lain during the day and then refrozen. The
roads could be treacherous in the dark even when it hadn't
snowed.

Her phone chirped with a text. "When are you going to
get here?" It was from Mitch, naturally.

She answered him with an "On my way."

There were only a few other cars on the road. Normal
people were home, wrapped up in blankets watching *The
Bachelor*. Light snow started to fall. She'd managed to
avoid driving in a snowstorm so far this winter, making
sure she was home or at Mitch's. She'd lost her talent for
driving on snow a long time ago. She'd only had her license
for one full winter before she'd graduated early and left for
San Francisco halfway through her senior year. Any skills
she'd had were long gone.

April felt her hands go clammy. She admonished herself. A few flakes weren't going to make the road slippery.

Suddenly headlights appeared on the road behind her. She'd just gone over a little rise, and the car behind was speeding downhill quickly. There was nowhere to get over out of the way. The roadway was already narrowed by drifts of snow on either side that would be as hard as a concrete wall.

April slowed, and the car came up even faster. At the very last minute, it pulled around her. Her heart rate slowed.

Cripes, that guy could have driven her off the road. Was he trying to make her have a wreck?

She was relieved when she pulled up to Mitch's ten minutes later. His house was brightly lit, and she could see from the chimney that he had a fire going. She wrapped her coat tightly around her and made a run for it.

Mitch had been expecting her. He was heating milk for hot chocolate.

"With or without?" he asked, holding the bottle of Baileys over her mug.

"Definitely with," April said. The warmer the better, the faster the better. Baileys would help.

"You're shaking. Are you okay?" he asked, dropping a dollop of the liqueur in her mug.

"Some jerk was playing chicken with me on Dowling Road."

"In this weather?" He indicated the flakes falling outside his window and put down the bottle. He put his arms around her and hugged her tight. Her feet came off the ground and a giggle squeezed out of her.

Mitch kissed her eyelids and handed her a cup of hot cocoa. "How about a bath before dinner?" he said.

This was the worst part of being with Mitch. The ride home. She had to leave his nice warm bed and get into the freezing cold.

"Stay," Mitch said, his mouth tight with the effort of keeping his eyes open. He threw a heavy arm over the down comforter, but she scooted out of his grasp. As her feet hit the hardwood, the feel of the cold surface made her eyes pop wide open. The sensation reminded her of when she was a kid and her foot had come out of her snow boot that had stuck in a snowbank.

She scooted back under the covers. "I've got to get home."

It was late. She steeled herself to throw off the covers again. Mitch beat her to it, tossing his side of the comforter over her.

She caught a glimpse of his bare back before he wrapped the extra blanket around his shoulders. Mitch staggered out of the bed, taking the top quilt with him. He headed toward the bathroom, she thought, but she didn't hear the toilet seat go up. A moment later, she heard her car start up.

She struggled to a sitting position and tried to gather her clothes without uncovering herself too much.

Mitch raced back into the room, yelping. "It's co-o-o-ld out there."

He sat down on the edge of the bed and belatedly put on his fur-lined slippers.

"Let the engine run for five minutes," Mitch said. "Or maybe ten."

What a guy. She'd been dreading getting into that frigid automobile. He was making her feel warm all over.

"Time enough for one more snuggle," he said, wrapping her in the quilt and gathering her onto his lap. He kissed her neck, but the tip of his nose was cold and she pulled away.

He fought her, trying to get her to lay down with him again. She pushed him off, placing a pillow over his head for good measure.

She said, "You're just making it worse. I can't stay. You know Charlotte won't fall asleep until I'm home. Their bed is practically in my face when I walk in the door."

"The barn is bigger than that."

She looked at the clock. "It doesn't feel like it at one in the morning when you are trying to sneak in like some kind of high schooler. I need to get dressed."

"Let me help," he said. He shook out her jeans and held them for her to put her feet in. Awkwardly, she lifted her butt and picked up one foot. Mitch tucked the quilt under his chin and reached his long arms around and grabbed her foot. April started to laugh. She felt like an overgrown toddler being dressed by her father.

"Quit wiggling," Mitch said, his voice muffled in her shoulder.

April giggled and stabbed her foot into the pants leg. The other was easier, and she stood up to snap them. Mitch popped her heavy sweater over her head.

"You're going to make a good dad someday," she said just as the mass of wool descended. The sweater had a huge turtleneck and her words were lost in it.

"What?" Mitch said.

She turned around to face him and kissed him. "Never mind. Just saying you take good care of me."

"You deserve it."

"And now you deserve a little pampering. Get back into bed. I'm capable of putting my shoes on. Thanks to you, the car will be nice and warm. Go on."

He obeyed, settling back on a pillow, crossing his arms behind his head. "Text me when you get home," he mumbled.

April put on her socks and boots and heard his breathing even out. He was falling asleep. She tiptoed through the door.

The snow had stopped, leaving only a slight dusting that blew away as she walked. No problem driving. This stuff was powdery.

Still, she pulled out too quickly, making the car fishtail at the bottom of the drive. Her poor Californian car was not used to its new big bad snow tires.

She turned on the radio to keep her company. A country-western station blared new country. She wasn't sure who. Kenny, Tracy, Chesney, Heaney. Something or other. They all sounded alike, but it was either this or the oldies station. She'd heard "I Will Survive" too many times this week.

April realized she'd never told Mitch about J.B. She'd have explaining to do when the news broke tomorrow. She'd blame him and his Three B's—bath, Baileys, back rub. He'd managed to obliterate her thinking mind within minutes of her stepping in the door. Perhaps a repeat performance would be required to remind him.

She passed only one car on the country road where Mitch lived and soon was at the turn to the major highway through town. She turned on her blinker, feeling silly as there was no one around to see it.

She did obey laws even when no cops were about. She'd been known to pay the bridge toll at the Delaware Water Gap even when the wooden arm was stuck in the upright position.

She'd always had a good relationship with the police before she moved back to Aldenville and met Officer Yost. They'd gotten off to a bad start her first day on her new job, and they hadn't recovered. Perhaps by obeying all the traffic rules, even when he was probably home, snug as a bug in his bed, she might win some karmic brownie points.

It was good that the roads were clear and empty. She was feeling so relaxed, her reaction times would be way off. Right now she wouldn't be able to sense danger. Whatever hormones Mitch had sent rushing through her body were making her feel like her skeleton had turned gelatinous. She smiled and glanced at the mirror, ducking away as she saw her reflection. She looked like an idiot, grinning at herself.

She couldn't help it. Being with Mitch, even for only a few hours at night, made her happy. Very happy.

A stop sign, with snow atop it like icing on a cake, loomed in front of her. She came to a complete stop. She was alone in the intersection.

She pulled out her phone. Mitch wouldn't get any real sleep until he knew she was home safe. She punched the message and sent it to his phone. "Home safe." A little white lie. He'd be able to get some serious rest now.

He took good care of her. The least she could do was return the favor.

She pulled onto the roadway. The terrain was so flat and empty that she could see the lights of the truckers on Interstate 80 just a mile or so to the east, driving on their parallel track. Maybe heading to the early morning markets in New York. Traffic moved swiftly. She enjoyed the feeling of company despite the fact that the cars and trucks were a mile away.

It felt good to have Mitch in her life. Had anyone ever cared about her the way Mitch did? By the end of their relationship, she and her ex, Ken, had led separate lives. He wouldn't have cared that she was driving alone late at night on a deserted road.

She'd thought she wouldn't like having someone to account to. But she'd been wrong. She liked calling Mitch when she woke up, during her lunch break and when she got home from work. They exchanged texts and IMs several times during the day. She thought she'd get sick of all the contact, but she never tired of opening her phone to see the smiling face he sent her or finding him online and getting a cheery "Hey!" from him.

She should have been to the Turkey Hill by now, and then the traffic signal. But she didn't see the bright lights. The road curved, and she realized she'd made a wrong turn. Nothing looked familiar. In the snow, landmarks were no longer recognizable. She must have turned off Mitch's road too early.

The hairs on April's arm tingled. She took in a breath and leaned forward, trying to guess where she was. The road was dark without many streetlights. Houses had been few and far between.

She considered turning around, but the snowbanks narrowed the roadway to two small lanes. She couldn't execute a three-point turn. If she tried, there was a distinct possibility that she'd end up in a ditch.

April felt a flutter of nervousness, and she swallowed hard to relieve it. This road would probably cross the valley parallel to the highway and bring her out to the other north-south road, the one that Deana lived on. She could easily find her way home from there.

She'd call Mitch. He'd reassure her she was on the right track. She reached for her cell and lost control of the wheel for an instant.

The car began to slide. Her headlights glinted off something metal ahead. She let the phone drop and made sure her hands were on ten and two just as her father had taught her. She gripped the wheel tighter and took her foot off the gas. She was careful not to brake. If the road was just a little bit icy, it would set her into a spin.

The bare trees along the side of the road were coming quickly at her. Her chest tightened. There was a line of brush on the shoulder, with a pine forest encroaching behind. She didn't want to go off the road. There could be a creek and ravine hidden under the snow.

Steer into it. Her father's voice came into her head. He'd taught her to drive. She saw a break in the snow cover, a gash all the way down to the mud. Her dad had told her that her hands would follow her eyes so it was important to keep looking straight ahead. Whatever was on the side of the road, she couldn't let it distract her now.

Her father's voice in her head was comforting. His teaching her to drive had been a nice time for both of them. He'd been a good teacher. She missed Ed. He and Vince had been gone several weeks and expected to stay in Florida for two more.

She pushed on the gas pedal and the car straightened. She skidded to a stop, half in the lane, half on the snowy shoulder.

As her lights illuminated the scene more, April's heart sunk. She *had* seen something off the road. The raw wound in the snow was tire tracks, half-filled with the latest accumulation. Someone had gone off the road like she almost had.

She flicked on her flashers. She leaned over her passenger seat and stared. Her headlights gave her a clear view. She could see where the car had left the road, but there were no footprints in the snow.

April listened but heard nothing but the distant rumble of cars on the interstate and the incessant burbling of a creek, which seemed to pay no mind to the dark and cold.

She opened her door and called out.

"Hello? Anyone there?"

There was no engine noise. Had the car been there long enough to have run out of gas? Or had it shut off when it skidded off the road? Snow had fallen on and off all night.

There was fresh snow in the tire tracks, but the accident could have happened anytime in the last couple of hours.

She heard a noise. A human sound. A groan. She stopped moving. The trees creaked in the wind. What had she heard? She couldn't be sure.

She got out, picking her way carefully. In the trunk of her car, along with a newly added forty-pound bag of kitty litter for traction and a folding shovel that Mitch had given her to dig herself out of ditches, was a high-powered flashlight leftover from the earthquake kit she'd carried back in San Francisco. Gone was the bottled water and rations. It struck her that an earthquake kit would be mighty handy in the event of getting stuck in a snowstorm, too.

An owl hooted in a nearby tree, causing her heart to pound and her feet to slip out from under her. She steadied herself. If someone was hurt inside that car, she needed to get help. She reached in for her phone, called 911 and reported the car off the road.

She grabbed the flashlight and stepped carefully across the frozen earth. She slipped once and cursed loudly. There were no houses along this stretch of road and no businesses. It was a wooded area with steep ravines and lots of undergrowth.

April held the flashlight over her head and caught a glimpse of the car at the bottom of a small embankment. She eased herself down, treading carefully. The snow here was crusty and slippery. There was no way to tell how deep it was without stepping through the brittle surface. She didn't want to end up knee-deep in snow.

April reached the back end of the car. It was nose down, surrounded by broken branches. She played the flashlight around until she found the driver's side. The car's front end was bashed in. The windshield had a point-of-impact break as though a head had hit it. She pulled on the door handle. The door was iced shut.

She circled, brushing away the accumulation on the windows, trying to see inside. It was light and powdery and flew easily away as soon as her mitten hit it, like tiny fireflies. She had the sensation that she was opening a secret cache. Like an archeologist brushing away sand to reveal the pharaoh's tomb.

It had to be a tomb. How could someone survive this crash? If they survived the impact, how could they stand the freezing temperatures?

She tugged harder and was gratified to hear something cracking. One last yank, girding herself against the ground and using all her strength, and the door gave way.

The nose-down position of the car prevented it from opening all the way. April squeezed into the small opening. There was no glass in the driver's side window. She could see a body tossed over the passenger seat like a no-longer beloved rag doll. She reached in to see if she could feel a pulse. As her hand wavered over the man's neck, a grunt came from his bloodstained lips.

April drew back her hand in shock. "Hey, can you hear me?"

There was no answer this time. April watched his chest and could see the rise and fall. His face was turned away from her, pushed into the plastic seat cushion. There was blood on the side of his face.

She thought about how cold he must be. Maybe the cold had helped him by slowing down his heart rate. Meant he didn't bleed out.

She tucked the flashlight under her arm and called the dispatcher back, her frozen fingers fumbling, barely able to push the last-called button. "There is someone alive in the car. I can see that he's breathing," April said.

"The EMTs are on their way. Are you visible from the road? You should be by your car."

April agreed to wait on the road.

She began to back herself out. Another sound, this time more like a sigh, came from the broken body. April couldn't leave him here alone. She had to offer whatever solace she could.

She moved back into position, squeezed between the door and the car frame. "I've called for help," she said. "They're on their way. Any moment now." She spoke softly.

His hand flopped like a fish, and she gasped. The movement seemed deliberate, not involuntary. He whispered something she couldn't understand. She tried to lean in further. The cold edge of the car cut her. He groaned again. April reached in to touch his arm, give him a bit of human contact. It wasn't much, but it was all she had to offer.

He was holding a business card. She loosened it from his fingers.

She realized there was no broken glass around him. None of the pellets she'd have expected to find from shattered safety glass.

She realized then that the side window wasn't broken out. It was rolled down. He'd been driving with his window down on a night when the weather was below zero. That didn't make sense.

Her eye caught the faded string braid on his wrist.

She backed up so quickly she hit her head on the door frame. "Ow!" she yelled before clamping down so hard on her lip that she bit it. She tasted the blood and felt her head throb.

She pointed her flashlight directly on his arm. The string bracelet was familiar. This was J.B., Kit's precious uncle. He'd lost control of his car, and he was hurt, bad. April looked to the road. She thought she heard help coming, realized all she was hearing was her own ragged breath.

She gulped, hard. Then she heard it for real. The siren that indicated that his rescuers had arrived.

"Down here," she yelled. She saw flashing lights. She climbed up the embankment a few feet, planting her feet and resting her back against a tree trunk. The night sky seemed to envelop her.

The clouds had moved on, leaving the clear night sky. So many stars. April looked up through bare branches and found Ursa Major. The order of the constellations, changing yet permanent, calmed her. The world was so vast there was no way to understand it all.

Like how J.B. had ended up in a ditch.

CHAPTER 8

April shined her flashlight so the EMTs could find her. One of them pulled her up from the embankment, his strong hand wrapping around hers. He told her to wait in her car and went down to see to their patient. The area was soon lit up with bright lights and the bustling activity of the people trying to save him.

April started her car and cranked up the heat. She tucked her hands in her pockets and leaned against the headrest. Her body ached from the cold.

As they put J.B. in the ambulance, April recognized one of the EMTs as the young woman who worked with Vince in Aldenville's volunteer fire department. She got out of her car and approached her.

"Is he going to be okay?"

"He's alive," she said grimly. She was stowing the equipment they'd finished with and didn't look at April. "Not stable, but alive."

"Did you find a driver's license?" she asked.

"The car registration. No license."

"That's not who he is. He's not that guy. His real name is J.B. Hunsinger."

She shrugged, her expression strobed by the flashing lights. "Our concern is saving his life, not identifying him. You can follow us to the hospital and talk to them there."

April got back in her car and pulled out behind the ambulance. They headed up the mountain to Lynwood General. The trip seemed to take only minutes.

She'd been born in this hospital but thankfully hadn't spent much time here since. Her parents were healthy and stayed away from doctors as a rule.

She went into the emergency room, the automatic doors making a whooshing sound as she entered. She found herself holding her breath, afraid to breathe in the sickness, the blood, the desperation that made people come to rooms like this. She heard a baby cry out from behind one of the curtains and winced.

April shook off her uneasiness. The best way to navigate places like this was to pretend like you knew where you were going. She kept her eyes straight, using only her peripheral vision to glance into the beds and see if the person lying there was J.B. The hospital was probably understaffed. No one challenged her.

He was in the last bed. The EMTs were talking to a doctor and a nurse. His breathing was labored. She saw again the family resemblance.

"Excuse me, are you with this man?"

April turned to see a nurse in the doorway. "I'm the one who found him."

"Please sit outside. We've not even begun working on him yet."

April backed out as the doctor and nurse approached his bedside. The young EMT fell into step alongside her.

"How's he doing?"

She shrugged. "If he has any family, I'd get them up here as soon as possible."

April stayed behind as the EMTs made their way back to their truck.

It was up to her to call Mary Lou. What was she going to say to her friend?

"Your brother, who you thought was dead, is dying." *"Sorry what I said about the meth house the other day, but now your brother is really, really hurt so you better get over here right away."*

April scrubbed at her face. She called Mary Lou. A man answered sleepily. "Who is this?"

"It's April Buchert, Peter. There's been a car accident. You should get Mary Lou up to Lynwood General as soon as you can. It's about her brother."

"What do you mean, her brother?"

So Peter hadn't seen J.B. this evening. April wondered if Mary Lou was keeping his visit secret. Not anymore.

"You should call Kit, too. And hurry. I don't know how long he's going to last."

She paced the foyer in front of the double doors to the emergency room. Icy blasts of cold, along with frightened people, came through every time the door opened. No one wanted to be in the emergency room.

Twenty minutes later, Mary Lou and Peter burst through the doors. They had thrown coats on over flannel pajamas and stuffed their feet into fur-lined boots.

Mary Lou stalked over to April, "What is going on?"

"It's your brother," April said. She looked for any sign that Mary Lou had seen her brother earlier.

Mary Lou stopped short and looked around the room

as if expecting a ghost to appear. "What are you talking about?" she hissed. "Didn't you get your kicks at my party? What's with you, April?"

The worst. J.B. hadn't gotten to Mary Lou's house. April took in a deep breath and talked as fast as she could.

"Your brother didn't die in that explosion last year. He's here in the emergency room. I happened on his car accident when I was going home from Mitch's."

"This isn't making any sense," Mary Lou said, her voice breaking with tension. She rubbed her upper arms as if she was cold. She looked to Peter. Her husband put an arm around her shoulder.

Kit and Logan burst through the doors. They were in paint-spattered jeans and sweatshirts.

"Mom? Dad? Where is he? Is J.B. okay?"

Mary Lou looked at her daughter with wide eyes. "What are you talking about? Your uncle is dead. You know that."

"Did you throw him out again?" Kit got close to her mother and spat the words at her. April took a step back. "It was your fault he was living on the streets and got involved with the meth gang in the first place. You wouldn't let him come back home after he rescued me from my bachelorette party."

Mary Lou shrugged off her husband's arm and took a step toward Kit. Kit stood her ground. Logan's eyes followed the two women, and finally, he moved next to Peter. It was obvious he was torn. Kit was his wife, Mary Lou his boss.

"Someday, Kit, you will understand what it is to make hard choices to protect your children. J.B. was a danger to you. I did what I had to do."

Kit's tears filled her eyes and dripped down her face. She pawed at her cheeks. "He was on his way to see you tonight. He wanted to come home. Instead, he ends up in the hospital. Did you kick him out again? If he dies, his death is on you."

Mary Lou started as though she'd been slapped.

A nurse came out of the cubicle where J.B. was. She gestured to April, motioning for them to come.

"Go see him," April said. "I know this is crazy. We'll figure it out later."

"We?" Mary Lou reared back. The look on her face cut April to the core.

Mary Lou's eyes were shiny with tears, and her jaw was trembling. Her lips had thinned, and she spat out her words. "You're not going to come anywhere near my family, April. I don't understand this, but I know one thing. You're not welcome in my house anymore. Stay away from us."

Mary Lou let the nurse lead the way behind the curtain. Peter and Logan followed. Kit squeezed April's shoulder as she went past.

They weren't in there for long when the nurse came out and closed the door. She shook her head at April.

"Sorry, he didn't make it."

CHAPTER 9

April drove home. The sun was coming up. She let herself in.
Grizz and Charlotte were up already, of course. She was
too spent to explain where she'd been, so she refused the
offer of breakfast and went straight to the shower.

When Ed and Vince had restored the barn, they had
not skimped on the bathroom. The marble shower was as
expansive as the front seat of a Cadillac, with showerheads
shooting water at parts of her body that had never been
attacked in quite that way before. Usually, in the spirit of
environmentalism, she turned off most of the extraneous
heads. Not today. She blasted them all, hoping to wash
away the stench of death and heartbreak. The heartbreak
of losing someone twice.

She fell asleep almost as soon as she climbed into the
loft, wrapped in her oversize terry robe. Even though it was
damp, she didn't take it off. She'd pay for sleeping with her
hair wet, but she was too tired to care.

She woke up several hours later, feeling stiff. She dressed quickly and came down the ladder. The clothes she'd left in the bathroom were neatly folded and placed on the floor. Charlotte drew the line at coming into the loft, but she couldn't resist picking up after April, no matter how often she asked her not to.

The business card that J.B. had given her was on top.

It was the card of a pharmacist, Dr. T. Adama, from a small chain located in Mountain Top, about fifteen miles away. That's where he'd told Kit he'd been living. This was the kind of place that J.B. would have frequented when he was shopping for the legal drugs that were needed to make meth.

April's curiosity was piqued.

She was due at Deana's in fifteen minutes. She still had half the filing to do. She called the funeral home.

"Hey, April, honey. Good morning."

"Dee, I'm going to be late today," she began.

Deana interrupted her. "Listen, I can't work on the files with you this morning. Why don't you come in later? I have an autopsy to do."

April's heart stopped. "An accident victim, from last night?"

Deana was cautious, never wanting to reveal too much. "All I know is the family is requesting one. I don't know anything more."

"It might be Mary Lou's brother."

"Her brother Gregg?" Deana asked. "He's in California, I thought."

April felt her exhaustion take over. This was too complicated. "I'll explain later when I come in to finish the filing," April said and hung up.

April fingered the business card. Why had J.B. given her

this? It was practically a dying declaration. It must mean something to him. Something important. While Deana found out how J.B. died, she could find out where he lived during the year he was supposed to be deceased.

She ought to go downstairs and bake something. This is the way it worked in a small town. Death came with condiments. Everyone would be making dishes for Mary Lou and her family. If Bonnie was home, she'd bake a huge lasagna. Suzi would probably make her lemon bars. Neighbors would bring over tuna casseroles and homemade nut breads. Rocky would go to HoneyBaked and bring them a spiral ham.

People would gather in Mary Lou's country kitchen, offering food and comfort. But April wasn't welcome there now. She'd find another way to bring solace to her friend. By finding out where J.B. had been.

She waved good-bye to Grizz and Charlotte, who were parked in front of the TV. A small child was sparring with Regis, both of them dressed in silk shorts. Regis looked like a leprechaun. Charlotte put down her knitting, the precursor to getting up and making her a late breakfast, but April held out a hand.

"I'll be out all day. See you tonight," she said.

"Meatloaf tonight, dearie," Charlotte called.

Half an hour later, she pulled into the Crestwood Center parking lot in Mountain Top. It was anchored by a grocery store. The drugstore was right in the middle. It was a national chain, one that had taken over most of the family-owned businesses that had been the norm when she was a kid. Avoiding the snow piled around the light standards, April found a spot not too far from the door.

The brightly colored aisles looked the same as the one she'd patronized in San Francisco and in Lynwood. It felt a bit surreal, and for a moment she wasn't sure where she was.

April walked to the back of the store. The cold remedies were under lock and key. A sign indicated that the store was complying with federal laws by limiting the sale of certain ones. The drugs needed to make meth.

The pharmacist-on-duty sign indicated that Dr. Adama was here. She looked beyond the counter into the glassed-off area where the filling of prescriptions took place and saw two people in lab coats, both with their heads down, concentrating on their work.

Why did J.B. have this business card? Was this someone who sold him drugs when he was buying? A pharmacist would be a good person to have on your payroll. Someone who could sell the legal drugs needed to make meth.

April took a deep breath. She'd have to be careful. If this guy was involved in something illegal, he wasn't going to be up front with her.

She was a few feet away from the patient privacy zone, trying to formulate a way to ask for information about J.B. without bringing up the drugs, when the customer in front of her cleared away.

"Can I help you?" a clerk asked, her eyeglasses bouncing on her chest, held there by a fancy beaded chain.

April glanced down at the card, even though she knew the name. "I need to speak to Dr. Adama."

The clerk was nonplussed. "Please step over there, to the consulting area."

April moved down a window, under a sign that read "Ask Your Pharmacist."

Ask what exactly?

A woman in a white coat joined April on the other side of the counter, wearing a professional, quizzical expression. According to the embroidery on the pocket, this was Dr. Adama. Dr. Tina Adama.

April was struck dumb for a moment. This was Dr. Adama? She didn't know what exactly she'd been expecting, but she definitely wasn't expecting a round-faced chubby woman who looked younger than she did.

"How can I help you?" the pharmacist asked. Her lab coat strained across her middle. She was in danger of popping a button or two.

"Do you know J.B. Hunsinger?" April asked.

Dr. Adama's eyes changed. She suddenly looked wary. Maybe she *was* involved with the meth making. Perhaps J.B. had burned her, too. Used her like he'd used his sister.

"Is he a customer of yours?" April asked.

Dr. Adama shook her head quickly, but April didn't believe her.

To the right of her, a small bent-over woman was quizzing the clerk about her medication. She was very deaf so the conversation was getting louder by the second. "I need my water pills."

Dr. Adama glanced their way. April was going to lose her if they didn't move along their conversation.

"Is there some place we can talk?" April asked. "A little more private."

Dr. Adama took a step away from the window. She glanced behind her. A large Brillo-haired woman stared at April from behind the glass.

"Why don't you state your business? I'm at work, as you can see."

State her business. April didn't know exactly what she'd hoped to find out. Why J.B. had given her the card,

of course. It was obvious that the doctor was lying, but
without accusing, she couldn't make her talk.

The Brillo woman was moving as if to come around and
rescue her friend. Time was running short.

"I'm a friend of Mary Lou Rosen's. J.B. was her brother,"
April began.

The pharmacist's eyes widened. Her skin paled quickly,
suddenly looking like the skin of an uncooked chicken. She
gripped the counter tightly, her knuckles going as white as
her face. Her coworker frowned in April's direction.

"Please don't tell his sister he's here. Alive," Dr. Adama
whispered desperately. "He's started over. He's doing fine.
Jimmy is a changed man. If you've come here to drag him
back into that life, I won't let you. We've made a new life
for ourselves."

Her friend caught the frantic quality in Dr. Adama's
voice and spoke firmly. "Tina," she said. "You need to sit
down."

They both looked down at her belly. The pharmacist
rubbed her stomach. At first, April thought she had indi-
gestion, but the way Tina Adama stroked the contours
of her lab coat, April realized there was a definite bump
under there.

Dr. Adama was pregnant. April felt a stab in her own
belly. She had to tell this pregnant woman, who obviously knew and cared about J.B., that he was dead. She
rolled around sentences in her head trying to find the right
words.

It wasn't going to be pretty.

April looked at the friend by her side. She tried to convey
to this women that she had bad news. "Can we go somewhere to sit down and talk?" she said, her voice softening.

The Brillo-haired woman took stock of April, looking

her up and down. April kept her expression serious, hoping she understood that this was for Dr. Adama's sake. The woman seemed to get it.

"Why don't you go into the break room, Tina?" she said. "Get off your feet for a few minutes."

"I don't know," Tina said, looking back at the office she'd left. "I've got a lot to do." Dr. Adama continued, her eyes going unfocused. "He's a new man," she said, the lines around her mouth softening. "I barely remember J.B. Jimmy is a sweet, caring, gentle soul."

April realized she was talking to a woman in love. A woman in love with a guy she didn't know was gone. She put a hand on her cold fingers, willing the woman to finally stop talking and look at her. Dr. Adama raised eyes to April. April gulped. This was up to her.

"There was an accident," April began. Dr. Adama waited for more information. April could see her making calculations. Which hospital? Where to go see him? Probably she was getting ready to call doctors she knew to tend to him.

April swallowed hard. There was no way to make this easier.

"J.B.—What did you call him? Jimmy—is dead."

The doctor gasped. She tottered and swayed like a skyscraper in a windstorm. Her coworker grabbed her. April's stomach sickened. She grabbed Dr. Adama's hands over the counter, trying to keep her in an upright position.

"Follow me," Brillo said. April avoided the eyes of Tina's friend, sure she wouldn't like what she saw there. She was ready to kill the messenger.

April and Brillo led Dr. Adama to a swinging door and into an employee lounge. A metal table sat in the middle of the room. A yellow laminate counter held a microwave and coffeemaker. Posters about employees' rights covered the empty wall. The water cooler gurgled, and Tina's coworker got them both cold drinks. The clang of the coins falling into the machine's chute made April jump.

"Thank you, Gloria," Tina said. "I'll be okay. Go on back to work." She grasped the soda can and regained some composure, although tears streaked her face.

"Who are you?" Tina asked when her friend had closed the door.

"My name is April Buchert, and I live in Aldenville."

From the stricken look on her face, she knew about Aldenville. "Was that where he was?"

April nodded.

"I was afraid when he didn't come home last night."

"Home? So you lived together?"

Tina rubbed her stomach again. "How did he die?" Tina asked quietly.

"His car went off the road."

Tina seemed to break apart. Her face caved in, and she slumped forward, cradling her head in her hands, leaning heavily on the table. She was silent for so long, April wondered if she should leave her alone and get her coworker back here.

When Tina did speak, her voice was thick with tears. Her chin quivered. "Oh God. I thought you were going to tell me he'd been murdered. Jimmy was afraid to go back to Aldenville."

"Why?" April asked. "He had family there. Family that loved him."

She shrugged. She was spent, the sadness making lines down the side of her mouth. "He said there were people there that wanted to kill him."

Tina sat back in her chair. She tried to cross her legs but gave up when her belly got in the way.

"How far along are you?" April asked.

"Five months. And yes, it's Jimmy's."

April ignored the sarcasm. She wasn't here to judge this woman's choices. She just wanted to know if J.B. had been happy. That was something she could go tell Mary Lou. "How did you two meet?" April asked.

Tina shifted. "About eighteen months ago, Jimmy came in here to buy cold meds. I scanned his ID. It came up as no-sale. He'd bought the same drugs at a CVS fifteen miles away earlier in the day. I was scared. I'd never had to refuse to sell to anyone before. I expected him to go ballistic. Instead, he smiled at me."

She smiled now, remembering. "He told me later he was so blinded by my beauty, he handed me the wrong fake ID." She laughed. "Beautiful was not something I'm usually called."

April could see he wasn't the only one smitten that day.

Tina continued. "He kept coming back. Never again to buy drugs. Just to see me. Once a week at first, then twice. He brought me coffee and a jade plant. He courted me. An old-fashioned word, I know, but that's what it was."

This woman didn't look like someone desperate enough to get involved with someone making meth. She wasn't model pretty, but she was smart and educated. J.B. must have been something special. April felt a pang at never getting to know this guy. He was special to Kit, to Mary Lou and now to Tina.

Tina went on. "I looked forward to his visits but didn't let it go any further. I knew what he was, after all. I couldn't kid myself into thinking he wasn't trouble. Still, he was a nice guy. You know how hard nice guys are to find?"

April nodded. God, how she knew. The relief of having Mitch in her life flooded her like a warm bath. Everyone had to find love in their own way. Tina and J.B. had found each other in the opposite of a meet-cute, but it seemed to work for them.

Tina leaned back, closed her eyes and crossed her arms over her stomach protectively. "He wasn't the picture of a meth maker. I got the feeling he was working off a debt of some kind. He said he never cooked the stuff, just bought the cold meds. He never used, and he said he'd stopped drinking the day he met me.

"Then, in a moment, everything changed. One night he showed up here, out back in the parking lot. He was waiting for me when I got off work." Tears spilled out of Tina's eyes. The realization that he would never be waiting for her again seemed to sink in even more. She caught a sob in her throat.

April touched her arm.

"He was a mess. The meth house had blown up. He'd been on his way back there, using one of the cars that they'd kept at the property. He saw the place go up, knew there were people inside and knew he was going to be wanted by the police."

April imagined how frightened J.B. must have been, to abandon his sister and his pregnant niece.

"I told him he could stay at my house until he got back on his feet. But I fell in love with him instead. We decided he could start over."

She looked April square in the face, as if daring her to deny that they'd made a good attempt at a new life. "He lived here as Jimmy Johnston, one of the fake identities he had used to buy meds. He got a job at the local lumberyard and went to AA every day. Eventually, he told me his real name and about his family."

She stopped; her words seemed to have run out. She'd wrung her paper cup into an unrecognizable sculpture.

"It's not true that his family loved him," Tina said. "His sister hated him. Even before the house blew up, she'd told him she never wanted to see him again. He was already dead to her."

CHAPTER 10

"She'd cut J.B. out of her life, away from her precious daughter. He sat here and cried that he couldn't see Kit."

"But he *was* in touch with her."

Tina's head snapped up. Her eyes, rimmed with tears, flashed. "He was not!"

April nodded. She was sorry she'd said anything. There was only so much this poor woman could take. "He came to her house last night. "

"To his sister's?" Tina asked. "He told me Kit lived at home." Her hand cradled her stomach, the touchstone. She was going to need all the strength she could muster to care for her baby now.

"No, to the new place. They're fixing it up to move into."

Tina's eyes became unfocused as she tried to take in what she was hearing. "I don't understand."

"Neither do I." April decided she'd said enough and told

Tina good-bye. She gave her her phone number and left the woman sitting at the table, feet propped up on another chair, lost in thought.

Tina said her name. April looked back as she got to the doorway. Tina had one last request.

"Let me know when the funeral services are. I want to be there."

April drove home, her mind spinning with what she'd learned. J.B. had been living as Jimmy Johnston with Tina Adama. He'd fathered a child with her. He'd fashioned a good life with her. A life of sobriety, a life where he was contributing to society. Perhaps for the first time in his life.

Too bad he picked the wrong time to return home.

Coming off Route 309 back into the valley, April realized she was close to one of the houses on the list of Mary Lou's foreclosures. She grabbed the sheet that was still lying on the seat next to her, along with the key to the lockbox. April saw the turn for the road up ahead and glanced at the clock. Not quite noon. Deana wasn't expecting her yet. She'd drive by and see what it was like.

Five minutes later, she was on a road that boasted a minicommunity. She couldn't see why it had sprung up in the particular spot on the road. Some developer's idea of an idyllic homestead, perhaps. More likely, cheap land.

The houses were all the same Cape Cod design, with two dormer windows. The one that Mary Lou owned was painted a royal blue. April walked up the front path, which was bare. Someone—Logan—had kept the snow and ice at bay. Salt crystals were underfoot.

She opened the front door and was pleasantly surprised to find the house smelled like air freshener. She'd expected it to be stale and musty. It was empty, and the windows couldn't have been opened in months.

She walked quickly, taking in the fake wood paneling and faux brick around the fireplace. The living room and dining room were in the front, and a kitchen stretched across the back end of the house. It had a nice breakfast nook with built-in shelves with a scalloped edge. She opened a cupboard and was surprised to find a mismatched set of plastic dinnerware. She opened more doors. There were pots and pans. The pantry held a box of coffee filters and garbage bags.

Upstairs, there were two bedrooms. The second one she looked in had a pile of clothing in the corner, as if someone had been planning to take unwanted items to the Salvation Army but had never quite made it. She'd have to tell Logan about it. It looked tacky.

This was an okay house, but nothing that really spoke to her.

Back in the car, she looked over the list of foreclosures again. There was one more on her way back. She made several turns, taking her to a part of town she hadn't been to in a long time.

She slowed, trying to find the next house that matched the picture. She wasn't sure if the tiny house dwarfed by the twenty-foot yews next to the front door was the one. She pulled into the first driveway that was cleared of snow.

The house was set far off the road. Spotting the river beyond, she understood. This was an old-time summer recreation spot, developed after World War II. Up the road a mile or so was a swimming hole her parents had used as kids. Before the lure of the Jersey Shore, Disney World and the Outer Banks, residents of Lynwood and Aldenville would spend their summers in cottages like this one.

As she got closer, the front of the house came into full view. It was cute, with gingerbread-scalloped eaves and clamshell shingles. Most likely about eight hundred square feet. Enough for one person.

April parked near the carport. She walked past the house into the backyard as far as the shoveled walkway led. The property ended at the riverbank. Summer was a long way away, but still she could picture a couple of Adirondack chairs facing the swiftly moving water. That view would provide her and Mitch a lot of entertainment.

April went back to the front door and let herself in. The house was one story, with a large sitting room, an eat-in kitchen and two bedrooms. Most of the appliances were old, but the wooden floors had been sanded and the rooms were a generous size. Ceilings were high. The house needed some loving attention, a fresh coat of paint and some grout cleaning, but the bare bones were good.

The back of the house contained its best feature—a sunporch with windows overlooking the sloping back lawn. A weeping willow, now bare, would fill the view in the spring.

April could picture herself working there. Her drafting desk, which she missed desperately, would fit right under the windowsill.

The view out the icy windows held her captive. The landscape was stark and unforgiving. The unbroken snow in the backyard had been furrowed by the wind into something resembling the pictures taken by the Mars Rover. It was impossible to tell how deep it was, but she could imagine falling into snow up to her waist if she walked on it. The river was churning with icy chunks.

Her mind drifted. She'd gone to Mountain Top to get answers for Kit and Mary Lou. She'd come back with information she didn't know what to do with. J.B. had been living quite comfortably just twenty or so miles away. He had a girlfriend. A new life. He was going to be a father.

How would Mary Lou take this?

She must have been more lost in thought than she realized, because suddenly she heard heavy footsteps on the wooden front porch. Her heart rate zoomed. She hadn't heard a car pull up. Her back was to the kitchen. She turned. The door opened.

She was frozen, all too aware of the isolated location. The lack of neighbors suddenly felt scary, not desirable. She saw a long black boot first.

"Miss Buchert," the voice said. "I recognized your car. Do you need some help?"

Officer Yost.

"I was doing just fine until you scared the bejesus out of me," she said angrily, coming through to the living room. Yost's boots were leaving puddles on the hardwood floor.

"I didn't mean to startle you. I keep an eye on Mrs. Rosen's properties for her. There's a real danger of squatters, you know. It's cold outside, and not everyone has a nice big place to live in like you."

"Knock next time," she said. He always knew more about her life than she wanted him to. How did he find her all the way out here?

He looked around the house. "You thinking about moving?" he said.

April was noncommittal. "I'm looking for a friend."

"Well, if your 'friend' wants a nicer place, Mrs. Rosen has a great one out on South Road." His air quotes were accompanied by a big grin.

"Thanks, I'll tell her."

April moved past him and went out the door. He followed, and she locked the lockbox.

"See you around," he said, getting back into his car.

"Hope not," April said under her breath.

Her cell phone rang as she was getting in her car. It was Charlotte. Yost waved as he backed down the drive. April didn't bother to return the gesture. She answered her phone, careful not to drive away and violate the hands free law.

"I'm sorry, April, dear, but I wondered if you'd be home soon." Charlotte's voice was soft and wispy.

April tried to gauge Charlotte's tone. She didn't sound desperate, just tentative. "I wasn't planning on it. I have to go into the funeral home and help Deana soon."

"Oh."

April knew that phrase. It meant something like "Oh shit," but Charlotte never cursed. She must need something. She never liked to bother April, holding April's workday sacrosanct.

"Do you want me to go to the store?" April prompted. "Are you out of milk?"

"We don't drink milk, April," Charlotte said.

She knew that. "It's just an expression."

"Oh. It's just that Dr. Wysocki's office called. He has a new prescription for Grizz. You know, for his snoring. We'll go to his office and get it ourselves."

"You will not!" April yelled. She moderated her tone. The idea of those two driving gave her the heebie-jeebies. And any cure for Grizz's snoring helped them all. "His office is right on my way home. No problem."

"Thanks, dear."

April hung up. Having these two living with her was like a full-time job. She reminded herself that she too would be old one day, and hoped that someone would take care of her. She considered this paying into a fund she'd collect from eventually.

Dr. Wysocki had to be close to retirement age. He'd

seemed old when April had visited their house as a kid. Violet was his only child from his second marriage. The scandal that had erupted when he'd married his young nurse seemed of another era, but everyone in town knew there were two Mrs. Wysockis and fought to avoid the awkwardness that could ensue if the two were in the same beauty salon or restaurant at the same time. Even now, nearly thirty-five years later, it was well known that Violet's mother did most of her shopping out of town.

Their Victorian on Main Street, painted authentically with forest green and maroon and cream trim, served as both clinic and home. The doctor's office was accessible by a side door off the wide driveway.

She let herself into the small waiting room. The air smelled astringent with overtones of unknown medicines. Despite that, she felt enveloped in a security blanket. Dr. Wysocki's way was gentle and warm. On many visits, one touch of his hand on her forehead or one kind question was all it had taken for her to feel better.

The room's gray carpet, salmon walls, mismatched chairs and end tables were so familiar she caught herself thinking about what flavor Tootsie Pop she'd pick on the way out.

There was no one behind the sliding window of the reception desk. The office behind the window looked deserted. The desktop was clear. Nothing in the inbox. No patient files waiting to be put back. April called out, "Dr. Wysocki?"

"In here," was the answer. April walked through the door into a short hallway. He was in a small exam room, washing his hands at the tiny sink.

He was a tall, slender man, stooped now as he rinsed. His hair was sparser than she'd remembered, white tufts sprouting in patches out of a scalp freckled with age spots. He had on a faded white lab coat and brown, wide-wale corduroys and Hush Puppies. Except for the lack of patients, it could have been a regular day at the office.

Dr. Wysocki smiled when he saw April. He reached for paper towels from a dispenser hung under the wall cabinet above the sink and dried his hands. Once finished, he put out a hand. She stepped forward to shake, but he pulled her into a hug.

"You look well, Ms. Buchert. Very well, indeed."

April broke off, feeling herself smile. She felt her blood pressure lower, her heart rate slow, her sore muscles relax. At the same time, she chided herself to eat better and vowed to start jogging.

"What are you doing here?" he asked.

"The Campbells asked me to stop by," she said. "Some kind of . . . ?" She blanked on what Charlotte had sent her for.

He led her back to the front, picking up a bottle at the receptionist's desk. It was marked "Sample, Do Not Sell."

He said, "Don't tell the drug rep I don't have many patients anymore. The Campbells and a few others don't want to have to find a new physician. I still get a few freebies and am happy to pass them on. This stuff is expensive."

Dr. Wysocki handed her the bottle. This close, April could see the fatigue. The skin under his eyes was dark, bruised and painful looking. She wondered if he'd retired because of his age or his health.

"How about a cup of joe? I have this complicated espresso machine, and no one in my family likes the stuff I make. I'd love to make you a cappuccino. As good as any one you'd get in San Francisco," he said.

April felt his loneliness. Deana could wait. "I'll be the judge of that," she said, following him down the hall.

His office was opposite the exam room, just behind the reception area. The first thing she saw when she walked into his office was not the fancy espresso machine but a huge picture of Violet that sat on his desk, facing out. It had to be her college graduation picture. She was beautiful, confident, smiling broadly in a manner that spoke to years of orthodontia.

So unlike what she'd looked like yesterday. What a waste.

Dr. Wysocki saw her reel from the picture. "I take it you've seen Violet since she came back."

April nodded. She had no clue what to say. "I'm sorry" seemed inadequate. "I'm sorry your A-student, athletic, homecoming-queen daughter is now an unrecognizable mass of humanity" sounded worse.

"You must be wondering how that happened."

April shrugged. She hadn't been able to imagine what could do such damage to a person. Cancer, years of anorexia, some odd aging disease.

She wasn't sure she wanted to hear the tale. She'd already been with someone so sad this morning. "Take a seat," the doctor said, indicating one of the two armchairs in front of his desk. "I'll make you a cappuccino, but only if you promise to listen to me."

This man had always been kind to her. When she'd thought she'd literally die of shame in high school, he'd assured her that was impossible. He taught her that having a gay dad was nothing to be ashamed of. That she would be okay. His kind words had gotten her through until she graduated early and escaped to college.

He fussed with his machine. His voice, always resonant and clear, was still strong. She had no trouble hearing him despite the fact that he had his back to her. She got the sense that it was easier for him to tell her this way.

"Right after college, Violet worked as a social worker in

Philadelphia. She loved it but when she turned thirty, she decided to go to law school. She said something was missing. She wanted to be able to contribute *more* to society. Can you believe that?"

He shook his head in wonder at the blind faith of his daughter. The machine made hissing noises, and he spoke over the sound as he tapped cups and moved levers.

"Law school was harder than she'd expected. Full of young bucks, kids ten years younger than her. Kids that didn't have to work for a living while studying. She struggled to keep up. It was all-consuming."

His hands stilled, and his back curved in defeat. His voice grew softer. "She started using . . . I don't think she knows what happened. Her memory of that time is gone." His shoulders sagged, and he cleared his throat. He turned to face April. "I can only guess, but I think in an effort to keep up with the young guns, she tried meth. Probably just once, to study all night."

"Meth?" When April was in college, kids used speed or caffeine pills.

He sat a cup of foamy espresso in front of her. His face was grave. She remembered this stare. She was about to get a lecture. She settled back in her chair. "Works great. Keeps you going for days a time. It's cheap and available. Violet took to it like a puppy to her mother's teat. Within three months, she'd dropped out of school, sold everything she owned. She stopped calling us and when we went to her apartment, she was gone. Dropped out of school, dropped out of life."

April's heart hurt for this man. He didn't deserve such heartache. He'd spent his life tending to the needs of others. Healing.

His eyes closed. "We found her after a year of searching, living in a ramshackle house in a bad neighborhood. She was living with a young mother. We found two toddlers eating dirt they were so hungry."

His complexion was gray. He glanced toward the ceiling. If April remembered correctly, the family kitchen was just above. Was Violet home? He clearly didn't want her to overhear his painful description.

"That was four years ago. She's been in and out of rehab five times. We finally ran out of money and brought her home. She's been sober eight months, but that's not enough. It takes a year for the drug to work its way out of your system. Relapse is a real possibility."

April had had no idea meth was so devastingly addicting. She'd read about it but had never encountered anyone directly involved. Now in Aldenville, typical small-town America, she'd been faced with the consequences twice in as many days.

Dr. Wysocki pulled an old-fashioned photo album out of a desk drawer and laid it open in front of April. It was full of newspaper clippings about the ravages of meth. Headlines spoke to its addictiveness. One article from an old *Newsweek* stopped her cold. Pages featured before and after pictures of meth addicts. Horrible images, women with sunken cheeks, hollow eyes with no light in them. The resemblance to Violet was uncanny.

April felt sick. The people looked like victims of a raging plague. They didn't look alive.

Dr. Wysocki said, "Methamphetamine's been around for a long time. It was legal once and touted as a miracle cure. It's probably what Dr. Feelgood was serving to the Kennedys and celebrities forty years ago."

April sipped her drink. She fought not to make a face. It was bitter. "Really?"

"Do you know how meth is made?" Dr. Wysocki asked. "It's unbelievably easy to manufacture."

He sat down next to her and turned to a page in his scrapbook. He'd printed out a webpage with a recipe. There was an array of the household items needed. Tanks of gas, like the ones used in a barbecue grill. Coffee filters, paper towels, rubbing alcohol, packages of cold medicine. All looking so ordinary.

"The recipes are online, for anyone to find. All the ingredients are legal, legitimate. It's the combination that makes the drug. And the addition of pseudoephedrine, which is available in over-the-counter meds."

April struggled to take it all in. How could something so insidious be so available? People were so fragile.

"A few years ago the government started regulating the sale of pseudoephedrine. Limited to two packs per person. Trying to stem the tide. All that did was force the buyers to travel to many different drugstores to buy what they need."

"This is what J.B. Hunsinger did," she said.

"You heard about that? Aldenville's very own meth lab?"

April nodded.

"Of course, it was all over town when it happened, and I felt terrible for the Rosens. They've always been civic-minded people. But I was fighting my own fight. Fighting for my daughter's life."

He sat quietly, watching as April turned the pages in the scrapbook. Page after page of grief, horror and tragedy. Children were forgotten as their addict parents did whatever they could to stay high. She skimmed a story about toddlers searching for food, eating garbage. The more she read, the more furious April became.

It was hateful. How J.B. had been able to justify his involvement was truly not comprehensible. He had rationalized that he wasn't directly involved. He'd only bought legal substances, but he had to have known that what he was doing was making it easy for the gang to make meth. There was no way to justify that.

Dr. Wysocki's hand trembled. He leaned back in his chair, his left hand cradling the right. He closed his eyes. "The economy has made things worse. We used to have good paying jobs around here. We used to manufacture textiles, plastics. Union shops, with fair wages. All gone, overseas. What are people supposed to do?"

He scrubbed his eyes. "People are desperate. In my lifetime, I've never seen so many folks lose their homes."

April said, "My friend Mary Lou has been buying up foreclosures."

"That's good. Those empty houses can attract people making illegal drugs."

"Without heat? Water?"

"They're animals. They stay in a house for a few months, then move on. There's plenty of inventory to pick from."

He leaned forward. "Tell your friend to be aware. The real damage comes later when the houses are left behind, now contaminated with the drug. The walls get infested, the water supply can be ruined, the well a pot of stewed sewage."

April promised to tell Mary Lou. As soon as she was talking to her again.

Silence grew. April felt like the doctor's information was overwhelming. The doctor was up against a nearly impossible foe.

He closed the book, putting it back into the drawer. April saw the distinctive shape of a gun in his desk. She drew back. How desperate would Dr. Wysocki have to be to use that?

"You and Violet were friends once," he said. "Right?"

April nodded.

"She doesn't have many friends here."

April said, "We ran into each other at the IGA and the council meeting."

"She only goes out with that woman, Paula. They met in Officer Yost's support group. "

"Good she has someone," April said.

"Yes, but it's worrisome. I'm always afraid that she'll find those kinds of people again. She needs more contact with non-addicts. I'd hoped that when she came home, she'd reconnect with her old friends here."

So that was why he'd invited her in. A campaign to befriend Violet. She wouldn't be able to turn him down if he asked her outright. She tried to stave off his request. "We only spoke briefly," April said.

He shut the drawer hard. "I know she's not the same girl. If I could show you before and afters of her brain, you'd see holes in it. She's missing huge swaths of memory, of reason. The longer she can stay off meth, the better chance she has of real recovery."

Dr. Wysocki covered her hand with his. "Can you hang out with her? Do you still say 'hang out'?" He laughed, but there was no mirth. He had nothing left to give. The healer was asking for her help to heal his daughter.

She couldn't say no, but she couldn't imagine spending time with Violet. They had been out of touch for more than twenty years. She searched for some bone to offer him. "I could invite her over for dinner," April said. The Campbells wouldn't mind. "Charlotte would love for a chance to fatten her up."

He smiled. "That would be good. She needs that. But I'm hoping for more. She needs to find something that excites her as much as taking meth. What do you do you for fun?"

"My friends and I stamp."

"I don't know what that is. Some kind of arts and crafts?" he asked.

"Yes. And it can be therapeutic, in its way." April knew it sounded lame, but she did believe stamping had saved her life more than once.

"Would you mind taking Violet with you?"

There it was. The request she couldn't refuse. April agreed. He stood and gathered her to him, patting her back. She said her good-byes to the doctor, promising to make arrangements with Violet soon.

Deana opened the door for April. "Hey, come on in. I'm sorry I don't have much time to help you with the files. You know where you're at, right?"

Mark hurried past. He gave her a quick smile. His tie was pulled down, and his hair had been mussed up. If April didn't know better, she'd have thought these two had engaged in a little afternoon delight. Baby making.

"What's going on?" April asked.

Mark was the one to speak first. "Busy day. Deana has the autopsy, and we've got two viewings tonight and a funeral tomorrow. Someone's got to pick up the slack. Know anything about embalming?"

April took a step back. Deana frowned at her husband. "Not funny."

"I'm going. I'll be back in an hour," he said. "Tops."

April got out of Mark's way and let him pass. He stopped and kissed Deana on the cheek. "Not to worry, we'll get it all done."

She kissed him back. April loved the way Mark balanced Deana's seriousness with his lightheartedness. He would get the job done but without the personal toll it seemed to take on Deana.

"Let's go downstairs. I'll get you started, and then I have to get back to work."

"Fine with me," April said. As they walked down the stairs, April couldn't get Dr. Wysocki's sad visage out of her mind. "Where's stamping this week?"

Deana was the unofficial secretary of their stamping group, often doing the scheduling and sending out reminders. A group of true artists, they were often hard to corral. "Tomorrow night. Rocky's."

April remembered that Rocky had mentioned making display samples for the Ice Festival to showcase the new stamps she was designing. Stamps she had barely begun. Well, Violet would have to join in.

She turned on the lights and went to the right, to the old file room. April sighed. The pile of paperwork that she'd been dealing with seemed to have grown since the other day.

"Do you think it would be okay if I brought a guest?"

Deana looked at her oddly. "I guess. It's not like we send out engraved invitations."

April said, "The thing is, Dr. Wysocki got a hold of me and I agreed to bring Violet to our next meeting."

"Violet? Is she out of rehab?" Deana asked.

"She is. Do you know what happened to her?"

"Yeah. Sad." Deana glanced at her watch. "I've got to get back."

"Did you finish the autopsy yet?" April asked.

Deana's gaze fixed over April's ear. "Haven't started. That's where Mark is going." She shifted and her eyes met April's. "You didn't tell me you were there. At the hospital last night."

"I haven't really had a chance. Mary Lou told you?" April asked. Her stomach tightened. She didn't like the idea that Mary Lou had gotten to Dee first with her version of events.

"I had a long chat with her. She's devastated, of course."

"I'm sure," April said.

"She's awfully mad at you."

April sighed. "She doesn't have the right to be. I'm the convenient target for her heartache. I was the one who called the ambulance. I nearly saved his life. Almost. Somehow the fact that I talked to him while he was alive and she didn't is eating her up."

"But she did."

"She did? So he got to Mary Lou's?" April's spirits lifted. She'd feel so much better if she knew J.B. had made it to her house before he died. "I couldn't tell which direction he'd been coming from."

"I don't know about that, but I saw them earlier in the day. She was talking to him at the gas station."

"When?"

"Well, it was right about dark. But you know how brightly lit that Turkey Hill station is. I could see them clearly. I didn't realize it was him until I read the accident report and saw the make of his car."

"Well, that's something," April said. At least Mary Lou saw him.

"If that was the last time she saw him, she's going to be very mad at herself," Deana said. "They were fighting. In fact, the only reason I noticed her in the first place was because her car was parked at a weird angle, and she was yelling at this guy. I thought she'd been hit and was fighting with the driver."

"And that was J.B.," April said.

"It was." Deana stood, flexing her knees. "I've got to get ready. You'll be okay?"

April nodded. She grabbed a box of files and went into the new room. She turned on the light. The cremains closet was closed up tight. She listened for Deana's footsteps and heard her reach her work space in the bowels of the house.

April opened the cabinet. J.B.'s box that did not hold J.B. was still on the shelf where she'd left it. She remembered her righteous indignation and the strong feeling that he didn't belong here. But it wasn't even J.B.

So who was it? She wondered if anyone cared. J.B. had been afraid to come back to Aldenville, afraid someone was going to kill him. Did his fear have something to do with what—who—was in that box? Did he know that someone else had taken his place?

April finished her work in several hours and went upstairs into Deana's kitchen. As she passed the back door, she could see that the sun had gone. It was another early nightfall. That meant it was cold out, too. She'd stop at Mary Lou's and tell her about Tina.

The kitchen was bright and smelled of roasting chicken and coffee. Mark was sitting at the table with a cup of coffee in front of him, staring at a glass jar. He looked up when she greeted him, clearly distracted. She started to put on her coat.

"I'm going to warm up my car. I don't have a lot of gas, but it's too cold not to.

"Let me," Mark said. He took her keys from her and snagged a knit hat from the hook. "Deana's on the phone," he said, pointing his head toward the office down the hall. "State police wanted the results of the autopsy. I can tell her you said good-bye."

"Okay, thanks." April took her coat off. Nothing worse than getting overheated and then going out into the frigid air.

April washed her hands at the sink and grabbed a paper towel to dry. The small jar sat alone on the table.

April leaned over the table to get a better look at the object Mark had had in front of him. It was an ordinary canning jar with embossed lettering on the side and a two-part screw-on lid. Deana's mother had used them to put up jam when they were kids. April remembered this kitchen sticky with strawberries and sugar.

They'd always helped until the summer they were thirteen. One misstep, an errant elbow and a little high spirits led to an eight-quart pot of hot, gooey jam spilled all over the counter, dripping onto the floor. April knew if she could see Deana's foot, she'd find the scar from the blob of boiling liquid that had hit her.

She picked up the jar with that paper towel and tilted it to get a better look at what was inside. The presence of the canning jar made the contents even more sinister.

A bullet. She shifted it again. Two. Two very small bullets.

Mark huffed back in the door. She heard him blowing on his hands. "I'd give it a good five minutes. You better get gas. You can't ride around in this weather on a quarter tank. Your lines will freeze."

He stamped his feet on the mat and stepped inside the door. When he saw what she was holding, his eyes narrowed. "April, that's evidence. Put it down."

She complied. "J.B. was shot?"

He tightened his lips, his chin tipping up. He wasn't going to say but she could tell she was right.

"But the windshield was broken. And the car was wrecked." April pulled out a chair and sat down. "Twice? He was shot twice?"

Mark nodded.

"It's a very small bullet," April said, flicking the jar with her finger.

"Probably a twenty-two," Mark said. She knew Mark hunted like most of the men in town, knew his way around firearms.

"Must have been tough to find," April said.

His pride for Deana won out. "Not everyone would have found it. The doctors were too busy with his head wound. That was enough to kill him, but he'd also been shot under his armpit."

The sound of her engine permeated her mind, and she remembered how little gas she had. April got up and said her good-byes to Mark. Once inside the warm interior of her car, she took a deep breath.

Someone had shot J.B.

Twice.

In a manner that was nearly impossible to detect.

CHAPTER 11

Murdered. Someone had shot J.B. and then pushed his car off the road. It wouldn't take much to get it down that embankment. Gravity was on the killer's side. As was nature. Once he was off the roadway, out of sight, his head wound, not to mention the freezing temperatures, would have killed him by morning if the bullets had not.

She stopped for gas at the Turkey Hill where Mary Lou had seen J.B. April had planned on telling Mary Lou and Kit about J.B.'s life in Mountain Top. They needed to know that he'd been happy. He'd been loved. And he'd fathered a child.

She didn't know how long it would take the state police to get to the Rosens once Deana had told them. If Kit was working on her house, she'd welcome April. She headed there.

There was no sign of activity at Kit's. The house was dark. April used the driveway to turn around. She'd take a chance and go by Mary Lou's. April knew Mary Lou wouldn't want to see her, but Kit might be alone there.

Mary Lou's house was ablaze, lights on in most every window. The wide driveway was full. All the family cars, plus a state police car. And the Aldenville police cruiser. Even Yost. The official notification was on.

April watched the window. She could see the back of a state policeman's head wearing the distinctive wool hat, covered with plastic to guard against the weather. Mary Lou and Kit were seated next to each other at the dining room table. Logan, Peter and Yost stood in the background, arms crossed at their waists like some kind of honor guard. Kit put her head on the table, and Mary Lou caressed her hair. It was a tableau of sadness.

April didn't belong there.

She headed home. Her phone yipped. Rocky had sent her another text reminding her that the Ice Festival was less than a week away and that they were stamping tomorrow. Were the stamps ready?

There was nothing she could do for Mary Lou and her family tonight. Telling them about Tina now would just be adding insult to injury. She would have to tell the state police, but for now she just wanted to go home and immerse herself in work.

The day had been long and full of surprises. Meeting Tina, hearing Dr. Wysocki's tale of woe, and finally learning about J.B.'s murder. A hell of a day. And the one thing that tied it all together was methamphetamine.

She pulled up close to the barn. She was kidding herself. She wouldn't be able to work until she'd told the police about Tina. She decided to make the call to the state police in her car. She wasn't sure Tina would have outed herself to the police, and she didn't want the Campbells overhearing. She talked to a trooper and gave her Tina's information. Once that was done, she felt she'd done all she could. She made the mad dash to the kitchen door, trying to outrun the cold. Inside, the place was unnaturally quiet. The TV was off.

Only one person had that kind of impact on Grizz. Mitch. He was on the couch opposite the two recliners. Charlotte and Grizz were laughing at something he'd said. He got up to greet her with a kiss.

"What are you doing here?" she asked. She dropped the bag from Dr. Wysocki on Charlotte's end table. Charlotte nodded her thanks.

"Not happy to see me?" he said with a smile. He knew his presence was always welcome. Especially since it meant Fox News was silenced for a night.

"I didn't notice your car," she said, returning the kiss and leaning into him for a brief moment. She took off her heavy coat and hung it on the hook. "Been a day. I want to talk to you."

"Sure, but the Campbells have been waiting dinner for you." He leaned in and spoke quietly.

"Waiting?" She glanced at the clock over the sink. "It's only five o'clock." Early, even for them.

Mitch grinned. "Give you plenty of time before bedtime to digest. Think of it that way."

She returned his grin.

The Campbells had gotten up and were heading to the kitchen table. April saw now that it was already set with Charlotte's best dishes and her favorite lacy tablecloth. Charlotte opened the oven door, letting out heat and the marvelous smells. She put a bubbling pot of stew on the table and a basket of biscuits.

April's mouth flooded with saliva. "I skipped lunch," she said.

"May I?" Mitch said. He pulled out a chair for her. He'd made this table for Vince and Ed and still acted as if he owned it.

Grizz tucked a napkin under his chin and dug into his stew. Charlotte glanced his way, and he put his fork down. She closed her eyes and bowed her head.

"Thank thee, Lord, for the food we are about to receive." Grizz looked at Charlotte. She was still moving her lips. He said gruffly, "Amen."

April laughed. She knew Charlotte only made him say grace when there was company. Looked like Mitch still fit that bill.

Charlotte passed dishes, and April felt her stomach rumble. She filled her plate and dug in. When Mitch asked her about her day, she shook her head.

"Tell you later," she said. She made eyes at the other two diners. "I don't want to spoil their dinner."

He raised his eyebrows but backed off when he saw she wasn't going to talk. Mitch honored her inability to make small talk tonight and so led the conversation, asking the Campbells about their day. Charlotte launched into a detailed version of her favorite soap opera, alternating with Grizz telling Mitch how easy the college championship version of *Jeopardy!* was compared to the real version. Mitch was leaning in, earnestly agreeing with Grizz.

April was happy to let them talk. She listened with half an ear, feeding her body with Charlotte's good cooking and her soul with the mundane details of life. The fact that nothing out of the ordinary happened in this place today was a good thing.

"I've got a surprise for you after dinner," Mitch said.

April glanced up to find she'd missed some conversation. Charlotte was smiling at her. They'd all finished eating. She mopped up the gravy in her bowl with her biscuit.

"I already had one big surprise this week. I'm all surprised out. Unless it's snickerdoodles," April said. She looked hopefully over at Charlotte, who shook her head.

"Sorry," Charlotte said. "The surprise has nothing to do with me, dearest."

Mitch excused himself, then came back to the table carrying the pink satchel that contained her chain saw.

He plopped it on the empty end of the table, causing plates to rattle. Charlotte jumped up and started clearing. April grabbed the stew pot. It was still warm but not hot. She placed it on the stove.

"Not exactly a surprise," she said. "I knew this was coming. But tonight?"

"Time for your chain saw lesson," Mitch said, grinning from ear to ear. He carried the butter dish to the refrigerator and put it away. Grizz watched the activity, sucking on his teeth.

"Really? Now? Outside? Isn't it like five degrees out?"

"Come on, we don't have much time left before the festival. I want you to get in some practice."

Mitch handed her her heavy down coat and plopped a hat with earflaps on her head.

"You like the Elmer Fudd look, do you?" April said, catching a glance at herself in the door window. She shifted the hat so the fur lining was snug, finding herself seduced by the warmth.

"You look good in anything," Mitch said. "Bundle up. We're burning daylight here."

She put on the coat. "Daylight? It's black as a womb out there." April held out her arms, Frankenstein style. "I can barely move my arms." She saw Charlotte smile.

"You'll do fine," Mitch said.

A spotlight on the roof of the barn lit up the delivery of cordwood Mitch had had dropped off. The wood that Grizz had chopped by hand was neatly stacked under the lean-to roof that kept it dry. A brand new pile stood next to it.

"I want you to get a feel for using the saw. Chopping wood is easy," Mitch said, placing a log onto the concrete pad.

"Wait. I need to tell you about my day. I didn't want to say anything in front of the Campbells, but . . ." She hesitated, seeking out his eyes. He was her touchstone. If she could share her news with him, she could bear it. "J.B. was murdered."

Mitch listened, his face grim. "Oh no. That's going to be hard on his family," he said.

"Yeah."

She told him the rest. They were quiet for a few minutes. She leaned against him, but his face felt as cold as the ice he wanted her to sculpt.

"I know what you need," Mitch said. "Power tools."

He picked up the chain saw.

"Aren't you afraid I'll chop off my foot?" April asked, taking the chain saw from him. She was surprised at how heavy it was. She grasped it with two hands and felt it balance out.

"Go for it," Mitch said. He pulled a set of goggles over her head and settled them on her face.

She turned the switch and felt the tool jump to life in her hands. The blade cut through the first piece of wood easily. To her surprise, April found wielding the chain saw exhilarating. She liked the way it vibrated, sending shock waves up her arms and down to her toes.

She split all the wood in the pile, took off her goggles and looked for more. Her face was warm and her fingers tingled.

Mitch barked a laugh. "I knew you would take to this."

"I like knowing I could split the firewood if I needed to. How hard can ice sculpture be?"

"A lesson for another day. Let's go back inside. I'm freezing." Mitch jumped in place. "Being out here doing nothing is killer."

Reluctantly, April followed his instructions on wiping down the chain saw and put it away. She wasn't cold at all. She was looking forward now to working with the ice.

Back inside, they took off their layers of outdoor gear.

Mitch leaned in. "You look beautiful right now. Your cheeks are rosy from the cold. You sweated a bit and it's making little curls along your neck," Mitch continued, his words buzzing in her ear. He trailed his finger along her nape. She felt a corresponding flush throughout the rest of her body.

Mitch leaned away, still looking at her as if they were alone. April was too aware that Grizz and Charlotte were watching. Grizz was back in his recliner but had muted the TV when they'd come in. They clearly wanted a report.

April said, loudly enough for everyone to hear, "I really liked using that saw."

Grizz grumbled, "Firewood should be split by hand."

"No one's taking away your job, are they, April?" Charlotte asked from the kitchen. She cast April a significant look.

"Nope, I'll stick to wood cut by you, Grizz. Otherwise we'd freeze to death in here."

She thought she was laying it on a little thick, but Grizz cheered up.

"How about a game of cribbage, Winchester?" Grizz said, pushing up out of the recliner. "You owe me a rematch, if I remember right."

No one doubted Grizz's memory when it came to

cribbage. He and Mitch had played before, and Mitch had won—a rare spectacle.

Mitch agreed. "Boy, if I have to get my butt kicked, you're the man to do it."

"Damn straight."

Charlotte tsked at the sound of profanity. A timer went off. She leaned over the oven and brought out a cookie sheet. Suddenly, the barn was filled with the smell of sugar and vanilla. April couldn't believe it. Snickerdoodles. Charlotte had whipped up a batch of April's favorites while they were outside.

April looked around. This felt like family, she realized. A crazy thought. She hadn't known any of these people a year ago, and yet here she was feeling the warm fuzzies for them.

Living with the Campbells had been a crash course in what kind of people they were.

They were good people.

The phone rang. It was Ed and Vince, reporting that it was sunny and seventy in Florida.

Charlotte spoke to Vince first. Grizz grunted a few words, then went to set up the cribbage board. April got on the line and assured Vince his parents were doing okay. Then she was passed over to Ed.

Her father's voice boomed. He was excited. "Great news, Ape. Mrs. H. called from Rome. The painters are finished with the east wing drawing room. You can go into Mirabella and work your magic. The guys will be ready for you by Thursday, probably."

Mirabella was the house restoration job they'd been on for the last six months. It would last another year. April's part, stamping on the walls, was intermittent and had been slowed by the discovery of termites in the beams.

Work! That great four-letter word. She was happy to be

going back to work. A paycheck couldn't be too far behind. She'd have to do double duty on the Ice Festival stamps, but she could manage. She'd get started tonight.

Money coming in meant she could really afford her own place. She added looking for a rental to her growing to-do list.

This particular family unit—Grizz skunking Mitch, Charlotte washing cookie sheets—was about to be broken up.

April excused herself and went up to the loft bed early. She needed to do some work on Rocky's stamps. Mitch and Grizz were still playing, so she climbed up, listening to the two men count points. It was nice background noise.

April opened her sketchbook. She pulled her lap desk closer. Rocky wanted wintry stamps. She tried sketching the bare branches, snowflakes. She was already tired of winter. The time to draw for winter was in summer when snowflakes were charming designs, not the cause of stress and discomfort.

She tossed her sketchbook aside. This was why she couldn't be a stamp designer. Creativity on demand was not her strong suit. She needed inspiration. She squeezed her fingers, trying to relive the tension that had taken up residence in her hand. In her interior design work, she used the architecture, textiles, even fashions of the period to play off of. She had no trouble presenting the client with dozens of drawings to chose from.

April turned to a clean page, turned off her mind and just let her fingers draw.

When she looked down, she realized she'd sketched the murder scene. The bare trees, the rolling road, the ravine. J.B.'s car, nose down, nearly hidden by the evergreens.

Someone had shot J.B. up close and pushed his car off

the road. Shot him with a small gun. A lesser coroner might not have found it. Given that the other deputy coroner was a veterinarian, there was a good chance that the two small bullet holes would have been overlooked.

J.B. had known the person who killed him, that seemed evident. Clearly, someone was angry that he'd returned. Or perhaps someone had followed him from Tina's house? Someone from his old life who didn't want him to return. But who?

If there was any of the gang left, maybe they had to silence him. J.B. could identify them. Maybe he had been blackmailing them.

But Yost had said there was no meth making going on. It could be more personal. She didn't know if J.B. had had a girlfriend when he'd lived in Aldenville. A jealous husband? A jilted lover?

She had a lot of questions. She'd go to Kit's in the morning and find out more about J.B.

April heard footsteps on her ladder. Mitch's head popped into view. She realized the barn had gotten quiet.

"How's it going?" he whispered, perching on the ledge. She scooted close to him. He put an arm around her, and they sat, legs dangling. She could see the lights were out except for a low one over the kitchen sink. The Campbells were two mounds on their bed.

"Your sister's not going to be happy with me. I can't design worth a crap. I'm totally distracted by J.B.'s murder," she said.

They were quiet for a few minutes. He spoke first. "I hate the idea of being in a box on a shelf in Deana's place. Promise me never to cremate me," he said finally.

"Really? You're such an environmentalist. Isn't it the most green way to go?"

He shook his head. "I've got five acres of ground. Find

a spot for me out there. No vault, just a plain wooden box and me. Compost."

"All right, all right. Enough gruesome talk. I didn't know you were so against cremation."

"You've got a lot of learn about me, Buchert," he said, kissing the end of her nose and swinging his legs toward the ladder. "But it'll have to wait for another day. You've got work to do. Even I need some beauty rest."

The next day, April drove out to Kit's new house. Even under the present circumstances, Kit had limited time to get the house in order. She would most likely be there.

April was relieved to see her car in the driveway. Kit answered the front door when April knocked. Her face was pale, and she was chewing on the tie from her hooded jacket. She glanced up at April, then dropped her gaze.

April felt her pain. "I'm so sorry about your uncle, Kit. Truly."

Kit let April put her arms around her and placed her head on her shoulder. April stroked her hair. Kit hiccupped. After a moment, Kit used the heels of her hands to swipe at her eyes. She took a step back.

"The state police were at Mom's for hours last night."

"You must be exhausted," April said. She waited for Kit to continue. Something else was working on Kit. She didn't look just sad, she looked ashamed. "Were they really hard on you?"

Kit's face reddened. "One of them said it was a shame J.B. came back to Aldenville to see me."

April felt her anger rise. What a stupid thing to say. "Kit, you couldn't have known he would die."

"I shouldn't have asked him to come."

"J.B. came back because he wanted to. He knew the danger."

Even as she said it, April wondered, did he? He knew he could have been arrested, but did he expect to be murdered? He came after dark so no one would see him. He snuck into town but then showed himself at the gas station. Deana saw him there. Who else saw him?

Were those the actions of a man who feared for his life?

Kit's face crumpled. "I blew it. I really blew it."

"Blew what?" April walked her over to the kitchen where the chairs were still set up from the night J.B. visited. She pushed Kit into one and sat across from her. She patted her knee and tried to get the girl to look at her.

Kit wouldn't look up. Her forehead was creased in pain. There was something she wasn't telling April.

"Hey," April said softly, hooking a hair behind Kit's ear. After what she'd said to her mother in the hospital, the kid had no one to talk to. "Look at me. I'm not going to judge you and tell you you should have done things differently. I already know you did the best you could."

Kit sat back in the chair, shuddering as her crying stopped. Her voice had dropped to a whisper. "I could have changed the way this turned out."

She leaned forward on her knees. April stilled herself, waiting for Kit to continue. The girl had something to get off her chest.

Before she could begin again, there was a firm knocking on the kitchen door. The house had a breezeway between the kitchen and the garage, and they could see a figure in the dimly lit space. Officer Henry Yost came in, doffing his hat. Great timing, as usual.

"You two ladies out here by yourself?" he said, looking

through the kitchen into the living room. He stepped around a folding table full of wallpaper tools as he checked for other people. Who did he expect to find? J.B. come back from the dead? Again?

"More questions, Officer Yost? Can't it wait? Kit's not really in a good place right now," April said, standing next to Kit and gathering Kit to her side.

He held up a hand. "I know that. I'm not here to interrogate her. Her uncle is not my investigation. Of course, I'm doing what I can to help them, but this is the state's gig. I'm just here as a friend of the family." He patted Kit on the back. "I promised her parents I'd keep an eye on things."

There was an awkward silence. Yost didn't seem to notice he was interrupting. He loomed over the two of them. Kit was beyond being a polite host, and April had never felt the need to coddle Yost. She wished he would just go away.

Instead, he looked around the room. "How's the remodeling going? You kids have been putting in the hours on this place. You plan on being here late again tonight?" he said.

Kit said, "Logan'll be here with me."

"Well, I'll drive by later, just to check up on you."

April saw her opening. She got up and moved toward Yost, crowding him to the front door. She wanted him to get the hint that he was not needed there.

Once they were in the living room, out of Kit's hearing, April asked, "What do the police think about the shooting?"

Yost looked her in the eye. "They think J.B. Hunsinger was in the wrong place at the wrong time."

Yost tipped his hat and left.

April squinted after Yost. There was no way the police

thought this was a random shooting. He wasn't going to share what he knew, though. Not with her.

She wanted to hear the rest of what Kit had to say about her uncle. She had an idea that she knew what was troubling the girl.

CHAPTER 12

*April came back into the kitchen. Kit had picked up a scraper
and was poking halfheartedly at the wallpaper. She wasn't
removing much, but she probably felt like she was trying.
April found another flat blade and joined her at the wall. She
pulled off tendrils of the paper. It was just like peeling off a
sunburn without that awful pain when you've gone too far.*

Working side by side in silence, April composed her
thoughts. Kit was hiding something, something she was
afraid had gotten her uncle killed. April thought she knew
what it was.

"Did you see J.B. before the night he died?"

Kit's hands flew up to cover her mouth as she emitted a
small cry. Small as a newborn's.

She shook her head, her hair swinging and hiding her
face. April turned to face Kit, who put her blade to wall
and rubbed harder.

"Kit, I saw the box that you made for J.B.'s cremains. It's beautiful, full of life and spirit. Whoever made that box was happy, jubilant, not sad."

Kit's fingers clenched the blade so tight that her knuckles turned white.

"You knew he was alive when you made that box," April said. "When everyone else thought he was dead, you knew he was alive."

"No, I didn't."

Kit shielded her face and scraped harder. Bits of drywall flew from under her blade. She was going to seriously damage the wall if she pressed any harder.

April stilled her hand. "Look at me."

The burden of carrying around this secret dropped Kit to her knees.

"Does Logan know? Your mother?"

"Only Logan. J.B. said I couldn't tell anyone."

Kit's lashes were dewed with tears, and she fought to control her trembling hands. She picked at a piece of glue stuck to the wall.

She stopped, her eyes going out of focus. When she spoke again, her voice was thick with tears, and she stopped after each syllable.

"About a week after the explosion, J.B. came to the back door. I was so glad to see him. I let him right in. I went to call Mom, but he stopped me. He said people, bad people, were looking for him. It was too dangerous for him. Said he would go away for a while, but he would come again."

April said, "And did he?"

She nodded, her fingers entwined. She pulled on each one as if to crack the knuckle, without success. "Just after Christmas. He was clean and sober but needed a little more time before he could see my mother. He'd hurt her so much over the years, and he really wanted to make up for what he'd done. He wanted to have his one-year sobriety pin before he came back to us. He was working through his twelve steps. His anniversary date would have been March first."

Six weeks away. He'd gotten so close. April said, "Did he mention Tina?"

At Kit's blank look, April realized she hadn't told her about her uncle's girlfriend. She didn't think Kit could handle that information right now. Still, she had a right to know.

"He was living with a woman," April said.

"A friend?"

"More than a friend. She took good care of him."

Kit smiled. "That was obvious when I saw him. He looked so good, didn't he? I mean, he was well fed. His hair looked healthy." She laughed at April's reaction. "Well, it did. He used to have great hair." Her voice broke. "I hope my kids have his hair."

April decided to wait to tell Kit about Tina's pregnancy. They should meet first.

"Did she love him?" Kit asked.

April nodded. "Seems like they loved each other."

Kit closed her eyes. "So he had a little peace."

"Yes."

Kit surprised her, grabbing April by the shoulders. Her eyes were shining, and her mouth was set in a grim line. April wondered what happened to the happy woman she'd first met when she'd returned to Aldenville. Kit had been through a lot since then, and it showed on her face.

"I want to know who killed him, April. Not knowing has left a giant hole in my heart. It hurts to breathe."

Kit went quiet. April gently extricated herself and wetted a paper towel with cold water and handed it to Kit.

She wiped her eyes and sat on the floor. April pulled up a plastic bucket and sat down.

"I'm a mess. I need to know what happened." She looked at April. April couldn't look away from her desperate face.

"What happened the night of your bachelorette party?"

"What do you mean?"

"You said at the hospital . . ."

"My mother has a lot to answer for." Kit's eyes filled again. She hiccupped and caught her breath. April let her calm down before gently prodding again.

"Your party—what happened?"

"It was the weekend before the wedding. I got drunk. My girlfriends, who were driving, got even drunker. Logan was out at his bachelor party in the Poconos. I called J.B. to come get me and sneak me back into the house."

April could imagine the rest. Mary Lou would not have been happy with an underage drunk bride-to-be.

Kit picked up her sweatshirt string and twisted it in her fingers. "I didn't know he'd been drinking. He drove us into a light pole on Main Street. Mom and Dad had to come and get us. We were okay, although I had to go to my wedding with a fat lip. Mom didn't let him explain. She just threw him out."

April winced. That's when his life on the street began. And soon after that, he got involved with the meth gang.

"She was so mean that night. Stood by while he packed his stuff, then took him to the bus station. Told him not to come back. I wanted him at the wedding, but Logan took Mom's side. He thought J.B. was a bad influence. Everyone wanted me to stay away from him."

She gave April a shy smile. "But we managed to stay in touch."

"How?"

Her body relaxed, and she leaned her head back. "J.B. loved spy stuff. He had me reading Ian Fleming and watching James Bond movies when I was a kid. He taught me how to do secret writing and would leave me notes all over the house. We had our own code.

"It was just for fun until she threw him out. But then I was desperate to hear from him. The day before my wedding, I found a chalk mark on the tree outside my window. I knew what that meant. Spies use them all the time to indicate a message is in place."

She leaned forward. "I had to search, but I finally found the drop. He'd left a wedding gift for me in an old metal milk crate in the shed."

April wasn't that familiar with spy protocol. "So he would leave a mark somewhere and then leave you a package?"

"Or a message. The thing is it was always in the same spot. If I saw a yellow mark on my maple, I knew to check the shed for something from J.B."

April understood now. "And that's what you did, after the explosion?"

Kit looked forlorn. "I thought he was dead like everyone else. When I saw the mark on the tree, I thought it was an old one at first. I never went out to the shed. Then he came by the house when I was there alone."

"So you knew he was alive?"

"Yup. He had to take that chance and show himself to me. After that we used our system."

The girl had a lot more gumption than April had given her credit. "So how often have you two been in touch in the last year?"

"Only a few times. Then Mom found this place. I wasn't happy about it. I was worried that would be the end of my notes from him. Once I'd told J.B. where to find me, I felt better."

And then he came here and was murdered, April added silently.

Kit was thinking along the same lines. "If I hadn't brought him here . . ."

"Let's think about this. Did he have any other enemies? What about old girlfriends? Did he do other illegal stuff? Maybe his accomplices?"

"No, he was never on the wrong side of the law. I mean, yes, traffic tickets and a DWI, but never anything serious. Yost tried to help him, keep him out of serious trouble."

Officer Yost was always looking out for Mary Lou's family.

Kit said quietly, "I don't think my uncle was making meth."

April was quiet. She knew Kit didn't want to believe. "What if I found out he was?"

"I don't think he was a saint. Believe me, I know he wasn't."

"But Kit, Officer Yost, your mother, they think he was involved with the meth house."

"It all leads to the same place, doesn't it? I want to know my uncle. Good and bad. It's who he is . . . was." Kit laid a hand on April's arm. "Just find out for me. Find out who did this to my uncle."

April had one more question to ask Kit. "Did he get to your parents' house that night?"

Kit shook her head sadly. "Nope. My mom said she never saw him."

April left Kit's wondering what else J.B. had left behind for them to find. A trip to Mary Lou's shed was in order. But first stamping. And like J.B., she'd have to wait for the cover of darkness.

*   *   *

Later that night, April pulled into the drive of the Wysocki
house on Main Street. She'd worked all afternoon on
stamps and had a dozen ready. She hated working that fast,
but she had to admit she liked what she'd come up with.

Violet's dad was standing with her in the doorway
behind a full glass storm door. He held the door open and
gestured April in.

"Hi, Dr. Wysocki," April said. She peeked into the
kitchen. She and Violet had done homework at that breakfast bar. It had been shiny and new back then, and they
had spun the stools until Violet's mother begged them to
stop.

Dr. Wysocki handed April a still warm batch of brown-
ies. "My wife made these for you to take to your meeting.
Have fun, girls."

He gave Violet a peck on the cheek and a little push.
April remembered their first day of first grade; Violet had
greeted the new teacher like a peer. No one had had to
shove her out the door in those days.

Violet crossed her legs under herself on April's car seat
and bounced her knees incessantly.

April's phone rang. It was Deana.

She said, "Just so you know, Mary Lou is here, at
Rocky's."

April hadn't expected that. It was so soon after J.B.'s
death. And the news of his murder.

Deana understood. "She wants to be around us. She wants
to lose herself in stamping for a few hours with people who
love her."

"I've already picked up Violet," April said, stealing a
glance at her passenger. She wasn't paying attention to her
call. "I promised to bring her. Besides, I have the stamps

we're going to be working on. Rocky will be without samples for the Ice Festival if I don't show."

"I know. I just thought you'd want a heads-up."

"Thanks," April said. Deana was always looking out
for her.

She drove to the end of Main Street, but instead of turning left toward Rocky's, she kept going. Mary Lou was at
stamping. Her husband was probably at the council work
meeting. This was the perfect time to go by Mary Lou's
house and see if she could find out whether J.B. had left
another message for Kit the night he died.

She pulled up to the big two-story a few minutes later.
Yards here were big, well over a half acre. The houses had
been built for ultimate privacy, with few windows overlooking their neighbors. The house to the right had a tall
wooden privacy fence surrounding it. She parked in the
drive. The shed wasn't visible.

Violet roused herself. She looked out her window and
said, "Is this it? The house is so dark. Are you sure this is
where we're supposed to be?"

"Hmm," April said. "I thought it was here. Let me go
around the back and check. Maybe they're in the basement.
Stay in the car."

April turned the corner at the back of the house. Motion
detection lights came on, startling her. She threw up her
hand to shade her eyes. She glanced back to see if Violet
had noticed. She couldn't see the car from here so she pre-
sumed Violet couldn't see her. She picked up her pace. She
had to get in and out of the shed before Violet—or someone else—got suspicious.

April walked toward the shed. She guessed this was
where they stored the snowblower because the brick path
leading to the little building was completely clear of snow.

Still, she felt eyes on her. Probably just Violet. She tried

to look as if she was on a mission. She rehearsed an excuse
in case a nosy neighbor stopped her. She'd say Mary Lou
had asked her to get something from the shed. Some kind
of tool. An auger.

What the heck was an auger? She had no idea.

She got up to the outbuilding. It was big, at least ten by
ten. It sat on its own concrete pad at the far end of the property, a couple of football fields away from the house.

A big padlock sat on the hasp of the door. April blew on
her hands. Mary Lou's backyard was exposed to the wind,
and she was getting cold fast. The lock was a combination style. She grabbed it, trying to remember Mary Lou's
birthday, hoping the combination was that easy.

The lock opened in her hand. It hadn't been closed.

She let herself in. The space was full and had a chemi-
cal smell from the bags of fertilizer that were stored there.
She picked her way past the snowblower and various shov-
els. The lawn mower was under a tarp.

She saw the metal box right where Kit had said it would
be. The kind that used to sit on porches in her mother's
youth, when milk delivery came with the territory. She
opened it but could see nothing in the dim light coming
from the one window. She reached her hand in, praying no
spiders were living inside.

"April?"

April's heart stuttered. The lid dropped on her hand, its
edge sharp. She yelped and turned.

Violet stood in the doorway. "What are you doing in
here?"

April tried to look casual. "I was looking for Mary
Lou's spare key. Sometimes she's late to her own stamping.
But I guess it's not here. I'll call Deana and see where we're
meeting. Let's go."

Violet sighed but didn't move. April let her fingers

explore the inside of the box. She felt something plastic and
pulled it out. It was a tiny cassette tape.

J.B. had left behind another note of sorts.

She stuffed it in her pocket and led Violet back to the
car.

Rocky's studio was brightly lit. April opened the front
door, knowing that Rocky left it unlocked on nights they
stamped. She held it open for Violet, who was lagging
behind, her feet shuffling on the cleared walk. She was so
thin she had to be extra cold but she moved as though summer humidity had stolen her will.

Violet felt like an extra appendage. But April had made
a promise to her father, and Violet needed help today, not
next week or next month. April believed in the power of art
to heal. She knew that if Violet had a creative outlet, her life
would improve. Whether or not it would keep her off drugs
was something to be seen, but April knew it couldn't hurt.

April felt her own step quicken, hearing the noise of
her friends in the back of the house. She wasn't looking
forward to facing Mary Lou. She just hoped she wouldn't
make a scene. She pulled her cart behind her, letting it
bump over the hardwood floor of the living room, leading
Violet into the converted family room.

She looked back to see Violet's reaction as they entered.
Rocky's studio was a sight to behold. The entire back wall
was covered with a mash of images, found objects and art-
work. Rocky's specialty was collage, and she treated her
wall as a canvas. It was always evolving as Rocky swapped
out pictures and hung up new treasures. April noticed a
rusted farm tool, some kind of hook, had been mounted
near the middle.

Violet's eyes had widened appreciatively.

The other two walls were taken up with shelving, closed
and open, and drawers to house Rocky's raw materials. A

long white marble countertop ran under the window. For their stamping nights, Rocky set up two plastic eight-foot tables in the middle of the room and brought in chairs from the dining room.

Rocky was pouring wine. Deana, Suzi and Mary Lou were already seated and hard at work. The tables in front of them were scattered with inks, embossing crystals, paint and brushes. April dumped the new stamps she'd created in the middle of the table.

They greeted April as she entered. "Hi, everyone," April said. "Do you know Violet Wysocki? Deana, of course, you do."

Rocky and Suzi, being a year or two older, had been a different year in school and probably didn't know Violet then. But everyone knew Dr. Wysocki. Including Mary Lou. Suzi said hello as Rocky sat Violet down next to Deana.

"Welcome," Rocky said.

Violet gave a little wave, and Suzi smiled tentatively.

"Violet's never stamped before," April said. "She's been going through a bit of a rough patch. I thought she could use some ink stains on her fingers."

April tried to catch Mary Lou's eye to greet her, but she kept her head down.

"Like the rest of us," Rocky said, splaying her fingers for Violet to see. The tips were layers of color. "This is how we can tell our kind," she said, speaking in a robotic, alien voice. "We look for telltale markings."

Violet laughed, putting her hand over her open mouth.

"You here to learn how to stamp?"

Deana and April exchanged a glance. April hid a smile. Rocky saw a potential customer. Someone she could sell Stamping Sisters stamps to, or better yet, someone who

could become a salesperson for her. April could see the
wheels turning in Rocky's brain.

April spread out the prototype stamps she had carved
for the Ice Festival. Bare tree branches, ice crystals, a background stamp with a freezing rain pattern. She was proud of
what she'd done. Not cliché but still recognizable as winter.

Rocky looked through the designs, nodding her head in
approval. "This isn't a typical stamping night for us, Violet. Usually we work on our own projects. Tonight, Deana
and Suzi are helping me out. I need samples to display in a
booth at the Ice Festival. Samples that show people how to
use Stamping Sisters stamps."

As she was talking, Rocky stamped out the image of a
tree branch. She went over it with the glue pen and dumped
a pile of embossing powder on it. She brushed off the excess
and showed Violet the result.

The tree looked etched onto the paper, the embossing
playing up the delicate lines. Violet ran her finger over it.

"Cool. That looked easy," she said. She looked around
at the table and picked up a stamp. Rocky pushed an ink
pad toward her.

"Just play with it. Have fun," Rocky said. April smiled
at Rocky, grateful to have her friend take Violet under her
wing.

Suzi grabbed the largest snowflake stamp. She took a
red velvet scarf and she sprayed it with a fine mist of water.
She laid it on a board and placed the stamp underneath.
She stood up and applied a hot iron, leaning her whole
body into it. Soon the image of the snowflake appeared in
pink relief on the velvet. She repeated with smaller flakes
and held up her finished piece.

"That's beautiful," April said. She'd never burned out
velvet with a stamp. She was going to have to try. The

fabric looked exotic. She could see making a throw for her bed.

Deana gave her a smile and showed her the epoxy necklace she planned. She'd stamped out an image that would be made into a pendant. April smiled back. She was feeling good. If her friends produced these beautiful items from her stamps, Rocky would be able to drum up some interest at the Ice Festival. People would want one of each, she hoped.

Small talk prevailed as the group got used to their guest. Violet put her head down and experimented with what Rocky had given her. After a few minutes, her fingers were flying. April felt a bit of relief. Maybe the old doc had been right. This was just what Violet needed. Stamping could make her re-entrance into a normal life easier.

Rocky and Suzi asked about Violet's life. Violet talked about going to college at Villanova and living in Philadelphia. She skirted the last couple of years, but only April seemed to notice.

April found the brightly colored paper that she'd picked up at Kit's house in her stamping bag. She brought it over to Rocky.

"What is it?" Rocky asked, holding the circular paper up to the light. The color was a deep teal blue.

"Don't know exactly. I just figured you could use it somewhere. The color and texture are amazing."

Rocky stood and went over to her wall. She pinned the gaily colored paper just over her head, right next to a California fruit crate label that April had given her a few months ago. April walked back to her seat. Violet looked up as she sat down and caught sight of Rocky's addition. She took in a breath.

April ventured a momentary look toward Mary Lou. The shadow of J.B.'s death was etched on Mary Lou's face. She was trying to lose herself in the stamping. Her fingers flew as she turned out card after card. She was ignoring April's stamps and working with her own. Silently, without so much as a glance in April's direction.

The cassette tape in her coat, direct from Mary Lou's shed, weighed on April's mind. What would she find on it? She realized she didn't have a tape recorder that size. It was a microcassette. Kind of old-school technology. J.B. must have had one. April made a mental note to ask Tina.

Mary Lou was right. April was messing in her life. But Kit deserved answers. Answers to questions that Mary Lou seemed hell-bent to ignore.

Conversation stalled. Every topic seemed fraught. Their usual fare, the recounting of a run-in with the produce man at the IGA who insisted on singing the Chiquita Banana song if you put bananas in your basket, or an account of an argument with Claire the postmistress who periodically "lost" a bag of mail in her tiny post office, seemed inappropriate. Usual opportunities for much imitation and dissection, tempered with plenty of laughs, now felt hollow.

Complaining about the inequities of life seemed petty compared to what Mary Lou was going through. And while a different death might have brought out a run of fond memories or funny anecdotes, J.B.'s led to nothing but pain.

Violet was oblivious to the undercurrents. She took to stamping like a kid with her first set of finger paints, happily creating colorful images. Her cards had a cartoonish character with an underlying sweetness.

April considered calling it a night. It was early, but Dr. Wysocki couldn't complain. She'd had Violet out for nearly two hours. She was clearly enjoying herself. He'd be happy about that.

She just had one more stamp to finish carving. April looked over to Deana and signaled with her head that she'd be leaving soon.

Mary Lou looked up, perhaps sensing April's decision. She turned her attention to Violet. "Aren't you one of Yost's girls?" Mary Lou asked.

April was surprised. She'd thought Mary Lou had decided to ignore them both.

Violet started, her blue eyes widening. As devastated as her face was, her eyes took up most of the real estate there. She was a living rendition of one of those waif paintings sold in front of the IGA, if the waif had a hand in front of her mouth to avoid showing her broken teeth.

"Yost?" April asked. "What's a Yost girl?" Why would anyone want to be a Yost girl?

"Henry leads a program for . . ." Mary Lou stopped and looked at Violet. "At-risk women."

"It's a recovery program," Violet said. She sounded defensive. "Not just women."

Mary Lou said, "You heard him talking about it at my house. The Anvil. Isn't that what he calls it?"

Violet looked down at the card she'd just made. The reminder that she was different from them seemed to take the steam out of her. She laid her stamp down and scrubbed at the ink on her fingertips. She pushed the card away and sat back.

To April's surprise, Violet looked Mary Lou in the eye. "It's true. I'm a former crystal user. I'm trying to stay clean any way I can."

She stood and asked Rocky where the bathroom was. She left the table, her head held high.

April turned to Mary Lou. "I understand you're mad at me, but do you have to pick on Violet?"

Mary Lou threw her stamp down in disgust. "What were you thinking, bringing a girl like that here?"

"A girl like what?" April looked directly at Mary Lou.

"She's Dr. Wysocki's daughter. You must know her parents. I think they might even go to your *church*."

April spat out the word "church" as though it were a place for brewing batches of eye-of-newt stew. Rocky hid a smile.

Suzi chimed in, "April, I can see the girl needs a lot of help, but we're not drug counselors. What if we say the wrong thing? Besides, don't you think some of us have been through this enough with our own families? That we've had enough rehab and addicts to last us a lifetime?"

Suzi was looking at Mary Lou when she spoke and tears were forming in her eyes. April realized Mary Lou had never been confronted by the results of her brother's actions so tangibly.

"Sorry, her father asked me to help her."

"My dad?" Violet was in the doorway. "I thought *you* wanted me to come."

"I did," April stuttered. "I do."

"I'd rather not be in the presence of someone who uses meth," Mary Lou said. Her voice was imperious, cutting through all the chatter.

Violet ran from the room. April wheeled to face Mary Lou. "That was not necessary. She's turning her life around."

"Something my brother never got to do."

CHAPTER 13

They drove in silence, tires occasionally bumping over lumps of snow. Even though it was early, the town was quiet. Winter evenings were spent inside. April could see TVs on in all the houses they passed. What did folks around here do in January before television? Those had to be long nights.

"What's up with that Mary Ellen?" Violet asked.

"Mary Lou? I'm sorry that she was rude to you. She's just found out her brother was murdered."

"Not that. I know about her brother and that sucks. Still."

April turned in her seat. Violet was staring straight ahead, her fingers picking at a scab on her elbow. "Did you know her brother?"

"What? You think all addicts know each other?"

April struggled to explain, "No. Aldenville's a small town. I thought maybe . . ."

Violet opened the car door. "You thought maybe I bought my meth from his gang."

April leaned over to stop her, but Violet was quick. The seat belt buckle flew back with a thunk. "I didn't mean . . ."

Violet climbed out and stuck her head back through the open door. "My father had no right to ask you to babysit me."

"No, Violet, it wasn't like that."

"And for your information, Henry Yost saved my life."

An old yellow car with black racing stripes was parked in front of the Wysocki's house, illuminated by floodlights over the detached garage. April recognized it as a Ford Torino, seventies' version.

"That's a cool car," April said. "That your boyfriend's?"

"Just a friend."

April said, "Okay," and laughed, but Violet didn't join in. "I hope you'll think about stamping with us again," April said. "Just because your father thought it was a good idea, doesn't mean it's not."

Violet didn't answer. Her eyes were on the house. Would she confront her father? April didn't think he deserved her ire.

"Give us another chance. It's usually a lot more fun. And it can be very gratifying. Spiritual, even."

"Sure. Fine."

Violet's attention was on the front door. She was eager to get inside. She seemed a little nervous leaving her friend alone with her parents. Maybe Dr. Wysocki didn't like him.

April let herself into Mitch's with the key he'd given her.

"You're early," he called. Mitch was working at his dining room table on his latest design for his next Hope House. He'd built one home for a low-income family and was planning three more.

She kissed the top of his head. "Stamping was a bust," she said.

His attention had slipped back to the project. She could see she had interrupted his flow. She looked over his shoulder. This one was a four-square with two master suites on the upper floor. He was designing the bathroom, playing with cutouts of bathtubs and sinks.

"Go back to work," she said.

"I'm at a bad stopping point," he explained.

"That's fine," she said. April stripped off her layers of clothes and pulled off her boots. Mitch had lit the fire in his woodstove, and the room was toasty. His shag rug felt good under her feet.

"Want to watch a video in a few minutes?" he asked. "I've got the newest Jason Bourne thriller."

April considered. Watching a guy race around trying to remember who he was and what he'd done in his past didn't sound enticing. She got up to pour herself some wine.

"No, work on your house plans. I'm going online for a while."

He worked, humming quietly. She logged on to the website of the local paper, hoping to find some information about who J.B. had been working with.

She couldn't let Mary Lou's anger stop her. If April wanted to look into J.B.'s death, nothing could stop her. She had Kit's blessing, and that was all she needed.

She wondered if Violet had been lying to her. Her time in Aldenville didn't overlap with J.B.'s, but still the meth community couldn't be that big.

The local paper didn't have much in the way of online archives. She couldn't find an obituary for J.B., but she did find a police report about the explosion. It gave the name of the other deceased meth maker, Ransom Conway. A few lines explained that the house had burned to the ground. It gave the address.

She opened the map site and found the location. It was a rural route address so she couldn't pinpoint the exact spot, but she saw the general vicinity. It didn't look like much more than empty land with a sprinkling of homes. A vestige of a once thriving town, the site of a sawmill. It was several miles from town. She hadn't been out that way in years. From Mitch's house, it was directly across the valley behind the small mountain that loomed in his back window.

A search of Ransom Conway brought up nothing, just a few phone book listings for Conways. Impossible to know if anyone was related. She jotted down the numbers. She'd try them tomorrow.

She moved the map to the north end and found the river she'd been at yesterday. She followed it until she found the spot where the cottages were. She pictured the place she had looked at yesterday.

April closed the computer and got up, stretching. She found dirty dishes in the sink and started washing.

"Don't do those," Mitch called. "I'll get to them later."

"I'm just trying to keep busy." Keep from talking, if she was honest. She didn't want to hash over her day. She'd had enough of Mary Lou.

She washed the dishes despite his protests, feeling the comfort of the dull routine. When she was finished, she wiped down the counters. She hadn't had a sponge in her hand since the Campbells moved in. She missed the mind-less, rhythmic action. The kitchen reminded her of her other needs.

"I saw a nice rental property," she said quietly.

She walked over to where he was working at the

dining room table, drying her hands on a paper towel. She couldn't find the nice thick cotton towels she'd gotten him for Christmas. Probably out in the garage under a power tool. The top of the table was littered with bits of wood and carving tools. His scroll saw was behind him, against the wall, where the buffet should be.

Mitch didn't look up. "I told you there's plenty of room for your stuff here. You're practically living here as it is."

"No," she said. She was firm but gentle.

Mitch stopped, the tone of her voice getting his full attention. April felt like she'd swallowed a cotton ball. She knew what she was saying was right, but she didn't want to upset Mitch.

"Come in here," she said. "We need to talk."

"Those words are never good," Mitch said. But he got up and joined her in the kitchen, his face grave. She prepared coffee and set the pot on to brew. She used the Guatemalan roast, his favorite.

"You sure look at home here," he said, watching her put the coffee beans back in the refrigerator and take out the creamer. She opened the cupboard and got down two mugs.

She set his favorite in front of him. "I love your house, Mitch, and I like being here with you."

The L word. She backed off using the word "love." They hadn't said that word to each other. It was loaded, indicating a commitment she wasn't sure she was ready for yet. She'd only been divorced from Ken a few months.

Right from the beginning, they'd been so comfortable with each other, so happy to be in each other's company. They felt it. She knew she felt it and knew he did, too. They didn't need to say "I love you" to each other.

"But . . ." he said. "I hear the 'but' in there."

April sat, leaning on her elbows. She wanted to touch

him, but he was leaning on the counter across the room. "I've barely lived by myself. I went from my parents' house to my dorm to living with Ken."

Mitch winced at the mention of her ex-husband's name. "What about the barn?"

She didn't want this to turn into an argument. "Even before Grizz and Charlotte arrived, that was always Ed and Vince's place. Not mine."

He lowered his gaze. The man had the best eyelashes, long and lush. It really wasn't fair. She wanted to reach out and stroke his cheek, but they needed to settle this once and for all. They couldn't always distract themselves with touches.

She said, "I know you don't understand. You've been living on your own for so long. I need to make a home for myself. Complete with girly touches, if I want. Lace curtains, doilies."

"Do you have an objection to my décor?" Mitch said, eyes sweeping the kitchen as though seeking out its faults. The roller shade in the small window over the sink was a dull white. A reciprocating saw sat on the counter, and his small butcher block was covered with glue stains. A grease-stained paper towel had missed the garbage, despite the orange Nerf hoop that was perched above the opening.

She followed his gaze and laughed. Mitch joined in.

"I know it could use a woman's touch. That's where you come in," Mitch said.

"Getting my own place is not about your lack of style." April drew in a deep breath. No more joking around. She had to make him understand.

He seemed to be gathering his thoughts. "Being on your own can be lonely."

He'd been living alone for quite a while before she moved back to town.

She let herself speak what she knew to be true. Her voice came out soft and slightly quivery but gathered strength as she spoke. "I need a sanctuary, one that I built for myself. I need to take some time, listening to myself, to my body and my mind. I feel myself crying out for a dedicated space."

Mitch took her hand. She'd been keeping her distance, afraid that touching him would make it harder to say. But something else happened. His fingers twining through hers reminded her that Mitch wanted what was best for her. He had her best interests at heart all the time. In a way that no one else did. He wouldn't object to her moving into her own place.

His fingers tightened around hers. She couldn't read his expression. Finally, he smiled.

"You want me to help you look?"

She smiled. "Not just yet, but thanks."

April set out about ten the next morning with the address she'd found. A look at maps online had given her a good sense of where the house that had blown up had been. It was in the Aldenville town limits but several miles away from Main Street.

She wasn't sure what looking at the property where the meth explosion had happened would tell her. But someone had to know something about J.B. The neighbors might be helpful, telling her who'd lived there. People tended to stay in place in Aldenville, so someone was bound to know who'd owned it. Maybe someone remembered the guys who went in and out of there last year.

The roads in that part of town were sparsely populated and full of bends and dips. Fun to hit at sixty miles per hour. She and Deana had driven these winding roads as high schoolers. For April's sixteenth birthday, Ed had given her a 1987 Chevy Cavalier. It wasn't a sweet ride, but it functioned most of the time. When things got rough at home, she would get in the car, pick up Deana and just drive. At April's house, once Ed had left, life had been unpleasant. Bonnie had been so miserable. Things weren't a cakewalk for Deana, either. There had been a period when she was unable to reconcile teenage life with living in a funeral home. They'd needed their driving sessions.

This road looked sort of familiar. She slowed, looking for some landmark to tell her where she was. A scarred mailbox, listing to one side, had the address in gold and black lettering that she'd been looking for.

She opened her car door and got out. She blew on her hands and stomped her feet. It was nuts how quickly the cold permeated her layers of clothes. She wished she'd thought to bring a thermos of coffee.

This was the place. The wind howled across the empty lot. Scraggly pine trees rimmed the property. The remains of an old foundation were barely visible as the snow sunk along the perimeter, leaving the imprint. Next to it, a pile of debris rose like a mass grave topped with snow. She couldn't tell where a driveway might have been. Unbroken snow lay across the front yard in deep drifts. No one had been to the site all winter. There was nothing for her to see here.

April looked to see if anyone else was around. To her right, April could make out smoke coming from a chimney, and she smelled wood smoke. A little home was tucked into a copse of now bare trees. In the spring, it would be obscured from view.

There were no sidewalks, so she drove to the house with the smoke.

A woman opened the door, shielding a toddler, who insisted on seeing who was on the porch.

April spoke quickly, before the door closed. "Hi, I was wondering if you knew anything about the Conways. They used to own that place up the road." April pointed.

"It wasn't the Conways, it was the Farrell house. But no one's there now."

"The house burned?" April said. The woman didn't seem to mind that her superheated house air was leaking into the outdoors. April could only imagine how isolating winter was for this woman.

"Yeah, that was like a year ago," she said. Even though she was distracted by the twisting boy in her arms, she was clearly desperate for adult conversation. "My husband has been trying to buy the land for us, but there are no living relatives."

"There's no one?" April asked. "So who owns the land now?"

She shrugged, giving her boy a shot at freedom, which he promptly took as she loosened her grip. "It's in probate court, going to take forever."

Her attention strayed as her toddler dropped down out of her arms, squirted around her legs into the house and came back carrying a cat. The woman moved her hip to block her son's path. She let the storm door close. "No, no, Brandon. Sparky has to stay inside. You, too."

The boy dropped the cat and tried to make a run for the outdoors. "Sorry," she said as the front door closed. April could hear the indignant cries of the young boy as she walked away.

April stood on the porch and looked out at the road. There was a farmhouse across the street. She knocked on that door, but there was no answer. She got back in her car and drove a quarter mile to the next visible house, which sat up on a rise.

She drove up, parking in the driveway alongside an

old Suburban. A red snow shovel leaned against the open garage door, and inside she could see a large woman, dressed in knit pants and a sweatshirt, pushing a broom. This looked more promising.

She looked up when April pulled in, and came out to greet her.

"Can I help you?" Her face was red with exertion. The driveway was swept free of any snow accumulation, and the garage was so clean, April would have eaten in it.

"Are you selling something? I don't want anything. If you're one of those religious nuts, just be aware. I'm guaranteed a place in heaven putting up with my Marvin all those years. Not that I expect to see him up there."

She stopped and scowled at April.

April suppressed a laugh. She couldn't imagine Marvin getting the best of this woman. Maybe she hadn't been this feisty when he was alive. "Not selling anything. Just wondering about that lot. I heard it was for sale," April said, pointing.

"Are you one of them? Those druggies?"

"No," April said emphatically. "I'm April Buchert."

"Okay, then. I'm Jeanie. Jeanie Justice." She leaned on the broom handle. Her eyebrows knitted. "You don't want that piece of ground. People make drugs there. Terrible stuff. Horrible chemicals that leach into the ground. I'm worried about my water being contaminated. I've called the county, the DEA, the EPA. Someone has to do something. I drink nothing but the bottled stuff now."

"But didn't the meth making end when the house blew up?"

"I don't think so," she said in a singsong way. "Look over here."

She led April up her driveway, through the garage and out a small door in the back wall. Her backyard looked

over the house April had just visited. April could see a
swing set in the yard of the house with the harried young
mother. Just beyond that, in the pine trees she could see the
old foundation.

"They bring a trailer and park it there."

April was doubtful. "But how do they get in? I didn't
see any tire tracks from the road. The snow hasn't been
touched."

Jeanie pointed again. "ATVs. They come through the
woods. Usually at night." She shook her head. "They're not
there all the time," she said. "The trailer comes and goes."

April squinted, shading her eyes. This was big news.
Maybe J.B knew that the gang was still making meth there.
Maybe that's what got him killed.

Jeanie turned and went back in the garage. April followed. "Have you told the police?" she asked.

"I can take care of myself." She pointed to a rack of
shotguns mounted on the wall. "They don't bother me."

April drove straight to the Aldenville Police Station. She was
excited. She'd tell the chief that meth was still being made
out there. This could lead to finding J.B.'s killer.

The police station was located in the back of the munic-
ipal building, a fancy name for the old hotel that housed the
mayor, borough council offices and the police. A tiny sign
directed her to the right door.

There was no one in the office. She heard voices that
seemed to be coming from the upstairs meeting room. She
climbed the stairs as she'd done the previous week for the
council meeting.

A poster on the door depicted a blacksmith with a red-
hot pair of tongs in his hand. Across the top read, "Anvils."
This was the place.

A twenty-cup coffeepot had been set to brew and the smell wafted out, energizing April with the caffeine particles on the air. A small woman with tight gray curls greeted her at the door. Her face was youthful, but the steel-colored hair and the polyester 1970s-style pantsuit pegged her as middle-aged. These clothes were never going to be sold as vintage. They were just old.

"Coffee?" she asked brightly. This woman didn't look like an addict, unless fondness for out-of-style clothes was an addiction.

April accepted a cup. "I want to make sure I'm in the right place. Is this the support group run by Officer Yost?"

She got a mischievous glint in her eye. "The one-size-fits-all twelve steps or however-many-steps-you-need support group? That's us."

She slapped on a name tag and handed one to April, along with a fat blue marker. Her name was Paula Glanville. Under her name, she wrote, "Gambling."

April raised an eyebrow.

"Aldenville isn't big enough for its own Gamblers Anon meeting, so I come here. There's lots of AA meetings. Alcoholics aplenty," she said with a smile, "but gamblers, not so much."

In San Francisco, any given night, April could have found a dozen twelve-step meetings for any vice. Some vices, she was sure, that the good people of Aldenville had never even heard of.

But this woman didn't look like a gambler. "You?" April asked, fighting to keep the surprise out of her voice. She didn't want to insult the woman.

Paula nodded, her face turning cloudy. "Putting that casino in the Poconos was the end for me. I was there every day after work. I lost my job, my house. My parent's house, really," she corrected.

April winced.

"Oh, they're dead. Still, it had been in the family for six generations."

April hid her reaction better this time. This woman was determined to keep up her callous cheeriness. April didn't want to ruin her effort.

Paula greeted newcomers and offered coffee as they filed in. A pretty woman in leather boots and a full-length mink ignored the cup and found a seat next to a middle-aged guy in a flannel shirt and down vest that strained over his belly.

"Sex," Paula muttered, using her coffee cup to camouflage her mouth.

"Pardon?" April was at a loss. Was she suggesting those two . . . ?

"Sex addict. He's online poker. And porn."

April watched the room fill. She looked for Violet. No sign of her yet. There were at least a dozen people here. That was a lot of heartache for such a small town. The kind of pain that was spread around. No one got off easy with an addict in the house. Wives, boyfriends, kids, parents, all impacted. If Yost was helping them, he was doing a good thing.

Paula was wearing earrings shaped like anvils. She caught April staring.

"The anvil is the symbol of this group. We take our totems seriously."

April gave her a questioning look.

She pointed at the poster. "The blacksmith uses heat and tools to mold the shape he needs. He has to be able to pound and land his blows solidly. The anvil is the support. You can't have change without the anvil."

Yost entered with Violet on his heel. Paula turned to pour him a cup of coffee and doctored it with hazelnut-flavored creamer. He stopped dead in front of April. Violet veered off just in time to avoid stepping on his heel.

He wasn't happy she was there.

"New recruit, Paula? Haven't I warned you about picking up strays?"

Paula giggled, missing Yost's displeasure. "No, silly. She found us. She's got a problem with . . ."

Paula's expression turned inquisitive as she realized April hadn't said what her addiction was. She waited for her to fill in the blank.

Yost got there first. "I know what her problem is. I don't think there's a twelve-step program for interfering with police investigations."

A couple in matching ski jackets, complete with dangling old lift tickets, approached Yost, interrupting his attack on April. Something about a broken vow. He held April's eyes for several long seconds before he turned away. She was on notice.

"I've got a police matter to discuss."

"Well, since the council frowns upon overtime, you're going to have to wait. I'm not on duty for another"—he consulted his watch, pulling the pocket piece out slowly—"ninety-five minutes."

April frowned at him. "I'm serious."

"So am I."

She talked fast before he could stop her. "I was out at the meth house site, and the neighbor told me she sees people going in and out of there, making meth."

To her dismay, Yost laughed. "Let me guess. In a shiny trailer, right?"

April nodded.

Yost leaned back against the wall. He was in civilian clothes today, a neat sweater over a pair of blue jeans. Looked almost human.

He raised his voice, playing to his crowd. "And did she tell you about the other shiny things she sees? That float down from the sky? And shoot flaming arrows at her place?"

April shrank back. Crap. She'd found the neighborhood nut job.

Yost wasn't finished humiliating her yet. "That's our Jeanie. She loves a new audience. She must have seen you coming a mile away."

"All right, I get it. Sorry to have bothered you."

"No problem, Miss Buchert! Why not stay for the lecture? Today's topic is about moderation." His tone was smarmy, as if he had much to teach her and she had much to learn.

Then Yost leaned in and spoke quietly. He didn't want to be overheard this time. "Have you been talking to Dr. Wysocki? I saw you go in his place the other day. That man is obsessed. He thinks just because his daughter got hooked on meth, it's everywhere."

"Listen," April said, her patience gone. "Why don't you just go do your job?"

His face hardened and his voice turned menacing. "I do my job, day after day, year after year. What do I get? Some city council member who thinks he knows more than me about how to keep this town safe, telling me I need to work fewer hours or be replaced by the cops next door. No one knows this town like I do. It's been my life for thirty years. I know where all the bodies are buried."

He turned on his heel and approached the podium set up in the middle of the room. April let herself out.

CHAPTER 14

April sat in her car with the motor running. Yost had embarrassed her in front of everyone. She felt awful.

So Jeanie was a bust. The neighbors had told her exactly nothing. She knew no more about J.B. than she had before she went out there.

Yost's group had her thinking about twelve-step programs. J.B. had been in AA, according to Kit. People going through them had tasks to do. April couldn't recite every one of the steps, but she was familiar with at least one.

Amends. Her college roommate had looked her up several years after graduation out of the blue, apologizing for the number of men she'd entertained in their room when they were freshmen. She was going through Alcoholics Anonymous and had to make amends.

Is that what J.B. had been doing? Trying to make up to his sister and his niece? Someone else? Conway's family? Maybe someone hadn't liked his apology.

April reached for the gearshift to put the car in drive. Her hand brushed against her coat pocket, and she felt the small plastic cassette tape. She'd nearly forgotten about what she'd found last night in the shed. Now all she needed was a player.

Her phone chirped. It was Tina. April looked at the phone in disbelief. Talk about timing.

"Just the woman I wanted to talk to," April said. "Do you have a microcassette player?"

"Umm . . ." Tina was clearly caught off guard. "J.B. had one, I think."

"Good, I'm coming up to get it."

"Okay, I need to see you too. I'm at home."

Tina gave her directions to her condo. She lived in a converted garden apartment. April was able to park out in front and quickly walked to the second floor unit. A wreath of glittery snowflakes greeted her. Next to it was a tin banner of a Dickensian choral group. They held a sign that read, "Welcome. Home Is Where the Heart Is."

April wondered if Tina would feel the same about her house now without J.B.

Tina answered the door. April rubbed her feet on the snowman doormat, but after spying Tina's off-white carpets, she took off her boots.

"Oh, April," Tina said, gathering her in for an awkward hug. "I'm glad to see you. Do you have any word?"

"Word?" April straightened. Tina's eyes were bright with hope.

"On the funeral. I thought you came to tell me about the arrangements."

"What? No, Tina, it all just happened the day before yesterday." She softened her tone when she realized how fragile Tina seemed. "I mean, the family's still dealing. I was hoping that you had that recorder."

Tina didn't answer, didn't offer to take April's coat or invite her in. She wandered back into her living room and sat down. She'd obviously been sleeping on her couch. The back cushions were on the floor, and a fleece blanket had been tossed over the arm. She straightened the remaining cushions and settled against them. April sat on a rocking chair opposite and looked around.

The house definitely had a woman's touch. The furniture was dainty. Queen Anne–style with turned legs and faded velvet upholstery. The décor relied heavily on flowery prints and an overuse of pink. She had a breakfront full of Disney characters and another with a collection of bird figurines. The white brick fireplace was filled with candles in their original plastic wrapping.

It was hard to imagine a guy as tall as J.B. getting comfortable and watching the tiny TV tucked into the corner of the room.

Tina moaned. "I'm sorry. I know I'm being a pain."

"It's been a terrible week." April saw Tina's dark circles. The woman was clearly on the verge of a breakdown. "Are you getting any sleep?"

"Not much."

"How about the microcassette?" April asked. "Do you have J.B.'s tape player?" She felt sorry for her but the tape might hold the key to J.B.'s murder and that would help everyone.

Tina's head lolled against the back of the couch. She waved away April's question. "I just wanted to see him one last time."

April looked away. Tina's grief was palpable.

"I tried calling the hospital, the morgue, the state police. No one will tell me where he is."

April could understand the need for closure. "I'm not your best ambassador right now," April said. "Mary Lou is practically blaming me for his death. It's going to break her heart when she learns he was living here with you for the last year."

Tina's brow furrowed. She sat up straighter. "She told him to never come back. It's her own fault."

April didn't want to argue with her. She wanted the tape player and to get out of here. She looked around to see if Tina had found it and set it down somewhere. The coffee table was covered with baby books. No sign of what she'd come for.

She stood to get a better look into the kitchen. It was yellow with a daisy theme. She could see a sink full of dishes and a crumb-laden Formica counter. Tina was having a hard time dealing.

"Mind if I look for the recorder?" April said, inching toward a hallway. She could see three doors. Two bedrooms and a bath perhaps. Maybe one was an office.

Tina shrugged and grabbed a pillow and hugged it. She wanted to say more about Mary Lou, it was obvious, but April had heard it before.

The hall was lined with school photos. April realized as the child in the pictures got older that it was Tina herself. She glanced back to see her lying prone on the couch. There had been no pictures of J.B. anywhere.

She peeked into the master bedroom. There was no sign that a man had been living here. No clunky watch on the nightstand, no *Popular Mechanics*. She thought about the way Mitch had spread himself all over his house. His presence was everywhere.

J.B. had lived a very small life, even after he found sanctuary.

The small second bedroom was set up as an office, with the kind of white gilded furniture that April had lusted after when she was a young girl. A computer was set up and the doors had been removed from the closet, which housed filing cabinets and shelves with technical magazines and college texts.

April opened drawers, rifling through the contents. She pushed aside current bills, staples, rubber bands, feeling for the sharp edge of a recorder. Her fingers felt something about the right size that turned out to be a box of checks

She fingered the tiny tape in her pocket. She should tell Tina about it. Maybe she knew more about what J.B. did. She looked around the room one more time. Nothing.

So far all she'd found that belonged to J.B. was a guitar pick. No guitar, just the old pick. The recorder was probably in his pocket when he went off the road and died. He seemed like a guy who'd gotten used to taking up very little space in the world.

Tina'd said they'd been happy, but really who knew? He'd gotten sober. His infatuation with Tina might have been over. She'd rescued him and he felt grateful. April had only her word that it had blossomed into something more.

April thought back to the night he'd come to Kit's. He'd been nervous, jittery. Was he worried about being picked up by the police? Or was he a man about to leave his girlfriend?

Maybe his trip back to Aldenville had been an attempt to reconcile with his family and move back.

CHAPTER 15

The phone rang, startling April. It was on the desk in the
office. Tina didn't answer and the answering machine
kicked in.

"Tina? Are you there? There's someone here trying to
buy cold meds. I got a quick glimpse of the license. It had
an Aldenville address."

Gloria, Tina's coworker at the drug store. She hung up
when Tina didn't pick up.

Jeanie Justice was right after all. Someone was making
meth, or at least trying to, in Aldenville.

April went back out to the living room. Tina was snoring gently. She let herself out and raced to the pharmacy.
This could be lead her to people who knew about J.B.

Gloria was working the counter. There were no custom-
ers in the store. April walked right up.

"I was just at Tina's," she said. "I heard your message. Is
the person still here?"

Gloria shook her head. "She took off as soon as I tried to take her license and scan it."

"Darn it," April said. "What did she look like?"

"Kind of ordinary. Medium height, brownish hair. She said her kids were real sick and she needed several packs. I believed her until she got so skittish about her ID."

"You didn't see her name?"

"No, just caught the Aldenville on the address."

April banged her hands on the counter. "Too bad."

"You just came from Tina's?" Gloria asked. "How is she today?"

"Not great. Sleeping on the couch."

Gloria nodded. "I've been over there every day but she barely knows I'm there."

"Did you ever meet J.B.?" April asked.

"Never. She never even mentioned him until her pregnancy got too noticeable. She hasn't had many boyfriends, so she knew she had to explain that."

That made sense as J.B. was trying to keep his identity a secret. April wondered what J.B. had thought about going public once his girlfriend was pregnant. Was he happy or scared?

April thanked Gloria and went back home. She had more questions than answers now.

The morning of the Ice Festival, the sun was making a weak appearance. The rays were threaded through gauzy clouds that covered the sky like a layer of tulle. But the forecast was for sun that afternoon. No precipitation on the radar. And that meant the Campbells would be gone for the weekend. April jumped out of bed, wanting to wish them farewell. She didn't want to sleep through any part of having the barn to herself.

Grizz was already outside, warming up the car for their trip to Scranton. Charlotte had laid out ham sandwiches, homemade cookies, dried apples and bananas. A thermos of coffee was topped off with half-and-half. There was enough food to feed a family of six traveling by horse and buggy rather than two people driving an hour and a half. Even if Grizz never topped thirty miles an hour the entire trip, they'd be there before lunch. If they got caught in a blizzard, they'd be able to survive for a week.

She gave Charlotte a hug. "Have a nice time," she said.

"We will," Charlotte said. "It's been too long since we've seen Maisie and Don. I'm sorry we won't get to see you win the Ice Festival trophy, though." Charlotte packed their sandwiches into an old-fashioned plaid cooler.

April laughed. "You've got such high expectations. I'll be glad just to get through the day."

Charlotte grabbed her face. "You're going to do just fine. I saved you a sandwich," she said, closing the lid, eyes sliding to the refrigerator. April wriggled free, grabbed the handle and walked Charlotte out to the driveway. Grizz was tapping the wheel impatiently.

April waved to them out until they were out of sight and skipped back into the house. She had sheets to wash and piles of newspapers to recycle. She thought for a moment about leaving the barn doors open, to give the place a good airing. Having three people in this space in the dead of winter was good for no one. She shivered and decided against it.

April had worked at Mirabella all day yesterday. She was ready for some fun.

She was waiting outside when Mitch came to pick her up around noon. The sun was out fully now, and the steady drip of melting snow cheered her.

"Ready, Freddy?" she asked, getting into his Jeep almost before he came to a complete stop.

"You're in a good mood," he said, leaning over for a kiss. "I like it."

"This is going to be fun," she said. "I can feel it."

Aldenville was a small town made up of a small commercial area and miles of surrounding land. Main Street was a two-mile stretch bookmarked by six churches and the VFW hall. Several small businesses, a tea shop, the bank and the Brass Buckle Inn still dotted the street, but many had moved out to the busy highway that ran mostly parallel. Main Street had been left to return to its roots of sleepy small town thoroughfare, with one traffic light to break up the drive.

The Whispering Willows Park was in the middle of town. It had a community pool with a locker room, one park for little kids and another for bigger ones. A Little League and Babe Ruth field took up the rest of the acreage.

Today, it had been transformed. Gaily roofed booths had been set up along what were usually the first- and third-base lines of the Little League field. That was a testament to how frozen solid the ground was. The baseball league was particular about their field and usually allowed no one on it during the off-season.

Fake snowflakes, as big around as a tire, hung everywhere. Kids dueled with plastic icicles while their parents sipped from cups shaped like glaciers. A snow machine made redundantly abundant snow, better for the snow-person-making contest. April laughed when she saw the gender-neutral title.

The festival had already begun. At the far end of the park, an ice rink was crowded with skaters. Mitch and April jumped out of the way of an overzealous roller making his snow-person's head. He had a Dowling Nursery hat on. Suzi waved a carrot as she urged him on. Mitch scooped up loose snow and tossed a snowball her way. She easily ducked it.

Tantalizing smells were emanating from a food tent. Next to it, a twenty-one-and-over beer garden was drawing a crowd already. In the tents, large heaters were working hard to provide some level of comfort to the outdoor revelers.

In the middle of the park were blocks of ice, as tall as April, waiting to be carved. Mitch took his huge duffel of tools over to their station. The contest didn't begin for an hour or so, but he would set up. April had one stop to make first.

She carried her portfolio over to Rocky's Stamping Sisters booth. She had finished one more collage late last night. She was happy with the icy scene and wanted to make sure Rocky gave it a prominent place.

Rocky's little booth was warm. She had a propane heater on full blast. April reached down and felt the rays toast her fingers.

"Is that thing safe?" April asked.

"Sure it is. Just be careful and don't knock it over."

April edged into the booth, avoiding the little heater.

Rocky tossed her hair back and examined April's creation. "Oh, this is good." Rocky said, "How do you like this idea? *Guinness Book of World Records.* We're going to make the largest card ever."

Now April understood the enormous roll of craft paper that covered the front counter and trailed down, ending in a plastic storage box. Rocky had laid out stamps and inks and made up a sign that read, "Be a part of history. Put your mark on the world's largest greeting card."

April smiled. Rocky had a flair for the dramatic, but

drama alone didn't amount to sales. "You're going for a record?"

"*Guinness Book*, here we come. Why not? I'm going to put Stamping Sisters on the map—one way or the other."

"Good luck," April said. She backpedaled before Rocky could involve her. The success of Stamping Sisters was important to her, too, but she wanted to focus on Mitch's project today. The ice-sculpting contest was due to begin at one. The artists had three hours to complete their piece before the judging.

Mitch walked by, pulling a wheeled cart with their tools behind him. "Let's go, Buchert. Time to make the donuts," he called.

"Here goes nothing," April said.

Rocky shoved her out of the booth. "Just coo admiringly every once in a while. That's all men need."

"Got that figured out, do you?" April said.

Rocky smiled enigmatically. Her love life was a well-kept secret. "Stay warm," she said. "You know the first signs of frostbite, don't you?"

April shook her head. She felt a small spark of panic. She was going to be standing in the middle of all that ice for hours. Of course, there would be no propane heaters in the sculpting area. "What are they?"

"How should I know?" Rocky laughed.

April waved Rocky's joke away and followed Mitch. She joined him just as the rules were being explained over a loudspeaker. The contestants were to work in teams of two with each person contributing something to the design. The finished pieces would be judged on workmanship and "wow" factor.

The judges were introduced. There were several familiar faces. Mary Lou's husband, Councilman Peter Rosen, stood with hands clasped behind his back. He was wearing a gray wool overcoat with a velvet collar and a blue scarf Mary Lou had knit tucked in the lapel. April recognized the guy who owned the local supermarket and a woman from her mother's church. And Officer Henry Yost.

April leaned into Mitch's shoulder to avoid being overheard. "That blows any shot we had. We don't stand a chance with Yost judging," April said. It was unfair how often Yost popped up to ruin her day.

The judges moved off into a heated tent to wait out the contest.

Mitch shrugged off her worry. "We're going to be so head and shoulders above the rest, that he won't have any choice, even if he chooses to be the Russian judge. Besides, your design is going to knock 'em dead. We've got wow factor up the wazoo."

April kissed him. If only she had as much confidence in herself as he did. She knew what made a good graphic element and what would be easy to carve. The design was deceptively simple but striking. But she didn't know if it would translate into ice.

Two entwined hearts. She'd been hoping the romantic element would appeal to the judges. Not so much Yost, though. She had never seen any evidence of a heart in him.

"I'm going to finish setting up," Mitch said. "Why don't you go suss out our competition?"

April looked at the circle of sculptors. There were a dozen teams, forming a circle with the blocks of ice facing out. "What would I be looking for? The best chain saw? The biggest bicep? The raddest chisel?"

"I think there's coffee for us in the tent, smart ass," he said good-naturedly.

That sounded more like a job she could do. "Okay." She leaned in for a kiss.

Three teams down from their station, April was surprised to see Logan. She nearly didn't recognize him. He had a hood on and a scarf covering his mouth. April tapped him on the elbow.

"Logan! Where's Kit?" April looked around for signs of bundled-up babies in the spectators that walked past. She saw plenty of snowsuits, but none looked familiar.

"Back at Mary Lou's. They'll be here for the award ceremony. What are you doing?" he said.

"Coffee run."

"I'll come with," he said, checking with his partner, who nodded.

Inside the tent, a big urn of coffee was set up for the participants. Yost and Councilman Rosen were talking. Logan didn't acknowledge his father-in-law. Logan followed April, and they silently filled up paper cups that bore a local insurance agent's logo. He bundled three packets of sweetener, tearing the tops with his teeth.

"I didn't know you did this." She pointed to the sculptors.

He took a sip and nodded. "Kit's uncle taught me. He used to win this every year, back before his hands got too shaky."

April poured cream into Mitch's coffee. "J.B. was an ice sculptor?"

The more she knew about this guy, the more she thought she would have liked him. Maybe he drank because he was a creative soul, one whose fragile essence couldn't hold up to the daily pressure of life.

"He was jack of all trades, master of none," Logan said bitterly.

They walked back to Logan's station and he handed
over his second cup.

Logan's partner pulled up his goggles. April realized
she'd met him at Mary Lou's party. It was Buck Sienstra.
She reintroduced herself.

"You here with Winchester?" Buck said, glancing over
at Mitch, who was engrossed in laying out his hammers and
chisels. He polished each one before setting them down in
a pre-designated order. Mitch's superstitious side was coming out. April started to head back and see if he was at all
interested in the hot drink. Buck's words stopped her.

"You're the one that found J.B., right?" he said.

"You knew J.B.?" April asked.

He nodded. His mustache caught the coffee, and he
wiped it off, stroking his face with force, his thumb and
forefinger moving in opposite directions.

"Sure, competed against him for years. Now, this
guy"—he punched Logan lightly on the arm as though he
didn't want to hurt him, just take him down a peg—"he's
not as good at the artistry, but he's strong as a bull."

Logan grinned and put his head and shoulders down
as if he were going to tackle him. Buck held him off with
one hand.

Buck got serious. "I heard he was murdered." He banged
his chisel against his metal toolbox. The sound was loud
and ominous. "He never should have come back."

Logan nodded, his face darkening. "I told him not to."

April looked at him. His mouth was twisted. She hadn't
realized he'd been with Kit when she saw J.B. around
Christmas. Given Logan's position as Mary Lou's number
one yes-man, she wasn't surprised by his reaction.

April sensed Buck knew more than he was saying. "So
you think that gang was after him?" she asked.

Logan was saying something. April tuned him out and

moved closer to Buck. She wanted to hear what he had to say about J.B.

To her surprise, Buck laughed. "Gang? There was no gang. Who told you that?"

Logan jumped in. "That's what J.B. said. He told Kit he'd gotten involved with the Cretins. They made him get their drugs."

April nodded.

Buck snorted. "That's a laugh. The Cretins don't operate around here. No, it was local yokels, that's for sure."

"But who?" All this time she'd thought it was the gang. She'd been picturing guys in leather jackets with tattoos. She remembered the box in Deana's cupboard. Whose cremains were those?

April asked, "Did someone else go missing? I mean it couldn't have been just J.B. and one other guy, making drugs and distributing them. It seems all J.B. did was buy the meds."

Buck shrugged. "Heck if I know. The guy who the police IDed that day was Ransom Conway. His mother lives over on South Road. She buried him. But I don't know every slimeball that lives around here. Could be that no one reported him missing because they didn't want him back."

"Whoever he was," Logan said.

"The way I heard it," Buck continued, "the cops found no intact bodies. The heat was too intense. Everything was gone. Two cars out front had legal registrations. The rest were stolen and had no papers. The two were registered to Ransom and J.B. The cops just sort of split up the remains and gave half to each family."

Wow. Stellar police work. April could see Yost chatting up a woman selling hot cocoa. It was Paula from the support group. Today she was sporting a sweatshirt with an anvil on the front. Always his cheerleader, it seemed.

Logan was shifting from foot to foot, still trying to join the conversation. He seemed to sense his opening.

"I clocked J.B. when he showed his face," Logan bragged. "Just hauled off and hit him."

April took a step back. No wonder Kit hadn't wanted her husband around when she met J.B. out at the Dowling Road house.

Buck said, "You're always going off half-cocked. J.B. was good people."

"If you like meth-making drunks," Logan said, eyes narrowing. He was showing off, trying to impress Buck and appear macho.

"You really don't know what you're talking about, boy," Buck said quietly. "That man had integrity."

Logan rolled his eyes. April reminded herself that he was a twenty-one-year-old father of twins who had probably never been farther from home than Philadelphia. Maybe New York, on a school field trip. He had no life experience outside this little town. He would grow up someday. At least she hoped so, for Kit's sake.

Buck said, "J.B. had standards. He had no choice."

April caught the sadness in the man's voice. "What do you mean, no choice?"

Buck lowered his voice. "He never specifically said, but I got the feeling he did what he did because he owed someone."

That was the second time someone said J.B. was in someone's debt. April stayed quiet, giving Buck the space to say what he wanted to say. She shot Logan a look, hoping to silence him.

Buck stroked his mustache again. "Sounds weird, I know, but J.B. never was a druggie. An alcoholic, yes. Even as a drunk, he knew the real danger was drugs. His mother had been a diet-pill junkie. She died of an overdose back in the eighties. Accidental, they said, but who knows?" He sipped his coffee again.

April's head tilted, and she stole a glance at Logan. Mary Lou's mother—Kit's grandmother—had been an addict and died with too many pills inside her. News to her. Logan's cheeks had two high, bright red spots. His lips were thinned. Looked like that was news to him, too.

April couldn't remember Mary Lou ever talking about her mother. Nor had Kit, for that matter. And the stamping group always spent time talking about family. Mothers were an intense—and frequent—topic of discussion.

"Kit's like that, too," Logan said. "Won't even smoke a doobie with me."

April fought the urge to smack a little sense into Logan. Kit had a lot of work ahead of her to turn him into a mature husband and partner.

April felt rather than saw Mitch looking for her. She'd better get his coffee to him.

"Good luck today," April said, shaking hands with Logan's partner.

Buck grinned. "We don't need no stinkin' luck. We got talent."

He yelled over to Mitch. "You're going down."

CHAPTER 16

An *air horn blew, and an announcer said there was five minutes* until the contest began. April hurried back to their station. She smiled when she saw Mitch. He was pacing the small space, muttering, swinging his arms in a wide circle. She'd seen this mode before. He was blowing off excess energy.

Mitch rubbed his hands together and took the coffee from her. His cheeks were ruddy—whether from the cold or excitement, April wasn't sure. She was feeling the butterflies in her stomach rise up, matching his level of anticipation.

"It's beautiful," April said, pointing to the slab of ice they'd been given to work with. She circled it slowly. The translucent ice gave the piece an ethereal quality already. She could almost understand Michelangelo's sense that he was freeing the object from the stone. She could practically see her design of entwined hearts inside.

She began to understand Mitch's excitement.

He handed back the coffee. "All righty then," he said. "Let's be ready to start the minute the timer says go. I've read and reread the rules. There's nothing that says you have to do an equal amount of carving compared to what I do. Just help me with the base. After that, you're free to go."

April drew back and looked at him. "I want to help." There was no way she was going anywhere. She and Mitch were in this together.

"I appreciate that, but once I get going, I'll be in the zone. There won't be much to do. You'll be free to wander the festival. Buy a corn dog."

"You know I hate corn dogs.

"Schmooze the judges. If you see Henry Yost, try not to piss him off today."

April grinned. "I try not to make promises I can't keep."

He kissed her cheek. "Find a place to stay warm."

Staying warm did sound good. Her fingertips were already aching from the cold. She wasn't sure she could feel her toes.

The air whistle blew again. The Aldenville Ice Festival Ice-Sculpting Contest had officially started.

He indicated a spot on the block of ice. "Put your blade right here."

April pushed down her safety goggles and started her chain saw. Her whole body felt the vibration. Tiny bits of frozen water spat out at her. She flinched. Mitch put a steadying hand on her back, and she made the cut.

She stood back. She could see the beginning of the entwined hearts she'd sketched. She'd nearly chewed off the inside of her cheek, but the sculpture was started.

Mitch rubbed his hands together and blew on them. He wore leather fingerless gloves, and April liked the look of them. But Mitch wasn't going to dally.

Without another word, Mitch put down his goggles and

got to work. He dropped into a mode of concentration that she knew too well from spending time with him in his wood shop.

She held on to her chain saw, waiting for Mitch to give her another chance at the ice. She was getting bored. And cold. Standing in one spot doing nothing was not helping her circulation. She couldn't feel her toes. She danced in place. Mitch glanced up. She stopped moving, guiltily. She was breaking his concentration.

April saw Mary Lou next to her husband in the judging tent. He was in the midst of a large group of people, smiling and shaking hands. She wondered when the next mayoral race was. He certainly seemed to be running for office.

Mary Lou caught April's gaze but looked away quickly.

Carving next to them was a young couple in matching plaid jackets. April admired the way they were working in tandem, moving in and out, each movement seemingly in sync with each other. It was beautiful to watch. Then the woman made a jerking motion with her saw. Suddenly a stream of profanities came out of the man's mouth. Their block of ice had shattered, leaving them with a pile of rubble.

The woman put a mittened hand over her mouth. April saw tears glistening before she looked away.

"Yes," Mitch said, pulling off his goggles, stopping his chain saw. His hand rose in a discreet victory salute. He leaned in close so she could hear him over the din. "They were our biggest competition."

"I thought we were in this for the fun," she said. She didn't like this competitive streak.

Mitch didn't say anything, just stood back and studied what he'd done so far. A sliver of ice from somewhere landed on the back of her neck, causing her entire body to shiver uncontrollably. She'd known Mitch would lose himself in the work, but she'd pictured herself stoically standing by. The reality was it was colder standing next to the block of ice than she could have imagined.

"I'm going to go in the tent and warm up," she said. Mitch's eyes never left his project. He pushed his goggles back down.

She blew him a kiss and walked around the circle of sculptors. It was impossible to tell what the sculptures would end up looking like, but some were taking shape. No one took notice of her.

April moved out into the Ice Festival, passing the casino booths. Violet's parents were manning the St. John Bosco Catholic Church's bake sale. Mitch would be bereft if she didn't bring him back a cookie or two. She had to wait for a family of six to make their choices. After minutes of back and forth, all four kids went for the Rice Krispies Treats.

Dr. Wysocki nodded at April and smiled warmly.

"Hi, April," Mrs. Wysocki said. "I didn't see your mother today."

"She's still on her honeymoon," April said. "She's gathering recipes in Ireland right now."

Mrs. Wysocki smiled. "In that case, I can't wait until the next women's fellowship potluck."

"What'll it be for you?" Dr. Wysocki asked.

"How about two snickerdoodles and a chocolate chip?" April said, pointing to the ones she wanted.

"On the house," he said.

"Oh, no," April said. "I can't do that. It's for charity."

He pushed away her money, reached in his front pocket and put a five in the till. "That'll cover it. We owe you."

April thanked him and walked away. Violet clearly hadn't told them what kind of reception she'd gotten at stamping.

As soon as she was out of sight, she poked her nose

into the bag and inhaled. The snickerdoodles were calling to her. She'd just have one. Mitch wouldn't miss what he didn't know he had.

She pulled out the cookie and bit into it. Yum. She was about to indulge in another bite when her elbow was jostled. The cookie fell to the ground and crumbled. April swallowed a curse and sighed instead.

"Sorry, April." Violet was at her side, looking furtive. "I don't want my parents to see me. My mother thinks I ought to be helping her in that booth."

She made herself even smaller and ducked behind a balloon seller. A pair of high-heeled leather boots crushed April's cookie and ground it into the path. April cringed.

Still, she knew what it was like trying to avoid getting sucked into a parent's projects. The older folks in this town did most of the volunteer work. Her generation was falling way behind in that department.

"Got a minute?" Violet said. She steered them into a space behind the eating tent. It was a good spot, out of the elements and the sight line of Violet's mother. April could feel a little warmth coming through the wall.

Violet looked down at the ground, out into the crowd over April's head and back to the ground again. April was getting nervous. Their spot was a little isolated. Was Violet waiting for someone else? She pulled out her cell phone, checking the time, but mostly making sure it was on.

Violet's shoulders heaved, and April realized she was struggling to find the words she needed. She forgot her uneasiness and put her cell away. She waited for Violet to get the courage to say what she had to say.

"I want to thank you for taking me to your stamping group," she said, eyes down. "You didn't have to do that."

April was surprised and felt a ribbon of warmth unfurl in her for this poor woman. Violet's ravaged face and body gutted her. She was so far from the freckled-faced second-grader lisping through "Rudolph the Red-Nosed Reindeer" at the holiday pageant. *"Like a lightbulb,"* they'd shouted together.

"I enjoyed having you with me," April said.

Violet seemed to be tearing up. "No one's treated me nice since I came back. It was like everything I'd done in my life, college, buying my own place in the city, going to law school, none of it mattered."

Her voice got quieter, and the hubbub around them snatched her words away. She pulled off one bright blue mitten and shook out a pack of cigarettes. April leaned in closer so she could hear. "All I wanted was to keep up with the twenty-five-year-olds in my class. It was so much harder than I thought."

Violet shrank back against the tent, finding a space out of the wind to light up.

"What's done is done," April said, hearing her mother's platitudes come out of her own mouth. It was comforting in a way, bringing Bonnie into her thoughts. "You're putting all that behind you now."

April put a hand on Violet's shoulder, breathing in smoke. Violet swiped at her eyes with the other mitten.

"I wish it was that easy," she said.

April said, "You're not using, right? And you're going to your support meetings?"

Violet nodded. A group of loud teen boys went by, showing their love by hip- and shoulder-checking each other. One crashed into Violet's side, nearly knocking her over. He apologized and quickly moved off, telling his friends to jet.

Violet ground out her cigarette. She pulled April in for a hug. "Anyhow, I just wanted to say thanks for letting me stamp with you."

"I hope you'll come again," April said.

"I'm not sure your friends would like that," she said. Violet's eyes shifted to the crowd and she squared her shoulders. "We'll see."

She walked off with a flip of her mitten.

April reached down for her phone. It was not even three o'clock. She still had an hour before Mitch needed her back. She took a step forward, but her path was blocked.

Mark and Deana stood in front of her. "We've been looking for you," Mark said, mock sternly.

April put her phone away. The voice mail light was lit, but she had ignored it. They'd probably been calling her. It was hard to hear the phone ring in the din of the Ice Festival.

Deana said, "We're going for a late lunch. Care to join us?"

"*Halupki* and sausage rolls," Mark said, rubbing the front of his coat. "You know you want some."

He rolled his eyes. Deana nudged him and joined April laughing. The bite of cookie had just whetted her appetite. The sandwich Charlotte had left for her was long gone, eaten before Mitch had picked her up.

"I'd love to, but I'd better wait for Mitch. We'll eat later."

"We just went by there, looking for you. He said you should eat with us. He was working furiously. I don't think he wants to be distracted."

"Me? A distraction?" April tried on a femme fatale voice but dropped it.

Mark said, "Us manly men, we need our alone time, too, you know."

"For what? To do your nails?" April asked. "Nice try. I'm starving. If Mitch says it's okay to eat, then I'll eat."

She snaked her arm under Deana's and the other under Mark's, and the three marched toward the entrance of the food tent.

"By the way," Mark said, "the temperature is twenty-nine. Chance of flurries tonight."

April punched his arm lightly. "Thanks, Weatherman. Thanks for reminding me how cold I am."

The tent was warm. Not enough to take off their coats, but several large heaters were working hard to keep the frigid air comfortable. Planks of wood had been laid down between aisles of tables to serve as a sidewalk. The noise from the diners was loud. April communicated with Mark and Deana by hand signals.

They loaded their plates with carbs as if they were bears about to go into hibernation. Mark led them to a long communal table with three empty seats. They greeted the people around them and tucked in.

April was mopping her plate with bread when she looked up to see an unexpected familiar face.

Tina Adama stood in front of them. "Mind if I sit?"

Deana looked at April, clearly questioning. Mark jumped up and pulled out the bench he'd been sharing with April. He kept his hand on it so she wouldn't tip and fall off.

"I warmed it up," he said, indicating that Tina should sit in his place. He took his plate and moved to the opposite side next to Deana. She took his hand in hers. They both looked to April for answers.

Tina settled on the bench, unbuttoning her coat and taking off her gloves. She set them on the table and unwound her plaid chenille scarf.

April took in a breath. She hadn't told them about Tina's existence. She'd been hoping to tell Mary Lou first.

"Deana, Mark, this is Tina Adama." She leaned across

the table to avoid revealing her identity to everyone around them. She knew she could count on them for discretion. "J.B.'s girlfriend."

Mark's eyes went wide. Deana tightened her grip on her husband's hand but otherwise didn't flinch. April admired her ability to look unsurprised. Tina reached across to shake hands.

"We're so sorry for your loss," Deana said. Mark nodded and shook her hand.

April turned to Tina. "What are you doing here?"

"I saw a flyer for the festival at the drugstore. I knew that Peter Rosen was one of the judges." She saw the question in April's eye. "What? They've got a website you know, Rosen Realty. It's very informative."

April had seen the website. Plenty of pictures of Peter and Mary Lou, Kit and her brother. Even the twins. Information about their civic duties, their volunteer work. It was all laid out there in an effort to entice the buyers and sellers of homes. Everything a person would want to know about a family.

"I thought there was a chance I could meet Jimmy's people," she said, her eyes straying down. She settled a hand on the gentle curve of her stomach. April glanced at Deana. It wasn't easy to tell under the bumpy contours of Tina's down coat that Tina was pregnant, but something in the way her hand moved told the story. Tina could not stop touching herself.

Deana gave April a sharp look. April nodded slightly. Deana's eyes widened. Death of a loved one, pregnancy, all Deana's buttons were being pushed right now. She snuggled in closer to her husband. April knew she was hurting.

"I couldn't stand it if he was buried without me," Tina said, sounding more macabre than she'd intended.

Deana straightened. This was something she could help

with. Mark looked down at his wife as if he knew what she was thinking. They believed in the value of rituals surrounding the dead. They also knew the complications of families.

Tina shrunk down in her seat, swallowed by the wide quilted collar of her coat. Her face was even rounder than April remembered. The bulky coat made her look little and vulnerable.

"I haven't had a chance to tell the family about you," April said. "They might not be all that thrilled to meet you."

"She's carrying his child," Deana said loudly. April looked at her friend, knowing she'd decided to help Tina. Once she'd made up her mind, nothing stopped her, but she didn't know about April's doubts.

"I know that but . . ." April began. She lowered her voice.

Deana cut her off. "What is it you'd like to have happen?" she said to Tina.

Tina sat up straighter. Her hand clutched her stomach as she looked at Deana hopefully. "Just to be there. If they don't want to meet me, I won't make trouble. I just need to be present."

"Let's call Mary Lou right now. She's here somewhere. I'm sure she'd be glad to meet you."

April had to stop this. She wasn't sure Tina was who she said she was.

She put her hand over Deana's phone. "Why don't we just let Tina know when the service is? I'll make sure she gets to it. What do you think, Tina? I can even pick you up."

Tina considered.

Deana looked to Mark. He'd caught his breath through his teeth. "Looks like you won't need the phone," he said.

The three women followed his gaze. Mary Lou and Peter were making their way into the tent. In two more steps, they'd see them.

April stared at the plate in front of her, now empty except for her dirty plastic silverware. A lull in the conversations around them brought quiet. April heard Mary Lou call out to Deana and Mark.

"Peter has to eat and run," she cried, pointing at the buffet. She steered her husband toward the goodies. Her hand gestures made it apparent she'd seen the two empty seats next to Deana and Mark and wanted them saved.

April saw Violet and Paula seated on the other side of the tent, watching them.

Mary Lou started toward them, obviously not seeing April. Or ignoring her. And not knowing who Tina was. April felt her scalp turn hot despite the cold. This wasn't going to end well.

Tina stood up from the bench, nearly dumping April in the process. Her presence had been anchoring one end. April caught herself and stood, just as Mary Lou arrived.

"Oh," Mary Lou said, spotting April. She looked at Deana as if she was disappointed in her. She adjusted the brim of her floppy wool hat. April couldn't see her face very well now.

Tina took a step forward. April grabbed the back of her coat, but Tina twisted away. She'd obviously recognized Mary Lou.

"Hi, I'm Tina Adama. Your brother and I were involved."

Mary Lou's face had gone pale. Tina put out her hand.

"I'm happy to meet you," she said. "Jimmy talked about you all the time."

"Jimmy?" Mary Lou said stupidly. That was so unlike her, April knew just how flummoxed she was by Tina's presence.

"J.B.," April said. "Tina knew him as Jimmy."

Mary Lou recovered a bit, color returning to her cheeks. "And *you* knew this how?"

This was the woman April knew. Never without a come-back. April couldn't tell her that she'd been to Mountain Top twice in the last week, seen where J.B. lived.

"She's a pharmacist," she said, hoping to focus the attention back on Tina.

"Not a drug addict?" Mary Lou said. Her face said she didn't believe it. "A fellow alcoholic?"

Tina's mouth fell open. "Your brother was clean and sober when he lived with me," Tina said, her voice tight. Tina stepped around the bench and moved closer to Mary Lou.

The tinny music that had been playing stopped. The crowd noise died down some. The Ice Festival announcer came on to say that the sculptors had ten minutes to finish. He encouraged spectators to gather round for the judging. April had to be at Mitch's station before that time was up or they would be disqualified. It would take her half that time to get over there.

She looked from Mary Lou to Tina. They hadn't taken their eyes off each other's faces. J.B. had two strong women in his life, that was for sure. April suspected they were more alike than they knew.

"Lived with you?" Mary Lou said, her words clipped and cold. April felt another chill. It was her fault Tina was here. She'd brought this woman into their lives and now she wasn't even sure J.B. had loved her.

"Listen, why don't we get together and talk this out?" April said. "You can come to the barn a little later. After the Ice Festival. The Campbells are away, and I've got some great wine. We can talk . . ." She glanced at Deana.

Deana smiled at April. She liked the conciliatory tone

April was trying out. Mark's hands were crossed in front of his body, and he had on his neutral funeral-director face. Ready for anything. Peter was coming toward the table with a plate of food. He was grousing that he had no time to eat. He'd heard the announcement, too.

April glanced out of the tent. Streams of people were heading toward the ice-sculpting area. She would never get over there in time unless she left right now.

"I've got to get back," April said. "Mitch . . ."

Tina and Mary Lou ignored her.

"We'll be there for the judging," Deana said.

She started to move away. "Okay, how about it? Say, eight o'clock, my place?"

Mary Lou seemed to be waiting for Tina to agree first. Tina appeared to be thinking about it. She placed her hands on the front of her coat. One on top and one on the bottom, cupping her belly. Mary Lou's eyes widened.

The air horn blew a two-minute warning. April had to fly.

As she snuck through the stakes at the back of the tent, she heard Mary Lou say, "You're pregnant?"

CHAPTER 17

April raced back to their station, skidding into it seconds before
the final air horn sounded the end of the contest. She saw
Kit on her way to the food tent.

Mitch put out his hand to stop her.

The announcer said, "Chain saws down. Cutting tools
down."

"Glad you could make it," Mitch said.

She bent over to catch her breath. "Oh man, you won't
believe what's going on in the food tent. Tina, J.B.'s girlfriend, is talking to Mary Lou. Mary Lou just noticed she
was pregnant. I think I saw Kit heading there, too. It's
going to be a bloodbath."

She looked up. Mitch was not listening at all. He was
fussing with the blue tarp he'd thrown over his work. She
looked around the circle. The judges were making their
way around the circle. Peter Rosen must have skipped his
meal and taken a shortcut.

What was going on between Tina and Mary Lou? April couldn't stand the suspense. She strained to see the food tent. The sun had set quickly and it was completely dark. The lighting around the ice sculptures didn't put a dent in the black.

Mary Lou was bound to be unhappy when she realized Kit knew about Tina's existence. Because of April.

A round of applause brought April back to the contest. The first sculpture had been uncovered. April's breath caught in her throat as she saw an icy locomotive with realistic steam rising from the stack.

She put her hand through Mitch's arm. "Wow, that is something. Let me see ours."

"Not yet," he said, unhooking himself from her.

He was acting so weird. He must be really nervous, April thought. He walked several steps away from her and back again. He cracked his knuckles loudly. She remembered the treats in her pocket. Maybe if he stopped long enough to eat a cookie, he wouldn't implode before the judges got there. She tried to get close to him, but he stepped on her foot.

"Ouch," she yelled, louder than she'd intended, but her extremities were so cold already that his misstep really hurt. She hopped on the other foot, futilely rubbing her toe through her thick boots. "I was just trying to give you these cookies I bought for you."

"Careful!" Mitch warned. He ran behind her, making sure she hadn't rattled his sculpture. She'd gotten too close.

Tears sprang to April's eyes. Her big toe throbbed. Her face hurt from being outside in the cold all day. Mary Lou and Tina were having it out, and she wasn't there. Mitch had worked on his mysterious piece all afternoon without her.

"Pardon me for living!" she yelled.

Mitch turned back to her. "No, no, I'm sorry."

"We're here," Deana called. She and Mark were in front of them. Mark was filming with his little video camera.

"Smile for me," he said. "How about a picture of the happy couple?"

Mitch grabbed April in for a hug. She slipped on a piece of ice on the ground, her boots going out from under her. She lost her footing and began to slide precariously close to the statue. Mark reached in and grabbed one arm. Mitch got the other and they righted her.

She stood still, brushing off both men. Mitch looked at her pleadingly. He pouched out his lower lip. "Sorry," he mouthed. She took in a breath. All she wanted now was to go home.

"Where are those judges?" April said. She looked, but instead of judges, she saw the local TV station coming her way. Jocelyn Jones was the same reporter who had come to the corn maze event at Suzi's last year. The spectators shifted, following the news crew. Suzi and Rocky were in the crowd behind the reporter. April watched to see where the crew was headed. Probably going to film the winner for the six o'clock news.

To her surprise, they stopped at her station. Her heart skipped a beat. Had Mitch won? Her spirits lifted. She looked at him, ready to forgive him.

"April Marie Buchert," Mitch said. His voice sounded unusually loud. April looked at him. Behind him, the crowd was getting bigger.

The light on the TV camera came on, blinding April. She turned her head away. "What's going on?" She turned back, her vision slowly righting itself. The spots grew farther apart.

To her shock, Mitch was on one knee, in front of his piece, which was still covered. April looked to Deana and

Mark, who were grinning widely. Rocky elbowed her way to the front of the crowd.

The announcements that had been ongoing were silent, and she could hear Mitch's loud breathing. He was miked. She saw the black thing attached to his collar. She looked at the TV reporter. She waved, grinning widely.

"April Marie Buchert," Mitch said again. His voice was so loud, she put her hands over her ears. The cameraman raised his camera again.

"Get up," April whispered. She leaned into Mitch and tugged at his arm. "Please get up."

To her horror, her voice was amplified through his mike. Panic clawed at her throat. What was he doing? Had he lost his mind?

"What? I'm going to ask you to marry me." He looked bewildered. He pushed off one knee and stood, taking her hand in his.

She held her hand over his lapel mike. "What makes you think this kind of public proposal is what I would want?"

"Every girl likes a grand gesture." He wasn't getting how far off the mark he was.

"Not me. You should know that." Mitch's bewildered look felt like a stab in April's heart. He looked up at her, searching her face for the reason for her freak-out.

"Look, I appreciate . . ." she began, seeking for words that would mollify him. She didn't want him to look like a complete fool in front of the whole town.

The crowd was shifting, waiting for the next act. Mitch turned to his statue, pulling off the tarp with a hard yank.

"I want you to have this."

He swirled the tarp off with the uplomb of a bullfighter. The piece was revealed. The cameraman moved in. Jocelyn stood, microphone at the ready.

April's heart sank even further. The sculpture seemed

to be glowing in the dark. It was not her design, not her entwined hearts. It was a giant ring, with a huge faceted stone. An enormous diamond.

The crowd burst into applause.

"Are you kidding me?" April burst out. Mitch looked startled. He reached up for her hand, but she snatched it away. "That was supposed to be the marketing piece for our new Stamping Sisters line. You ruined it."

She caught Rocky's eye. Rocky was clearly torn between her brother and business. But she'd gone for the grand gesture, too.

Mitch stood and said plaintively, "I just wanted you to move in with me."

She seethed. She didn't trust herself, so she clamped her mouth shut and remained silent.

"All right," Mitch said, covering up the mike with his hand and standing up. He brushed off his knees. "I get it. You don't want to move in with me."

"Right now," April said through gritted teeth, "I don't even want to see you." She could just picture the evening news. She could hear that helmet-headed witch now. *"April Buchert thwarted her boyfriend's big proposal at the Aldenville Ice Festival today. Evidently, his six-foot-high diamond ring wasn't big enough."*

April faced Mitch, her back to the ring. She didn't even want to look at it.

Everyone had gone quiet.

She gathered every good feeling she had for this man and tried to channel them. It wasn't working. She could feel nothing but anger. But she wasn't going to fight with him in front of this crowd.

"Mitch, honey."

"I wanted to surprise you," he said.

"You succeeded. Can we talk about this later?"

Mitch studied her face. He drew in a deep breath, then exhaled mightily. He turned on his heel. "Sure," he said. He made a cutting motion across his throat. The bright lights went abruptly off. April blinked trying to adjust to the darkness.

She took a step and felt her foot land on something round. A piece of ice, a rock. She felt her feet go out from under her, seeking more secure ground. But not finding it. She found nothing but uneven slipperiness.

Arms windmilling, she lost her footing and fell heavily into the ring. It crashed into the ground, breaking into a thousand pieces.

April fought to right herself. Mark stepped up and helped her. Mitch hadn't moved, his face pale, his lips forming a perfect O. The noise reverberated, picked up by his mike. The crowd gasped as one.

April ran.

"It wasn't your fault," Deana said. *She and April were in* Rocky's booth. The Ice Festival was over. The Mitch and April show cancelled. She could just imagine the spectators getting a chuckle from the debacle. She'd be doing her shopping in Lynwood for the next month. Facing the checkers at the IGA would be too tough.

"Why didn't you stop him?" April said, looking from Deana to Rocky. "You had to know it was a bad idea."

Rocky put in, "My brother can be very persuasive."

April knew that better than most. But it was going to be her powers of persuasion that were needed. She had to convince Mitch that just because she didn't want to get engaged right now, just because she'd humiliated him in front of the entire town, didn't mean she didn't love him. She put her head down on the ledge and groaned.

Rocky pulled her giant card out from under April's chin. "You know what this means, don't you?" Rocky addressed her comments to April, but she was talking loudly so anyone could hear.

"No nookie tonight. The Campbells are away, but I know my brother. He'll need to a day or two to sulk."

An unwelcome voice joined in. "Best *laid* plans, eh?" Yost emphasized the middle word with a leer.

April glared at Rocky. She knew Rocky was just trying to lighten the mood, but really. "Does everyone know the Campbells are gone for the weekend?" She ignored Yost in the hopes that he'd go away. Instead, he leaned against Rocky's booth as if he were one of the gang, getting the scoop on the latest gossip. April turned her head away.

Rocky shrugged. "Winter doldrums. We don't have much else to talk about."

April sighed, toying briefly with the idea of moving back to San Francisco. She wouldn't, but now she needed her own place more than ever. One out of town. Away from the prying eyes. The fewer neighbors, the better.

Deana kissed her cheek. "I've got to go. Mark and I have a viewing tonight. Call me later."

April waved limply as Deana and Mark walked away. Behind her, Rocky packed up stamps and supplies. Yost finally got the hint and took off when April wouldn't talk to him.

Lights were going out as booths were dismantled.

"Can you give me a ride home?" April said.

Rocky said, "My truck is full."

"I'll take you home, April." The offer came from an unexpected quarter behind her. April thought she recognized the voice but couldn't be sure. She turned.

"You're right on my way," Mary Lou said.

That wasn't exactly true. April and Mary Lou lived on

opposite ends of Main Street. Not far, but still. The barn was ten minutes away from Mary Lou's house.

Rocky looked at April for an answer. She smiled encouragingly as though a reconciliation was on the horizon, but she hadn't been there when Tina showed up. April could see Mary Lou had something to say to her.

Mary Lou jangled her keys. "Come on, you owe me an explanation."

That much was true.

They walked in silence to Mary Lou's luxury SUV. She pushed a button and the car started, engine purring smoothly. As April got in, she could feel warm air already flowing. She rubbed her hands in front of the vents and felt her toes begin to thaw painfully.

Mary Lou was silent as she backed out of her parking space and got into the queue of idling cars waiting to leave the park. There were a lot of cars with the same idea and only one lane leading out. It was going to take fifteen minutes to clear. Twice as long as it would normally take to get home.

"I have never been so cold," April said, hoping the time in the car would pass quickly if she filled it with small talk.

Mary Lou held up a leather-gloved hand without looking April's way. April got the message loud and clear. So this was how it was going to be. She was doing a neighborly duty, nothing more. April settled back and looked out the window at the dark night.

When Mary Lou spoke, it was almost a whisper. The fight had gone. "My brother was all the family I had. Just him and Gregg. Our parents are dead."

April's breath caught. She was afraid to exhale, afraid Mary Lou would shut down again.

"He had so much potential, you know. He was the high

school quarterback, prom king, head of the Young Republicans. Smart, too. He went to Penn."

April hadn't known.

"He threw it all away when he became a drunk."

Her voice broke. In the glow of the elaborate dashboard, April could see that Mary Lou was barely keeping it together. She'd gripped the steering wheel so hard, she'd popped the side seam of her glove. A very pink finger was showing through.

"You have no idea the hell my brother put me and my family through. Thirty years of lies. He stole from me. He brought lowlife scum into my house."

April protested, "Tina's not a lowlife."

Mary Lou didn't seem to hear. "He broke every promise he ever made to me."

The bottleneck eased with cars going off in two directions and up the cross street. Mary Lou hit forty before she reached the intersection. April would be home in a few minutes. The pain in the car was palpable. She felt her own throat tighten as Mary Lou talked.

"He very nearly got Kit killed. He drove with her when he was drunk. That's when I threw him out of the house. For good."

The bachelorette party Kit had told her about.

"A few months later, he was arrested again for being drunk and disorderly. Caught taking a midnight swim in the community pool. Yost went easy on him. He was too lenient, to my way of thinking. Part of me was hoping he'd lock him up and throw away the key."

"Yost let him go?"

"Not exactly. He got him into some kind of alternative program. Henry kept tabs on him and let me know from time to time how he was doing."

Had J.B. been part of the Anvils?

"But you found out he was making meth?" April asked.

Mary Lou nodded slowly, her head looking heavy. "I ran into him at a Walmart in Bloomsburg. I was there picking up some things for Connor, when I was visiting him at college. J.B. was in the pharmacy section with a half-dozen packets of cold medicine.

"I didn't know what that meant. It just seemed strange. He was acting so suspiciously. I asked Henry Yost later why he was so squirrelly. He wouldn't tell me, but I found out from Connor. The college dorm was riddled with info about spotting meth makers."

But April was curious about the more recent time Mary Lou had seen her brother, the meeting she'd been keeping a secret. "The day he died, people saw you talking to him at the gas station," April said.

Mary Lou pulled off the road. April's breath caught until Mary Lou had stopped the car safely on the shoulder. She buried her face in her arms crossed on the steering wheel. Her shoulders heaved, and April heard her sobbing. She reached over and touched her back but wasn't sure Mary Lou even felt her hand. She left it there anyway.

The tears subsided, and Mary Lou lifted her head. "I did. I saw him get out to pump gas. I couldn't believe my eyes. I was so furious. I didn't let him say a word. I just yelled at him. My last words to him were so harsh." Mary Lou wiped her eyes and pulled back onto the road.

So she never saw her brother again? He never made it to her house after seeing Kit? It was so sad.

"And now, Tina's having my brother's baby. That's my family. That changes everything."

Mary Lou turned into the barn's driveway. The motion detector lights came on, but the barn was dark. April's car sat forlornly ahead of them.

"No Campbells?" Mary Lou said, peering into the barn's windows.

Mary Lou had to be the only person who didn't know she was alone tonight.

"They're off to his sister's. They don't drive at night, so they'll stay over."

Mary Lou looked pointedly at April. She got the hint and opened the car door. "Good night."

April left Mary Lou's car, wishing she had words to give to Mary Lou, but there was nothing to say.

CHAPTER 18

April held her phone, staring at the screen. She'd thought she'd heard the ping that meant a text from Mitch. Nothing. She scanned the barn. It felt empty despite the Campbells' furniture taking up most of the floor space. She'd never thought she would miss Charlotte and Grizz, but the barn felt terribly empty.

It was too early to go to bed, but crawling into her loft and staying there until morning was tempting. Her phone rang when she was halfway to the ladder. Not Mitch's ring. She plopped down in Grizz's recliner to answer.

"Hey, darling."

"Mom? What are you doing up?" It was just past seven, which meant it was after midnight in Ireland.

Bonnie laughed. "Just out to a pub." She sounded happy. "I got your messages. I'm sorry. I couldn't figure out the time difference. Clive tried to tell me." She laughed. "You asked me about a microcassette tape player."

April had called her mother when she couldn't find the right size player.

"I just remembered where I put the one I had. Look in the top drawer of my dresser, way in the back. I think it's in there. I once had a notion I'd write my family history, so I started taping memories."

That would be some document. April smiled. "That's a lovely idea, Mom. I hope you do more."

"How are you?"

She felt her mom's true concern about her welfare and it pierced her like a pin going in a balloon. She felt herself deflate.

"It's been a rough night. Today was the Ice Festival. Mitch proposed in front of everyone . . ."

Her face burned at the memory of Mitch down on one knee.

"Mitch asked you to marry him?" April heard her mother repeat the news to Clive. Clive clapped his hands.

"Hang on, hang on. I didn't say yes."

"Why the heck not?" Bonnie shushed Clive, who was hooting and hollering. Of course he would find the scenario wonderfully romantic.

April rubbed her cheek. What to tell her? "He didn't really mean it. He just wants me to move in with him."

"What's the problem with that?"

"I'm not ready."

Her mother was silent. April knew she was picking her words carefully. "Are you sure?"

"You of all people should understand," April cried. Her mother had to be pushed into marrying Clive. Without the threat of his deportation, April wasn't sure she ever would have. "Why would I want to get married? I just got divorced, for crying out loud."

Bonnie made a sound that sounded like a giggle. Must have been the connection.

"Darling girl, listen to me. You know how I felt about marriage. Well, I've changed my mind. Marrying Clive was the best thing I've ever done."

April heard kissing noises. Her mother and her husband were demonstrative in their affection for each other. She felt a pang of something too close to jealousy to suit her. Being envious of her mother's happiness was wrong.

"But Mom, it was an awful scene. He sprung it on me, out of nowhere. Got down on one knee in front of everyone at the Ice Festival. Used the PA system so the whole place heard. Even had his friend, that TV reporter, there taking video."

"He did what? Oh Clive, we missed a good one." Now Bonnie was laughing outright. Before she'd met Clive, April hadn't heard her mother laugh like that in years. Maybe in forever. It was lovely to hear but not at her expense.

"Mom, it was mortifying."

Her mother and Clive had obviously been drinking at the pub well past their usual limit. Bonnie snorted over the phone, a wet sound that made April pull the phone away.

Their laughter was contagious. April heard herself let out a giggle. "He had changed the ice sculpture we were working on. Made it into a giant diamond ring."

Bonnie roared. "A ring?"

"Huge. Taller than me." April laughed at the incongruity of it.

Her mother's laugh turned to deeper, and she fought to catch her breath. "That's a man worth keeping, April. Not too many guys would have the nerve to go through with that. In front of the whole town. Think how much he loves you."

April stopped. She hadn't thought of anything but her own humiliation. The fact that Mitch went to all kinds of trouble to set the whole thing up had escaped her.

Even though it was misguided, it was a phenomenal effort.

"Have you talked to him?"

Her mother knew her. Knew how she could dig in her heels when she was mad. "Call him. Let him apologize. Don't let it go too long."

April agreed.

"Have you been over to water my plants lately?"

April was silent. She'd forgotten completely about her mother's house plants all lined up in the bathtub. All she had to do was go over once a week and give them a drink. She hadn't been to the house in ten days or more.

"Go. Right now."

"Mom, it's wicked cold."

Bonnie insisted. "If you wait for it to warm up, my plants will be dead. That pothos belonged to your grandmother . . ."

April agreed and they hung up. As long as she was going to Bonnie's, she'd look for the tape player, too. There'd be no sleeping tonight anyhow. Maybe the tape would tell her more about J.B. She found it and pocketed it, grabbing her heaviest coat and pulling her boots back on. She opened the sliding barn door. Bonnie's house was only ten minutes away.

But she was parked in. Mitch's Jeep was pulled in behind her car. She felt her heartbeat stutter as he got out. He hesitated, then crossed the distance between them in several long strides. He stopped short of taking her in his arms.

"I'm sorry," he said, leaning in so his forehead touched hers. "I'm a jerk."

She stopped, thrusting her hands deep into her jacket's

pockets, feeling the plastic case the cassette was in. She'd heard what her mother had said. She knew relationships weren't easy, but they didn't stand a chance unless there was communication.

She turned away and opened the door. "Come in," she said. She took off her coat and hung it on the pegs by the door. He stayed in his until she insisted he take it off. She heard her mother's voice insisting Mitch was a keeper.

April moved into the kitchen. She leaned against the counter. She'd have liked to busy herself with wiping down the counters or doing dishes, but Charlotte had left the place immaculate. Mitch propped himself on the table. His head hung low.

"I'm sorry," he said. "That was a silly thing to do. I didn't think it through, April . . ."

She couldn't stand to see him beating himself up so. "I didn't mean to make you feel like this."

Mitch barked, "Like what? Like a horse's ass? I'd say that was all my doing."

"It's not about marrying you or not marrying you," she said. "I just want to have my own place for a while. I'm happy with the way things are with us."

Mitch crossed the room and stood in front of her. His eyes were misty. "I love you."

April felt a tweak of pain. Was he just telling her what he thought she wanted to hear?

"I don't need you to say that. I'm not looking for a grand gesture."

The moment they'd met six months ago, there'd been a connection. He was good-looking, creative and good with his hands. He believed in fair dealings and getting paid what he was worth. He had a great reputation in business.

Her parents liked him. Even the Campbells were held in sway by Mitch's charm.

He was everything she wanted in a man and a few things she hadn't thought to ask for.

"Did you even want to get married?" she asked. "I mean, we've never really talked about marriage." Her throat was full of rocks but she realized they'd skipped this step.

He'd heard plenty about her nightmare marriage to Ken. They'd celebrated her divorce. She knew his parents had an unorthodox marriage, miserable for the first thirty years and blissful for the past decade. He'd toasted with Ed and Vince every time a state added gay marriage to the legal side of the register.

But she didn't know what his views on the institution were.

"Did you ever come close to getting married before?"

"Once," he sighed.

April's heart stopped. Silly, unrealistic for a man in his thirties, but that wasn't the answer she was hoping for.

"Well, twice," he said.

Her heart sunk even lower. She glared at him. "What?"

"Melody Kingston asked me to marry her in second grade. There were Twinkies involved, if I remember correctly."

She slapped his arm. "Get serious."

He moved closer. His eyes were softened around the edges as if filling with tears. The wrinkles across his brow met in a deep V in the middle.

He let his grin fade. "I came close. My college girlfriend. We dated senior year and several years after. The time never seemed right. I wasn't ready. She broke up with me when I didn't deliver a ring one Christmas. I didn't know what I was waiting for until I met you."

April burst into tears. Mitch took a step back, surprised.

She buried her face in her hands. "I've ruined everything. I did it all wrong. Got married too young, stayed with him too long. Now you're ready and I'm not."

Mitch rubbed her back, waiting for her to finish before taking her face in his strong hands. One thumb caught a stray tear and brushed it away.

April caught her breath. Mitch didn't speak until she was looking into his eyes.

"I'll wait for you," he said.

His simple words delivered a jolt of electricity. She flung herself into his arms and smothered him with kisses.

She broke off and looked at him. "This doesn't mean I'm not renting a place of my own," she said. "Or that I ever want to see myself on the local news again."

He kissed her to stop her talking. She opened her mouth to his, catching his essence and savoring it. She was grateful he was still holding her. Her legs wouldn't have held her up anyhow.

"No one's home, right?" he whispered, his voice husky.

She heard the desire and felt herself turn to jelly. She nodded.

"Yes," she said.

"Then let's build a fire and enjoy it."

The Campbells' oversize furniture took up most of the living space. They pushed back the couch and moved a heavy coffee table out of the way and brought some pillows onto the floor. Mitch lit the fire. April poured wine. She turned out most of the lights, just leaving a small light on in the kitchen behind them.

They settled on the floor. They watched the flames lick at each other.

Mitch spoke first after they clinked glasses. "I never should have surprised you. I got caught up in the planning without really thinking about how you'd react. I had my fantasy."

"Fantasy's not a bad thing." She lifted her face to his and kissed him. They started slowly, savoring the sweetness between them. Things heated up quickly. April felt the fire on her back and heard the crackling. The taste of wine in Mitch's mouth was sweet and fruity. She closed her eyes and sunk into Mitch's embrace, lost in the sensations.

Much later, Mitch was stoking the fire that they'd let go out when the barn door opened with a large crack. April shot up, standing before she realized it. Mitch was airborne, too, nearly tripping over her. He stepped in front of her as if to protect her. A blast of cold air assaulted them.

"Who is it?" April croaked, her heart pounding. The light switch in the kitchen was flipped on. April and Mitch covered their eyes.

It was a warring Grizz and Charlotte.

"Dang blessed. We didn't have to get towed," he was saying. "I could have gotten it started."

"Good thing Scott came along when he did or else Vince would have found us next spring thaw," Charlotte fussed. She followed him in, carrying the cooler. It had to be a lot less heavy than it had been that morning, but Charlotte acted as if it were still full.

Grizz rubbed his face repeatedly. His other hand worried his scalp. His step was heavy as he moved slowly into the kitchen. Charlotte missed the table putting down the cooler. It landed on the floor. Grizz ignored her. He pushed the door closed behind her.

"Leave it," he grunted at his wife. April could hear the fatigue in his voice.

"What happened?" April asked.

Their heads spun to the darkened living room. Charlotte held a hand over her heart. "Oh look, Grizz, the kids are up."

April blushed. She twisted her shirt back around so she was wearing it facing front. She pulled her sweater over it. Mitch stood behind her. She heard the snaps on his fly connect. Each one sounded like a rifle shot to her.

"Where have you been?" April turned on the floor lamp. "Did you change your mind and decide to drive home tonight?"

Charlotte shook her head. Grizz frowned at the out-of-position couch and the pile of pillows on the floor as though trying to figure out how they had gotten there. He took off his shoes and got up to poke at the fire, muttering about wet wood.

April picked up the cooler from the floor and emptied the garbage out of it, mostly waxed paper that Charlotte had used to wrap their sandwiches and cookies. She rinsed the thermos, keeping an eye on Charlotte, who hovered nearby. She didn't like her color.

"Sit, please," April said.

Grizz had settled in his recliner without taking off his coat. Mitch scooped up pillows and returned the cushions to their rightful place.

Charlotte sat in her armchair, wrapping herself in one of her afghans. Her cheeks looked raw. "We needed gas. We got off the highway, but we couldn't find the place Grizz remembered. We made a wrong turn and had to detour because roads were closed with drifting snow."

She glanced at her husband. April could fill in the rest. Old man not prone to taking advice. Lonely roads. Blowing snow. Mitch looked at her and shook his head.

"The car just died. Finally, a young fellow on his way home from work stopped and called a tow truck for us. He brought us here. The car's stuck up there."

April looked at Mitch, whose face was grave. This could have ended badly. He reached out and rubbed her back, acknowledging her concern.

"When? Were you coming back from Scranton?"

Charlotte shook her head. "On our way up there."

"You were stuck in the car all day?"

Grizz grunted. Charlotte nodded and closed her eyes.

Mitch squeezed her arm. "Well, they're home now."

April decided he was right. False cheer was the way to go. These two didn't need anyone blaming them for their misadventure. "That's what counts. Are you warm enough?"

April went to Charlotte and put another blanket from the back of the couch over her legs. She knelt and rubbed the old woman's hands. They were freezing. "Are you okay?"

"Just tired," she said, eyes closing.

"Going to bed," Grizz said. With another loud sigh, he began taking off his belt. April knew the rest of his clothes would soon follow.

She'd have Dr. Wysocki stop by and check on them first thing in the morning. For now they needed rest. April turned the heat up and heard the furnace kick in. Of course that meant her loft would be unbearably hot within minutes.

Mitch read her mind. "You can stay at my place," Mitch whispered, steering April toward the door. "I just did laundry. You've got a change of clothes at my place." He grabbed her heavy coat from the closet. She picked up her purse and keys. She looked back at the couple, feeling a slight catch in her throat. She was so glad nothing had happened to them.

"Do you think they'll be all right?" she said.

Mitch looked around the loft. "Sure. I stoked the fire so it'll burn out. The flue is clear. They just need to rest."

"But . . ." April turned. "They've been through such an ordeal."

"All the more reason we let them get the sleep they need. Listen," Mitch said.

Both of them were already snoring. "You're right."

April tucked the blanket around Charlotte's feet and made sure Grizz had another blanket within easy reach. She turned off the floor lamp and turned on the light over the stove for a night light.

She and Mitch tiptoed out. They bypassed the big door and went through the kitchen, closing the door gently.

"Wake up," Mitch said in her ear. April opened one eye. Her face felt plastered to the pillow, and she wondered if she'd been drooling. She wiped her mouth surreptitiously. She had been deep in a dream that had vanished but left her feeling good. Or maybe it was Mitch's ministrations to her before they fell asleep that were responsible for the endorphins still in her system.

She slapped playfully in his direction, hitting only empty mattress. "Leave me alone, you sexy beast. I need some rest." She pulled the covers higher, reveling in the comfort of his warm bed. She never wanted to leave.

"April."

She lifted her head, hearing something in his voice that turned her stomach to cold stone. It wasn't morning yet. Her concerns about the Campbells came flooding back.

"The fire chief called." Mitch's face was grave.

"Is there a fire?" she asked, sitting up. She tried to remember if she'd heard sirens in the night. Mitch didn't answer her right away.

Mitch threw a Pendleton wool blanket around her bare shoulders, pulling it tight under her neck. He looked into her eyes. She saw compassion in his that frightened her, made tears spring forward. Her entire body shuddered as if trying to rid itself of the fear that possessed her.

"The barn," he said.

She wrestled from his grasp. "The barn. No way. That

place has been standing for the last hundred and fifty years. No way."

"Chief Islington called, looking for you."

She rooted around, looking for her clothes. Mitch grabbed a pile of clothes and handed them to her. She noticed he was dressed already.

She stepped into her underwear. "We never should have left the fireplace . . ." she stuttered.

Mitch pulled her close. "We didn't do this. It was an explosion."

That made no sense. She pulled back. She saw something else in his face. Something that spoke to a deeper tragedy.

"Grizz?" Her voice dropped to a whisper. "Charlotte?" The sight of them tucked under a homemade afghan crossed her eyes. She shut them, but the picture wouldn't go away. She looked at Mitch.

Mitch nodded. His handsome face was marred by a solemn reserve. "Chief said no one could have gotten out. That's why he called, to see who was at home. Your car was the only one in the driveway. The barn is burning now, fully engulfed, he said."

April bit her hand. A tiny noise leaked out of the side of her fist. More like a squeak but it hurt as if it had been torn out of her throat. "Why? How?"

"No one knows yet. Gas leak, maybe? Neighbors said it sounded like a bomb going off."

"Charlotte hated that gas stove . . ." April couldn't form complete sentences. "Do you think she started cooking? I bet she was making cinnamon buns. Even after the ordeal they went through yesterday, she'd be up early . . ."

She buried her face in his shoulder. "Is the chief sure?"

"I asked him that, too," he said. "There was no sign that anyone got out."

"Come on," Mitch said gently. "Let's go over there." He handed her her coat.

The scarf Charlotte had made for her was hanging around the collar of her coat. She sobbed when her fingers touched it.

Tears streamed down her face. "I've got to call Vince."

Mitch nodded. April sat heavily at his kitchen table. She rubbed the surface. So much like the one in the barn that he'd made for Vince and Ed before she'd come home. Now it was gone.

He handed her his portable phone. "I dialed. Just push talk if you're ready. Or you could wait until we know more."

She grabbed for his free hand, squeezing. He took the pain. She knew he could handle sharing her burden, and that knowledge gave her back her voice.

"I'm going to call now," she said.

The phone rang. She pictured her father and Vince sleeping in their Florida time-share, filled with bamboo furniture and brightly colored paintings. The opposite of the dark, dreary landscape outside.

After several rings, a sleepy Vince answered.

"It's April."

She heard him take in a quick breath. "What's happened?"

Calls at this hour were never good. April went on. "There's been an explosion at the barn. It's gone. I wasn't home, but your parents were."

Vince was a volunteer fireman. He knew better than April what an explosion could do. He groaned. She could picture him pinching the bridge of his nose, trying to take in what she'd said.

Ed came on the line. "April? Tell me. Vince can't speak."

She filled her father in. "Mitch and I are heading over there now. I'll call when I have more details."

She knew her father. He wanted to get off the phone to comfort Vince. She let him go.

CHAPTER 19

Mitch drove April home. The sun was just coming up, casting
a rosy glow. The snow glittered and sparkled. A fresh coat
overnight had turned the fields fresh and pretty again. When
they turned down the road leading to the barn, April let out a
cry. Smoke was rising from the spot the barn had occupied.

They couldn't get close to the place. Fire trucks littered the
drive. Early risers had stopped along the street and watched
from their cars. Even at this hour, word had spread.

They parked in the street. The driveway to the barn was
a couple of hundred yards behind them. From here, April
couldn't see the barn. She could smell the fire, though.
Ashes swirled in the air and lay over the snow like cinnamon. Icicles formed in the trees from the fire hoses. The
landscape looked like something from a horror flick.

The chief approached them. "There's not much left,"
Chief Islington said.

April swallowed hard. "Did you find Grizz and Charlotte?"

He nodded.

"We left them sleeping last night. They were exhausted from their day."

"They died without knowing what hit them."

April stopped him with a wave of her hand. Her stomach suddenly clenched, doubling her over with the pain. She heaved, unable to control the spasms that rose from her inside. Mitch held her hair back, but nothing came up but painful hiccups.

When she regained her composure, Chief Islington was indicating that they follow him. She grabbed Mitch's hand. The barn was usually visible as soon as they went around the curve in the driveway.

"Are you sure you want to see this?" Mitch said.

"I need to be able to tell Vince I was here. For him." She looked up where the barn had stood. The sky instead was wide and empty. "For them."

The barn was a heap of rubble. The river rock that made up the foundation and the fireplace lay scattered across the yard, tossed away from the house as if they'd been hollow. The beautiful clapboard that once graced a barn in Massachusetts looked like a pile of pickup sticks. April's heart ached for her father. And Vince.

"Enough," April croaked. She walked back to Mitch's car. She got inside. He turned it on to keep her warm. Rocky knocked on the window. She was carrying a huge thermos of coffee for the firefighters. Suzi arrived with coffee cake and donuts. Deana and Mark were close behind with a portable table, which they set up in the drive. Mitch joined them to help set up.

Deana pulled April out of the car for a hug, and April's

tears flowed freely. Mark put his arm around his wife, drawing all the women into his solid embrace.

April felt strength returning to her core. These good people would help her weather this. She would need all of them in the coming weeks. She broke off the hug.

April turned to her friend. "Deana, will you tend to the Campbells? I'm sure Vince would want you to. He and Dad will be flying in later."

"Of course," she said.

"I'm available for an airport run," Mark said quickly. "Just send me their flight information."

They huddled around Mitch's car, trying to keep warm and out of the way of the firemen and state police coming and going.

Logan was in the crowd of people that had gathered by the end of the driveway. He came forward to talk to April, his young face creased. He seemed to be trying hard. She felt for him. Comforting people who'd had a great loss was not something he'd had much practice in.

"Kit wanted to come," he said. "She's at my mother's, feeding the babies. Certain things I can't do. She wanted to know you were okay."

"Thanks, tell her I'm dealing."

A state trooper approached April and asked to speak to her. He moved her out of earshot from the crowd. She felt Mitch's eyes on her and heard Rocky questioning him.

"Are you the owner of the property?"

She shook her head. "My father, Ed Buchert, and his partner, Vince Campbell, are."

He wrote in his small notebook. "How long have you lived there?"

"About seven months."

"Do you know what's in the shed?"

Mitch took a step forward. The policeman held up a hand.

Mitch backed off, moving behind April. She felt a supporting hand on the small of her back and leaned into it.

"What are you talking about?"

"We found evidence of an illegal drug lab," he said. "Propane tanks, blister packs from cold medications."

April rocked forward on her toes. Her fists tightened. "Of course we had a gas grill. Who doesn't?"

"Ma'am, I need you to calm down."

"How can I?" she said angrily. "There was nothing like that in there."

The chief stepped in. "Listen, we've got a long way to go before we determine if this was an accident or deliberate. It's too soon to tell right now. I've known Ms. Buchert and her family a long time. Let's not throw around any accusations."

The trooper backed down. Had he expected her to confess? Maybe he wanted to see her face when accused. He'd picked up on something in April. Her guilt at leaving the Campbells alone last night.

"All right. I'll coordinate with the Aldenville police. Until we figure out the cause of the explosion, don't leave town. Leave word with us as to where you're staying."

April walked away, waving off her friends' protests and Mitch's pleading looks. She walked hard and fast. Where *was* she going to go? She had nothing but the clothes on her back. Her car was destroyed. Her stamp collection. Her tools. Her livelihood.

She sat down on the cold, hard ground and wept. Her tears felt scorching hot, burning her cheeks.

Mitch found her and pulled her to her feet. He put his hand underneath her coat and rubbed her back fiercely. She let him gather her close, and she held on to him.

Their respite was short.

"Where were you last night?" Henry Yost appeared in

front of them. April's tears came harder. He was the last person she wanted to see. She couldn't bear to see him taking pleasure in her misery. She kept her face buried in Mitch's shoulder.

"She was with me, Henry," Mitch said. His hand didn't stop its circular motion.

"Charlotte must have left the gas on. Pity those two old folks were all alone."

He didn't know when to keep his mouth shut. April pulled away from Mitch. She'd never had the desire to spit in someone's face, but Yost was asking for it. She felt saliva build in her mouth.

She forced herself to look away from Yost. Charlotte wouldn't want her to be that rude. She concentrated on the landscape beyond him and waited for him to tire of baiting her and go away.

Beyond his Smokey the Bear trooper-wannabe hat, April saw a car slow down in the housing development that abutted the barn. The street had a clear view of her ruins. The yellow and black Torino came to a stop. The driver got out and put his hands on the roof. The passenger leaned out of the window.

She recognized the orange coat. Violet. Did Violet have something to do with this? April needed to talk to her.

April reached into Mitch's coat pocket and whispered, "Your keys." Her fingers scrabbled, coming up with nothing.

"What?" he said, already patting his pants, coming up empty. "In the ignition."

Ignoring both men's questioning gazes, she raced up the drive to Mitch's Jeep, happy to see he hadn't been parked in by firefighters or gawkers. She maneuvered the car out, jamming it into four-wheel drive for better traction.

She made a right onto the road and another right into

the development. It consisted of only about a dozen homes, built in the mid-eighties. A giant cul-de-sac with one road in and out, shaped like half a racetrack.

April roared down the street, not finding second gear, double-clutching into third to knock down the rpms. The Torino was gone. She had just missed her.

She knew where to look for her. She took the road out to Main Street to the Wysockis' Victorian. There was no sign of the car. April climbed out of the Jeep and banged on the front door anyway.

Mrs. Wysocki came to the door wiping her hands on a kitchen towel. April could smell cinnamon buns baking, joined by undertones of coffee and bacon. She'd forgotten that it was a normal Sunday morning for most folks. She was so far away from that comforting routine of newspapers and multiple cups of coffee today.

"Where's Violet?" she asked. Mrs. Wysocki's step backwards told her she needed to moderate her tone. She dialed her urgency back a notch. "I need to speak with her."

"Come in," Mrs. Wysocki said, tucking the towel into her apron. "She just went out. She'll be back in a few minutes."

April followed her into her kitchen. Mrs. Wysocki had a small under-the-cabinet TV with the local news on and the sound off. Across the bottom, in the crawl, was news of the explosion. April turned away quickly. She couldn't bear to look.

Mrs. Wysocki had seen it. She took up a position by the stove. The linoleum in front of it had a worn spot. A matching one was in front of the sink. "I'm sorry about the loss of your home," she said stiffly. "Have you eaten anything? Some toast? Coffee? Stay for a minute. Doctor will be down in a minute, and I'm sure he'll want to see you."

April's stomach growled. She was nauseated from the

rush of adrenaline that was slowly leaving her system now. She sheepishly took a piece of toast from the woman, who sat her down at the breakfast counter. There were four plates set. A dozen eggs were on the counter, some of them already cracked into the bowl. Mrs. Wysocki was expecting two more for breakfast. Violet and her boyfriend.

The room was too warm, windows steamed from the baking. April bit into the toast. She was light-headed from the over here. A sense of disorientation took over. She could have been in Bonnie's kitchen, so familiar was this room to her.

Dr. Wysocki came in, his hair wet from the shower. He was wearing a pair of khakis and a well-pressed plaid flannel shirt. He was surprised to see her.

He glanced at the TV and she knew he knew. "I'm sorry about the barn. You okay? The Campbells?"

She shook her head. Mrs. Wysocki drew in a quick breath, and her husband moved close and put his arm around her.

April continued, "Someone made it look like a meth lab exploded."

"Not Violet." Mrs. Wysocki closed her eyes, her hand covering her bosom, like a woman in a silent movie. The dish towel acting as the lace hanky. This wasn't melodrama, though. She was truly heartsick.

"She's the only meth addict I know."

"Former meth addict," Dr. Wysocki said automatically, without his usual conviction. Mrs. Wysocki's hand fluttered.

April scowled. "What about her boyfriend?"

"She doesn't have a boyfriend," Mrs. Wysocki said.

April saw the recognition flash over Dr. Wysocki's face. "They would never . . ."

"Tell me where he lives."

"She doesn't have a boyfriend," the mother said, her voice breaking. "Honestly."

"Please," April begged.

"It's not a boyfriend," Dr. Wysocki said with authority. "It's that woman. Paula something or other."

From the Anvil group. That's who owned the Torino. She'd just assumed it was a guy. "Where does she live?"

"I don't know."

"I might . . . I did." Mrs. Wysocki turned away and rummaged through a tiered wicker basket on the counter. April saw PP&L bills and a notice from the water company. Mrs. Wysocki went through the pile twice before she dumped the contents onto the counter. Finally she found what she needed.

"Violet had me pick up some things at Costco for her a few months ago. Paper towels, that kind of thing. She drew me a map to Paula's house. I saved it in case I had to go back."

She produced a wrinkled piece of notebook paper, raggedly torn loose, and laid it in front of April. The main highway was sketched on it, and arrows indicated turns onto small roads. No names of the roads or an address.

"What's this?" April asked, pointing to a round circle that seemed to be a landmark.

"A silo," she answered.

Great. Silos were everywhere.

"What about this?" The initials RM were just above a turn arrow.

"Oh, I remember. She said I should turn at Redneck Mike's place."

Redneck Mike's was a well-known landmark in the valley. In the last century it had been a tavern, a stop for weary travelers. Now it was just a broken-down bar at a crossroads. April knew right where it was.

Dr. Wysocki had a strange look on his face. "What else did you buy for them, Celia?"

His wife was puzzled. "I don't remember. Coffee filters. That was when she had such a bad cold. I had to sign for some kind of medicine for her, too."

Dr. Wysocki's face sagged. All things used to make meth.

She grabbed the makeshift map and raced for the door. "I'll try to send Violet back to you."

Mrs. Wysocki made a noise that sounded like a sob. April glanced back to see Dr. Wysocki take his wife in his arms. Their breakfast company wasn't coming any time soon. April's heart broke a little. Mrs. Wysocki wasn't that different from Bonnie, or Charlotte, for that matter. Women whose kitchen was their domain. The domestic goddesses making their family a comfortable home. A nest, a safe haven. But it hadn't been enough to save her daughter.

April's phone was ringing. Mitch had called several times. She couldn't talk to him just now. She wasn't going to waste any more time. She sent him a text. "I'm OK. B back soon." That would have to do for now.

The church parking lots were full as April sped down Main Street. Yost was back at the barn, not available to ticket her. She floored Mitch's Jeep and was rewarded with a yip from the tires as she pulled out onto Route 93.

The road was free of traffic. She kept an eye out for Paula's Torino. Where had she and Violet gone? April wondered if Paula had been the woman at the pharmacy.

Passing the snow-covered fields, April felt as alone and desolate as they looked. She'd gotten the Campbells killed.

She got to Redneck Mike's and stopped. She held the map in front of her, trying to see where to go next. She was at the eastern end of the valley, close to where Interstate 81 crossed it, not far from the junction with I-80. The map pointed left, back toward town. It indicated that Paula's place was the fourth house after the intersection where Redneck Mike's stood.

She pulled into the parking lot of Redneck Mike's. It was a long building with asphalt-shingle siding, its few windows lit up with neon beer signs. At this hour, it was closed, and there were no cars in the parking lot.

April took a breath. She'd steamed away from the barn, so sure that Violet had the answers. She felt her body go limp. She wasn't sure of anything anymore.

Someone had tried to kill her. Of that she was sure. The Campbells had been innocent bystanders. That explosion had been meant for her. She was supposed to be the only one home. The state police would investigate, but that would take weeks or months.

April traced her steps mentally. What had she done to become a candidate for killing? She'd visited the site of last year's meth-lab explosion. What if that hadn't been an accident after all? The chief had said it was impossible to tell the difference without a lot of investigation.

She'd gone to look at houses on Mary Lou's foreclosure list. She'd found Tina.

Tina. April's heart flopped in her chest like a hooked fish. She stretched for the gas pedal. What if she wasn't the only one in danger? Tina had come to the Ice Festival yesterday, shown herself as someone who knew J.B. Worse, as someone who knew J.B.'s secrets. Anyone who had felt the need to shut up J.B.—and her—might have the same inclination to silence Tina.

She called Tina. No answer. She left a message but she had to warn her in person. Maybe that's where the Torino was heading.

She put the key into the ignition and hesitated. The road

conditions would be awful. She didn't know this end of the valley very well. This is where she had been when she'd gotten lost and found J.B.'s car. The image of J.B.'s car, crashed in the ditch, flashed into her brain. She could easily be next.

April took in a deep breath, forcing air down into her lungs. She took off slowly and gradually increased speed. After a couple hundred yards, she gained a little confidence that the car was not going to fly out from under her and go skidding across the two lanes. She held on to the steering wheel tightly and crouched over it, looking more and more like a grandma behind the wheel.

There was no time to waste. She found her way back to Tina's house. The sun was up, but the skies were gray with clouds and the house was dark.

She knocked hard on Tina's door, ringing the doorbell with her other hand. It wasn't sleeting up here, but gently snowing. The complex had the muffled quiet of a fresh snowfall combined with the normal hush of a Sunday morning. It was the perfect day to stay in bed. No one was stirring.

She heard nothing from inside Tina's. She looked for a light at the neighbor's but saw none. Tina was probably the kind of person to leave a spare key hidden somewhere close. April felt around the doorjamb and looked under the doormat. Nothing.

She saw no flowerpot or fake rock that could hold a key. She ran her hand around the "Welcome" sign. Nothing.

Frustrated, she pounded on the door again. If nothing else, maybe a neighbor would come out and see what the noise was about.

The door opened slowly. A blinking Tina stood in the crack. "Who is it? April?"

April rushed in. "You're okay?" she said. April pushed the door open and went in.

"Bad night," Tina said. "Sick."

The house smelled stale, like unwashed body, sweat with an undertone of vomit. Tina's pregnancy was not treating her well. But she was alive.

"I only just fell asleep an hour or so ago."

Tina sat on the couch and pulled her blanket up around her middle. She was wearing a man's flannel shirt over a voluminous brushed cotton nightgown. Her feet were covered with fuzzy sleeper socks with nonskid bottoms. She yawned.

April steadied herself on the back of the chair. "My house was burned down last night. I was so afraid for you."

"Me? Why?" She picked at a hole in the blanket, unraveling the loose weave.

"This all started with J.B."

Tina's eyes were fluttering. She was falling back asleep. April couldn't believe it. She was worried about Tina being in danger, but all Tina could do was sleep.

April felt her way to the armchair. It must have been goose down because she sank into it. She wanted to stay there, enveloped by the flowery fabric. Away from Aldenville. Away from the drama. This must have been the way J.B. had felt.

This was what J.B. was robbed of. Sanctuary.

Her mind clicked into overdrive. She had to find the person responsible.

She stood. Tina burrowed deeper into her nest of blankets, pillows and stuffed animals. She was too fragile to move.

"Will you be okay? I've got to go. Don't answer the door."

"Don't worry," Tina said, slurring her words. She was out.

A blanket slid to the floor. April stopped to pick it up and put it back over Tina. Under it was a man-size T-shirt. It was light blue with a large image on the front.

An anvil.

"Tina, Tina, wake up. What's this?"

Tina opened one eye. She grabbed the shirt and tucked it under her chin. Her fingers worked the fabric, and she brought it close to her nose and inhaled.

It was J.B.'s. He'd been a member of Yost's Anvil group. So had Violet and Paula. April had the connection she'd been searching for.

April ran to Mitch's Jeep and headed back to Aldenville to find the pair.

She consulted the map once she'd passed Redneck Mike's. She counted houses. Number one, a large two-story on several acres. Next to it was a century-old place, huddled close to the road. Probably it used to be surrounded by acres before the road went in.

A few hundred feet later was an old barn, a faded tobacco ad gracing its flank and daylight seeping through the missing boards. Was that number three? April wasn't sure. The map said four houses from Redneck Mike's.

She peered through the side window, murky in the cold. She recognized the next house. It was Kit's. She slowed. Was this number three or number four? She'd come in from the opposite direction than the way she usually traveled to Kit's. She'd never realized the kids were living so close to the bar.

April stopped across the street. She looked back and counted. The two-story, the farmhouse. Now she could see a ranch house tucked in behind a row of poplars.

Mrs. Wysocki said she'd brought the supplies here a few months back. The house had been empty then. In foreclosure.

Kit's house was number four.

She tried to picture the list of foreclosures that Mary Lou had given her. Was this house on it? She realized she'd seen coffee filters and paper towels in the other empty house she'd looked at. And that interestingly colored paper she'd found at Kit's had been of the same texture and weight as a coffee filter. One that had probably been used in the drug-making process, adding the different colors.

Someone was using Mary Lou's foreclosed houses as meth labs. It was perfect when she thought of it. No one was keeping close tabs on the houses. They were empty, isolated. The meth makers could move around, get in and out without too much fear of being caught.

Mary Lou couldn't have known. Did Logan? It was his job to keep track of the houses.

April remembered with horror the bags of garbage she'd seen in Kit's basement. Dr. Wysocki's article had talked about how much garbage meth makes.

April's heart plummeted. If that was true, toxic chemicals from the crystal meth were imbedded in the carpet, the wallboard, the insulation. The cosmetic changes Logan and Kit had been making would not keep the danger from seeping into their lives. Indeed, their ministrations to the house might have released the danger.

Who was she dealing with? People with no conscience. She'd believed Violet when she'd said she wasn't using. That she was trying to lead a better life.

April's mind flooded with anger. She coughed and sputtered as bile rose in her throat. It burned on its way up. How dare these people? Not just destroy their own lives but innocents like Kit and her twins. What kind of a person did that?

April thought about the fire back at the barn. Kit's house would be better off if it burned right now. Mary Lou had probably insured the place. Fire insurance would cover the cost of rebuilding. Nothing was going to help with meth cleanup.

April shuddered with revulsion as she realized how tainted the house was.

Kit's car was in the driveway. She was in there, trying to fix up a house for her family.

Another car, an old station wagon, was parked on the shoulder just past Kit's. She didn't recognize the car. It looked as if it had slewed across the roadway and stopped there. The driver had been in a big hurry.

April grabbed Mitch's keys out of the ignition.

If the killer had caught up with J.B. when he left Kit's house, or if he knew that J.B. had had contact with her, then Kit was in danger. Whoever killed J.B. did it to keep him quiet. Keep him from talking about what he knew

She had to have help. She considered dialing 9-1-1, but what would she say? She didn't think the state police would be too interested in her story. A strange car was not enough to raise up the possibility of a real emergency. She'd tried calling on the Aldenville police before and Yost had embarrassed her in front of his support group. But she had a real problem this time. Chances were he was still at the barn and the chief would answer.

She dialed the Aldenville Police Station. No luck. It was Yost who answered the phone. There was no time to be picky. She needed backup.

"Officer Yost? I'm at Kit's house. She's in danger."

She could hear him eating something. A noise like a slurp came over the wire and then a swallowing sound. Protect and serve indeed. Coffee-break time.

"Why do you think that?" The "little lady" was implied.

April lied. "I heard someone threaten her. The same

person that shot her uncle. Just please meet me over there."
She stopped just short of pleading.

April swallowed her pride. It felt like a giant hairball
going down her gullet sideways, scratching her all the way.
"Please hurry."

She hung up and tossed her phone on the seat. She hurried up the walk. The porch steps were icy, and April went
down, cracking her knee against the concrete. She felt the
impact all the way to her teeth. Using the wrought-iron
railing as a crutch, she forced herself up and listened. Kit
was in there with a stranger. Her breath formed icy clouds
around her, and her toes started to ache.

She paced the porch. It shouldn't take Yost more than
a few minutes to get here. She'd wait. Waiting was not her
strong suit.

A strangled noise came from inside. April stilled herself, straining to hear. Another sound like a yelp. She had
to do something. April banged on the door, leaning on it
for good measure.

The door swung open. April hesitated. This door had
been locked every time she'd been out here. She forced herself to take a step inside.

"Kit?" she called.

"You're lying," she heard. "A big fat liar."

April moved into the kitchen. Kit turned to her as she
heard her enter. April's heart was in her throat, but she was
glad to see Kit was alive. Kit's face was streaked and her
eyes were red.

"Tell him, April. Tell him my house is not a meth house."

Dr. Wysocki was standing in front of Kit. He was holding a gun.

"Dr. Wysocki?" April asked. She got a slight nod from
the man. "What's going on?"

"I came here to find my daughter. I'm taking her to rehab."
His hand shook. The gun seemed too heavy for him. His
complexion was gray, and he looked older than his years. He
should be enjoying his retirement. Instead, he was chasing
down a daughter who could not shake her deadly addiction.

"What's with the gun?" She wasn't worried that he'd
shoot Kit on purpose, but he was not in control of himself
right now. He didn't answer, looking at Kit with intensity.

Kit said, "He thought he was going to have to run the
meth makers off. From my house," she wailed.

April stepped in front of Dr. Wysocki. She kept Kit in
her peripheral vision. The gun was pointed at the floor. So
far.

"I'm afraid that part is true," April said to Kit. "That's
why your uncle came when he did. He wanted to see
the place for himself. He was going to warn you or your
mother. I couldn't figure out why he'd come back. It was
too dangerous. He knew who was behind the meth making.
He knew if he ever stepped foot in this town that he'd be
killed. But he came anyway."

Kit was crying hard now. "I got him killed," she said.

"No you didn't. It's not your fault. Or his. It's the people
behind the drug making. That's who's to blame."

Dr. Wysocki let out a groan. The gun came up to his
eye level. His breathing was shallow. She wondered if she
should call his wife or an ambulance.

April moved a step closer. "Could you have done that?
Run off your own daughter with a gun?"

He looked up at her with bloodshot eyes. "I will do anything to keep her away from that awful drug. She's practically dead now."

April's throat closed up as she was reminded of all this
man had lost. A beautiful daughter, a serene retirement, an
old age free of anxiety.

He started to cry, his thin shoulders shaking with the effort of holding it all in. Kit went to him and put her arm around him. She looked at April with huge eyes, her own problems obviously roiling around her mind.

"Dr. Wysocki," April said, gently starting to disengage his fingers from the gun. "Do you know where Violet is?"

He shook his head. His fingers retightened around the gun handle. They heard a car crunch on the snow in the drive. Kit's head popped up quickly. April had to pull back her chin to avoid getting clocked.

"Oh, that's Yost," she said.

"Did my mother send him?" Kit sounded confused.

"No, I called him to help me when I thought you were in danger. I'll just tell him we're okay. No need for him to come in," April said, moving to the front door. She caught sight of Yost getting out of his personal car, parked across the road.

That car. In that spot. That was the car she'd seen when she'd left the night J.B. had visited Kit. The night J.B. died. Yost had been here.

Yost got out of his car. He was dressed all in black. He looked up and down the deserted road and pulled his ski mask down. April's heart plummeted. This was not the face of the friendly neighborhood cop trying to stay warm.

She ducked below the window in the door and reached up and threw the deadbolt.

Of course. Yost was the mastermind. He had access to Mary Lou's foreclosures. He had access to the vulnerable addicts like Violet and Paula. He'd stopped J.B. for a DWI, Paula for kiting checks. Violet's parents had given her to him to cure. His Anvil group was just a front for using people.

April looked for something to block the entrance. She pulled over a wooden sawhorse, recognizing the futility as soon as she did. But by balancing it on two back legs, she was able to jam the lock. It wouldn't hold for long, but she'd gained a little time. To think. To get help.

"Kit, take Dr. Wysocki and go down in the basement. I'll get rid of Yost."

"Why?" Kit pulled up Dr. Wysocki, who was staring at April as though she'd lost her mind. April wheeled her arms, hustling them to the stairs in the middle of the hall.

"That's who killed your uncle. He's the guy behind the meth making."

CHAPTER 20

She pulled open the basement door and shoved Kit and the doctor down, protesting. "Stay there until I tell you it's all clear. I'm going to get rid of him."

Yost hadn't come to the door. April looked outside and could make out a figure circumnavigating the backyard. Being a good cop and looking for trouble? Or making sure she was alone with Kit.

Kit's phone was on the counter. She grabbed it and called the police station again. She looked out the slider in the kitchen to the back of the house. She lurched when she saw Yost answer his cell. He'd had the phone forwarded to him. She bent over so he wouldn't spot her.

She had to pretend all was well and forced herself to sound cheery. "False alarm, Officer Yost. I got here and there's no one here."

"Really? Because I see lights on."

"Just me. I found the spare key under the mat. Logan

and Kit must have gone to get something to eat or something. They'll probably be right back."

"Well, I can check around. Make sure there's no one lingering."

April clicked off her phone. She yelled downstairs to Kit. "Can you turn off the light?"

"It's dark."

"I know. I don't want him to know you're here. He doesn't know how much you know. He might think J.B. told you things about him."

She was speaking in a harsh whisper, trying to paint a dire picture for Kit without worrying her sick. She didn't need Kit to totally freak out on her. If Kit thought there was a chance she wasn't going to see her babies again, she might try something stupid.

April had to keep her contained and get rid of Yost. At least until the police arrived.

She called the state police barracks. "I'm at 461 Dowling Road. I see an intruder with a gun outside of my place. Please send someone."

That would take a few minutes. The key was to keep Yost outside.

She stood in the kitchen window, trying to catch sight of him.

She smelled gas. Oh God. He was going to blow them up. Just like he had Charlotte and Grizz.

She pulled open the window. It stuck on the icy track. "Yost!" she hollered. "Stop. I've called the state troopers and told them that you killed J.B. I told them how you blew up my father's barn, killing those poor old people inside."

Yost's voice was high and tight. "It's too bad Logan is such a crappy caretaker. He doesn't know the first thing about gas lines. He should have had PP&L come out and inspect this connection to the house. It seems to be loose. Anyone could just light a match and whoosh."

April glanced at the door to the basement. Kit was counting on her to keep her safe. Kit, the mother of two babies. April couldn't leave her trapped in the basement if Yost was going to blow the house up. But if Kit ran, where would she go that Yost couldn't find her? Yost would never know how much J.B. had told her. He'd have to kill her, too. She would never be safe.

April had to stop him. She yanked open the front door. "Officer Yost, can we talk about this calmly?"

Yost appeared out of the bushes. Her heart stopped, and she had to hold herself up in the door frame. He looked like a commando out of a comic book. He was always in costume, she realized. As a policeman. As a civilian. Now as a killer. Were these the same clothes he'd worn when he'd blown up the barn?

She closed her eyes to regain her equilibrium, and when she opened them again, he was right in front of her, lit by the porch light. Every woman's nightmare.

"Did you cook meth in this house?" she asked him.

"I don't cook meth."

She waved off his smug response, barely resisting the urge to smack his face. She would have to make nice with him at least until she could figure out how to get them all out of this bind.

"No, you just had your girls do it. How many of Mary Lou's foreclosures did you use?"

"Oh, you know that, do you?" He came across the threshold and shut the door behind him, not wanting any of the gas to escape. April could see his shoulder holster through his open jacket. She wondered if that was his only weapon. A creep like him probably had a gun on his ankle, too.

He was taller than she was by a good eight inches, and grabbing the gun before he responded was out of the question. She tried to calculate how long it would be before the troopers could get there. Mitch was at the barn without his car. Logan might be on his way but given his fascination at the barn, it was hard to know when.

"Yes, I figured that out. You were so helpful to Mary Lou, weren't you? You had every excuse to pop round. And with so many houses in foreclosure, you had your pick, didn't you?"

Yost shrugged, his holster riding up and down. He thought that she was admiring his guile. He was wearing a black turtleneck and an open leather jacket. Spy School 101. She wondered if she offered him a martini, shaken, not stirred, if he'd go for it. Yost. Henry Yost.

A noise from the basement reminded her that Dr. Wysocki and Kit were down there, in the dark. She cleared her throat to cover it. Yost didn't flinch. He believed she was alone. Good. She could lead him away. Get him out of here.

"And Violet? Did you kill her?"

"Violet is fine. Don't you worry about her."

"Isn't that what you do? Blow up people that you're finished with? Isn't that kind of your MO? J.B. was the exception. He came to town and you had to finish him off, make it look like an accident. He was the only one who could put you with the meth houses." She paused to let her accusations sink in before continuing her attack. "Why did you go after Charlotte and Grizz?"

He scowled. "That's on you. You told everyone you were going to be alone last night."

The whole town knew Charlotte and Grizz were away. After the ring reveal, everyone knew that she and Mitch were fighting. No one expected them to reconcile so quickly.

She was supposed to be home alone. Charlotte and Grizz paid the price.

"Before you came along, I could go about my business without anyone questioning. No one cared. I didn't sell the meth here in Aldenville. In fact, I kept drugs out of here. I wasn't lying that night at Mary Lou's. There are no drugs around here. And that's because of me. I keep this town clean. I was doing the town a favor."

The man had a seriously weird sense of chivalry.

April backed into the kitchen. She wanted him away from the basement door. He didn't need to know more people were in the house.

She sighed heavily. She could taste gas. It got into her nose and tickled it. She tried to calculate how long before the air got to dangerous levels. If Yost had done the same thing last night, maybe Charlotte and Grizz had been unconscious before the explosion. Small mercy.

Yost leaned in the doorjamb, his own gun still snapped in his holster. Gas was still leaking into the house.

She couldn't remember what happened to Dr. Wysocki's gun. Had it been in his hand when he went downstairs? Or had he laid it down? April scanned the kitchen quickly so Yost wouldn't follow her gaze. She kept him talking.

"Why? Why did you do it?"

"You were there. You heard. The borough council is eliminating my job."

"Pete Rosen was on your side. He might have changed a few minds. He only needed one or two."

Kit's hostess setup from the other night was still there—three folding chairs around a milk crate. J.B. had sat right there, eating kielbasa. She could see something metallic on one of the chairs.

April reached behind her, trying to feel for the gun. She didn't stand a chance in a quick draw, but maybe she could hold him off long enough for help to arrive. But her fingers touched only the plastic openings of the milk crate.

"The borough has been talking about getting rid of the police for years. It's inevitable. With budget cuts, it doesn't make sense to have a separate police force. I had to take care of my future."

April wondered how many other laid-off workers figured dealing meth was the way to go. Yost wiped his face with the mask he'd been wearing. He was sweating under his tight turtleneck.

"J.B. ruined things. He was calling it quits. He'd fallen for some chick. Wanted out."

His eyes lost focus. "Killing Ransom was an accident. I told the jerk not to be there that day, but he was probably tweaking and didn't know where he was. I hate users."

So he'd meant to kill J.B. but not the other meth maker. Nice to know he had standards.

He smiled, a look so reptilian she expected a tiny forked tongue to flick out. "I changed up my tactics. That's why I've only been using nonusers now."

April's eyebrows raised. "So Violet hasn't gone back to using?" That would be some comfort to her father.

"She's clean. I drug-test them. Paula kept her straight."

He cocked his head toward the middle of the house. The place was deadly quiet. They both heard the noise.

"Listen," April said, trying to make some noise.

Yost held up a hand to silence her. She protested, and he grabbed her by the upper arm.

"Quiet," he said and pushed her away.

She and Yost heard the footsteps on the basement stairs at the same time. He turned quickly. April jumped up from her seat, hand scrabbling for the gun. It wasn't there.

Yost yelled. "Who's there?"

April heard a car in the driveway and saw the red flashing light of the trooper car. She ran to the side door to unlock it.

When she turned back, Dr. Wysocki was standing with a gun pointed at Yost. Yost's hand hovered over his holster, but he'd hesitated. Even he couldn't shoot an old man in cold blood.

Dr. Wysocki didn't seem to have the same problem. His hand was trembling, but the gun was small and not heavy. He was close enough to do damage to Yost even if his aim wasn't true. But if he fired, the gas that Yost had turned on would surely explode, killing them all. April knew what was on his mind.

"Dr. Wysocki!" April yelled. "Hold on. Violet is clean. She hasn't used again."

Dr. Wysocki didn't react. His eyes were on Yost. He wasn't hearing her. She could smell gas more strongly now.

Kit's head appeared behind the doctor's. "Run outside," April said. "Kit, now."

The girl went out the front door. Yost watched her go, his eyes flicking from April to Dr. Wysocki and back.

If the state troopers came in right now, they'd see an old man with a gun pointed at a police officer. April was afraid that they would shoot Dr. Wysocki. She had to get him to put down the gun.

"Dr. Wysocki, he broke the gas connection at the intake pipe. You might not know this, but the house is filled with flammable gas. If you fire, we will all die in a fireball. Just like the Campbells," April said. "Don't shoot, Dr. Wysocki. Give me the gun."

Dr. Wysocki was not listening. "You got my girl involved with drugs again. I thought you were keeping her sober."

He pushed the gun to Yost's chest. "You deserve to die like a dog."

Yost's eyes widened. He hadn't heard the car. Now he could hear the low voices of the troopers outside. He grabbed the gun from the doctor's hand. The doctor was weakened by his grief and age, and Yost easily disarmed him. He took hold of the doctor and spun him around.

Yost gestured at April. "Come on, we're going out together. I'm not going to jail. You two are my ticket out of here."

The doctor was squirming in Yost's left-handed bear hug, but the policeman was restraining him easily. Dr. Wysocki bit his hand. Yost hung on, yelling.

He was distracted long enough for April to knock over a paint can. The white cupboard paint spilled, a long slippery trail insinuating itself around Yost's feet. The doctor released his grip on Yost's hand, elbowing him. Both men lost their balance and slipped, the doctor falling hard onto Yost. April pulled the doctor up and ran out of the house.

A trooper was waiting for them on the porch. He hustled both of them into the car where Kit was already huddled. Two other troopers stormed the house. Through the open door, they could see Yost wrestled to the ground. April let out a huge sigh. Her throat burned from the breath she hadn't realized she'd been holding.

"You okay?" Kit asked.

April checked with the doctor who was breathing hard but seemed to be fine.

"We're all good," she said. "All good."

CHAPTER 21

Unpacking didn't take long.

Even less time than when she'd arrived in Aldenville seven months ago. Then, she had pulled a small trailer of belongings behind her precious car. Now she had a box of hand-me-down kitchen stuff from Bonnie and a towel. And no car.

She was starting over. Again.

Mitch had dropped her off and gone to pick up the paint she'd ordered. She was wearing a sweatshirt of Deana's—of Mark's, actually—and a hand-me-down pair of jeans from Rocky.

April felt the tears welling up. She'd been lucky, she knew that. She could have been blown up in the barn as Yost had intended. Like poor Charlotte and Grizz. Vince would take a long time to recover from those unfair deaths.

Looking around and not seeing one familiar thing reminded her of what they'd lost.

A knock on the door broke through her pity party. She

wiped at her face with a paper towel and called out she'd be right there.

Violet, tiny, enveloped in her down coat, stood on the porch. She was out on bail, hoping to get into a drug program rather than jail. She'd promised to testify against Yost.

Her father was in the car. April waved to him. Violet held out a plastic tub. "My mother made cookies."

"Thanks," April said, taking the box from her. "Come in."

Violet took two tentative steps inside. "Nice," she said, her eyes traveling around the living room. The air was so cold April could see her breath.

April accepted the compliment without comment. "What are you going to do next?"

Violet shrugged. "I'm going to Scranton for treatment."

"Paula?"

"Gone. She disappeared the day after your barn . . ." She let the sentence end without her.

"Good." April nodded. Violet's eyes were black, hard to read "You'll come stamp with us again?"

Violet shrugged. "I'd like to, once I'm home from rehab."

A pounding on the back door startled Violet, and she was at the front door before April could stop her. April looked out the side window and saw the Jeep. "It's only Mitch."

"Hurry up, it's heavy," she heard Mitch say.

Violet said, "My father's waiting for me. We're going to rehab right now."

April hugged her quickly and opened the door. Violet passed through like a wraith. On the porch, Mitch was struggling with a big item. Instead of the paint cans she was expecting, he was carrying her drafting table.

"Mitch!" April said. She'd completely forgotten that her drafting table was at his house. She'd had the table since art school. It was ugly and heavy, being made of pressed board, but it was hers. The one Grizz had made her had been destroyed in the fire.

"Where do you want it?" he said, looking around. This was the first time he was seeing her new place. He did his best to keep his face neutral, but she saw the shock registering. This house was not going to be featured in the real estate section of the Sunday paper anytime soon.

"Um, anywhere?" she said, flinging her arm around the empty space. "How about in front of the window?"

He set it down, grunting.

"Do you mind? I need it facing the other way," she said. "So the light is at my back."

Mitch grumbled, although she knew he was mostly kidding. "Your chair's in the truck," he said. She raced out to get it, pushing it up the porch steps on its wheels.

She sat at her table, pulling herself close and rubbing the top. It was covered with the detritus of old projects: ink stains, doodles, even some ground-in glitter.

Mitch leaned against the door frame that led into the tiny kitchen. He crossed his arms and watched as she hugged her table.

"Happy now?" he said.

She looked up at him, his tone of voice unclear to her. Was he truly okay with her being in her own place?

One look and she knew he was. He was smiling at her, a smile that warmed her insides.

"I am. Very."

She got up from the table and walked over to him. He watched her, and she felt his love for her as he watched her move toward him.

"So happy to have my table. Even happier to have you in my life," she said. When she got close enough, she kissed his cheek and smoothed his hair. He smelled of wood shavings. She leaned into his neck and inhaled, filling her lungs with his unique scent.

He wrapped his arms around her. "Glad I could be of service," he said into her hair.

"Yoo-hoo, anyone home?"

She turned to see Rocky coming in the door. She had on hot pink leopard-spotted oven mitts and was carrying a big pan of something steaming hot.

"Is that lasagna?" April said, trying to snag a corner of the foil and turn it back.

Rocky moved it over her head. "Get away. You'll make me drop it. Again."

April went slack-jawed. Rocky just smiled.

"Don't listen to her, she didn't drop it," Deana said as she came in with a big bowl of salad. And then, as if it weren't obvious, she added, "We brought dinner." She looked for a place to set things down, settling on the small counter space in the kitchen. Rocky followed her, putting her dish on top of the stove. Mark waggled two bottles of wine as he came in the door.

"Brought my own corkscrew," he said. "And cups."

April leaned into Mitch's chest, watching her friends turn her place into a home. The windows steamed from their collective heat.

She was so lucky. To have this man and these friends in her life. She filled up with joy, her chest expanding. They would have a good bottle of wine, Rocky's famous vegetarian lasagna. They would laugh and play cards and get tipsy.

Someday, Mary Lou would talk to her, and she looked forward to being friends with her again. April would have to build her business back up, without any supplies. The stamp she'd made for Mirabella was at the job site, so she had work there for the next month or so. She would save up and buy more inks, more rubber. It would take years to rebuild the vast collection she'd had before, but she knew she could do it. Her career path would be a lot slower than she'd hoped.

Deana produced paper plates and cups. The house, the little river cottage, had come partially furnished, with an old kitchen table, metal with yellow pleather seats. There were only four kitchen chairs, but April pulled up her desk chair, and the five of them dug in. The lasagna was hot and cheesy, and Deana had managed to turn bag salad into something special with cranberries and Sonoma County goat cheese. Mark quizzed Mitch about ice sculpting. They all laughed at his account of April's horror when she saw the giant diamond ring.

There was a tentative knock on the door. April barely heard it over the giggling coming from Deana at Rocky's imitation of Mitch's proposal.

She listened. Again came the knock.

"Come in," she hollered, but when the door didn't open, she peered out the window. Night had fallen, and she couldn't see a thing. She flipped on the outside light and answered the door.

Mary Lou and Kit stood on the small porch. Suzi was behind them.

"Hello," April said as she moved inward so that they could get inside out of the cold.

Kit was pulling a black rolling cart. She looked at her mother and kissed April's cheek.

"Mom?" Kit prompted, looking at her mother, who had stopped in her tracks and was taking in the small space, which could have fit easily in one small corner of her four-thousand-square-foot home.

Mary Lou cleared her throat. "I want you to have this. I know you lost everything at the barn. Here are some supplies to get you started stamping again."

April knelt down and unbuckled the front of the case.

It was fitted with a heat gun, rubber, carving tools, acrylic blocks, and stamp pads. Dozens of inks and pens had their own designated space. The back of the case had clear plastic dividers and was filled with stamps.

Everything she needed to start stamping again.

Kit dove into a shopping bag and came up with an armful of sketchbooks that she shoved at April. "We bought the store out, can you tell?"

Suzi was smiling at them, but April's eyes were on Mary Lou. She tried to stand up but stumbled, slightly off-kilter with the addition of Kit's gifts. Mary Lou reached down and pulled her up.

"I want to thank you. You saved my daughter, my grandbabies . . ." Mary Lou's voice caught.

"Okay," April said, her tears clogging her throat.

"No, let me finish. I was wrong about you. I said hurtful things. I apologize from the bottom of my heart."

April went over to a box in the corner. She took out the small cassette tape that she'd found in Mary Lou's shed. She handed it to Mary Lou. "This belongs to your family. I shouldn't have kept it from you."

Mary Lou turned it over in her palm with her index finger. "Have you heard it?"

"No. I got Bonnie's tape player, but I haven't had the heart . . ."

"Can we do it now?" Kit said. "I want to hear my uncle."

Mary Lou blanched, but she nodded. The rest of the Stamping Sisters were looking at them. Mitch and Mark stood, offering Mary Lou and Kit their seats. Deana and Rocky cleared the table. Mitch poured them all a glass of wine. Rocky shared her chair with Suzi.

April set the tape player in the middle of the table and pushed play.

J.B.'s voice filled the small space. Mary Lou grabbed Kit's hand and squeezed.

This is to set the record straight. Tina has just told me she's pregnant. I'm about to have my own child, and I suddenly realize how precious that is. I'm sorry, Mary Lou. You were right. I didn't belong around your daughter or your son. I was a danger to them. I hadn't earned the right to be with them.

After you threw me out, I was living rough. In my car, out on the street. I was driving through Aldenville, mad at the world as usual. Winter was coming, and I didn't know how I was going to survive. Of course, that was all my fault. I rolled through the stop sign on Main. I had a forty in my lap and five more rolling around the backseat. I didn't see Yost until he was pulled up next to me.

I had so many traffic tickets, I knew I was going to jail for a long time. But Yost had another plan.

"You're coming to work for me," he said with that smug smirk of his. He knew he had me. I'm ashamed to admit this, but all I could think about was drinking. In jail meant no alcohol. Out of jail meant all the booze I could scrounge up.

You know now what the job was. Buying over-the-counter meds for his meth-making operation. He gave me a variety of IDs and an assortment of cars and told me to hit the road.

At first, I stayed drunk. Then I met Tina. And she saw beyond the drink, beyond the stupid guy buying OTC meds. She saw someone inside me. Someone I hadn't been for a long, long time.

*I told Yost I wanted out. I told him I'd disappear,
move away. He'd never see me again.*

*He called for a powwow at the house. I'd been
there earlier in the day, dropped off my truck.
Ransom was in a mood. He was using, getting more
and more paranoid and delusional. I knew he wasn't
to be trusted, and if I knew it, Yost knew it, too. He
would find a way to get rid of us both. All he had to
do was re-arrest me and throw me in jail.*

*I picked up a car and did some drugstore runs.
Yost generally showed up about three each day to
collect the day's output. I drove back to confront
him.*

*Instead, the house was burning. I could see the
smoke and the fire trucks from a mile away. I never
even went close. I just turned around and ran.*

*But I got lucky. I ran straight into the arms of the
woman who loved me.*

The tape came to an end. The room was silent. Mary
Lou and Kit hugged each other. April mopped her eyes.

J.B. had found a new family for himself. A new life.
Literally, with the baby coming. It was too late for Mary
Lou and her brother, but there was still a chance for her to
welcome Tina into her life.

April dished up lasagna for Kit, Mary Lou and Suzi.
Deana sat on Mark's lap, and April stood with Mitch,
leaning against the wall, watching them dig in. Soon the
kitchen was filled with laughter as the friends found their
way past awkwardness and hard feelings.

April knew family didn't always come as advertised.
The packaging varied, and sometimes it was hard to recognize. She'd learned to accept love in whatever form it
took.

Stamping Project

SUPPLIES

- *Light-colored stamp pad*
- *"Snowman parts" stamps*
- *Cardstock (five pieces)*
- *Snowman stamp*
- *Colored markers*
- *Scissors*
- *"Some Assembly Required" stamp*
- *Fancy paper (optional)*

DIRECTIONS

1. To create background, use a light-colored stamp pad to ink "snowman parts" stamps and press stamps all over the front of a piece of cardstock.

2. Use the same stamp pad to ink the snowman stamp and then press stamp firmly on a second piece of cardstock. Using markers, color in the snowman, and then trim the cardstock to rectangle shape.

3. Take a third piece of cardstock, cut a slightly larger rect-angle. Mount snowman rectangle on top.
4. Ink the "Some Assembly Required" stamp and then press stamp firmly on a small fourth piece of cardstock. Trim the cardstock to rectangle shape.
5. Finally, use a fifth piece of cardstock or fancy paper and cut a strip to measure ½ inch by the width of the card. Mount this strip of cardstock on top of the first piece of cardstock with the "snowman parts" background. Mount the snowman rectangle on top of the strip. Finish by mounting the "Some Assembly Required" rectangle on top of the entire card.